CW01046439

The Cornish Connection

Amanda James

PRAISE FOR AMANDA JAMES

Intriguing characters, mystery, a warmth that flows from the pages and a tempting taste of Cornwall. I loved it!
Celia Anderson

Nancy Cornish is a wonderful character; she's warm, funny and lovable. I adored spending time with her in The Cornish Connection *and I can't wait to see where her next cases lead.*
Chris Stovell

Everything I love in a book. A beautiful setting, a little mystery and a great story. This book really does have it all; a perfect summer read.
Lynda Stacey

Charlie believes in facts. Nancy believes in help from the other side. A psychic and a detective against a backdrop of Cornwall. What more could you ask for?
Anne Mackle – Books with Wine and Chocolate

A fabulous cosy mystery with a psychic twist that has such a heartwarming feel to it. A book that definitely has more to it than meets the eye.
Yvonne Bastian – Me And My Books

I can now say I am a super fan of Amanda James. I have read every single book of hers, all different genres, thrillers, romance, sci-fi, mediums, her repertoire is just unreal!
Zoé-Lee O'Farrell – Zooloo's Book Diary

For my Family

I wipe the flour from the counter with a soapy cloth and consider my hands. They look like a couple of boiled crabs. Old, boiled crabs. Red-rough, with stumpy fingers hinged on a mountain-range of knuckles, creases and cracks. I drop the cloth into the washing up bowl; hold my crabs up to the feeble early morning light leaking through the bakery window. Forty-three-year-old hands should look younger, shouldn't they?

'Depends, Nancy. If you were a lady of leisure, they might. But you're a good honest working woman. Hands in water, in flour, beating, stirring, kneading. What do you expect?'

I turn in time to see my grandma and namesake wag a finger and give a toothless grin. I open my mouth to reply, but the old lady pixilates and disappears through the wall. Great. My gran's not visited for months and then there's just a fleeting connection. Oh well. The cakes need to come out of the oven now. No time for chatting.

1

Chapter One

It's late afternoon, but the feeble light of morning hasn't put up much of a fight, preferring to slink away, hide in winter shadows – an apology for a day. Through the café window, I watch gunmetal-grey clouds muscle in over Padstow harbour, and a stiff wind bounce a fistful of fishing boats up and down on the water like rubber balls. Rain won't be far behind. The Whistling Kettle Café is empty now, apart from an old couple sitting opposite each other in the booth by the bay window nursing mugs of tea. Silent. Rheumy eyes flitting to the harbour, back to the tea and then harbour again, as if watching some invisible and very slow tennis match.

I wonder if they speak to each other when they're at home. Are they happy? Or are they quietly despairing about how their lives have turned out. Disappointment rendering them mute, fearful of the inevitable, yearning for what might have been. I remind myself that I can be too fanciful, and in this case too miserable. The old couple might be perfectly content and don't verbally communicate because they speak with their hearts. They know each other so well, just a touch of the hand, an angle of the head might be speech in kind.

Leanne, my young colleague, wipes down a table and stacks used crockery onto a tray. She's employing her usual vigour and under her energetic movement, her dark hair stuffed into a messy top knot, flops from one side of her head to the other, as if it can't make up its mind where to rest. She looks over at me and says, 'You get off now, Nance. She inclines her head to the old couple. 'We're not exactly run off our feet and you've done four earlies in a row.' She sets off to the kitchen, the top knot flopping, the crockery rattling like a set of comedy false teeth.

I smile my gratitude. 'I think I will, Lee. I could do with putting my feet up.' Truth is I'm knackered. I'm so looking forward to my three days off too.

'Yeah. See you soon, love. Enjoy your break!' Leanne tosses over her shoulder.

I bend to grab my coat and bag from under the counter by the till and when I look back up, the old couple have been joined by a young man dressed in a smart grey suit. He's staring at the old man and has shiny brown hair parted on the left and a face belonging to 1930s Hollywood. Very Fred Astaire. Except this man isn't a dancer. He's a messenger. Brown doleful eyes shift from the old man's face and lock onto mine.

'Please tell my son Graham he's made the right choice today… and not to be frightened. And please tell him, even though I never told him that I loved him, I always did.'

A hard gobstopper of emotion bobs in my throat and I take a few seconds to swallow it. Then I nod once. The young man smiles and is gone. He doesn't pixilate like Gran did earlier, but does the 'off switch' as I think of it. One minute they're there – the next they're gone. As if someone's flicked a light switch.

Disconnected.

A blessing, a gift, and an honour. I remember gran's words the first time she explained to me why I could see a Victorian lady sitting on our sofa. But today, today I wish I didn't have to pass on this message. I'm so tired, and for the last hour I've been picturing myself with a cuppa, a Jaffa cake or two and my feet up by the log burner. Has to be done though. It's my duty. No. *It's a blessing, a gift and an honour.*

With a heart as heavy as the clouds outside, I slide onto the booth next to the woman, startling her and the man out of their silent conversation. A winning smile is searched for, hopefully found and slicked across my lips. 'Hello. This won't take long…I don't want to upset you, but I have a message from your dad, Graham.'

Shock sends animation flushing through Graham's face – his mouth drops open and his bushy white brows raise to meet his tweed cap. 'My dad?'

'His dad's been dead nigh on thirty-years,' the woman says. Her eyes narrow with suspicion, her tone sharp as a lemon. Her name comes through to me. Settles on my tongue.

'I know, Marge.'

Marge's mouth copies her husband's. Then her hands jerk up puppet-like to cup both cheeks.

'And it must be a shock, but the thing is, it's not to me. I see spirits very often, have done since I was a kid. They sometimes come and say nothing, just pass by like, and wave, or smile. Other times they have messages. And your dad...' I look back at Graham who's now covered his mouth with a big gnarled hand. If my hands are crabs, his are lobsters. 'Your dad wants you to know you made the right choice today and not to be frightened. He says even though he never told you he loved you, he always did.'

Marge makes a noise in her throat that's a cross between a sob and a yelp and Graham's eyes brim with unshed tears. He pulls a big checked hanky from his pocket and blows his nose. 'Does he mean about what they said at the clinic this morning. About not having the chemo?'

I instinctively know the answer is yes and tell him so. Then I get up to leave. I feel even more drained after that. Marge puts a hand on my arm, looks up at me beseechingly. 'But will my Graham be alright? Will he get better without the chemo? I said he should have it. No point in just rolling over and playing dead. He has to fight.'

The slow tennis match the couple had been watching makes perfect sense to me now. Also making perfect sense, is the knowledge that Graham will be joining his dad before too long. But his passing will be peaceful – quick. As I look at the old couple so much in love after all these years, and so terrified of letting go, a gut-wrenching sadness overwhelms me. I take a deep breath. 'That's not for me to say. But make every day count and be thankful for your wonderful life together. And like your dad said, Graham. There's nothing to be scared of.'

'Thank you,' Graham says and holds his hand out. I take it, and crab and lobster do a short jig.

'It's my pleasure,' I say, and step outside. A fresh sea breeze hurls a spatter of rain at my cheeks which adds to the dampness already there. Then I stride up the steep cobbled streets as fast as I can, my breath coming in small huffs, my mind trying to blot out the pain in Marge and Graham's eyes. But once safe inside my little cottage, I allow my storm to break.

LATER, I MAKE stew and dumplings for dinner. It's one of my Charlie's favourites which we tend to have on a Thursday in winter. Charlie's a creature of habit and likes routine. Maybe it's to do with him being a DS. He likes order, logic, predictability – a set pattern to life. He says when he steps in the door and smells it cooking, all the stress of work gets left outside. Last week, he said that on the way home, he imagined me rushing about the kitchen, pushing my 'lustrous' red hair back from my forehead with a soapy hand, stirring the stew, laying the table. Then I'd turn to welcome him home with a smile as wide as the sky, my jade-green eyes twinkling my love for him. He's quite the poet when he wants to be. Which isn't very often nowadays. Work does tend to take over.

Sometimes I have flashes of what Charlie's up to at work. Earlier, in my mind's eye, I saw him chatting to his boss DI Abigail Summercourt. Their conversation was silent to me, but she gave him a manila work file. Poor love. He tries not to bring stuff home, but I expect he'll be working on it when he gets in. Abigail is ambitious, and I get the feeling she gets frustrated with Charlie. He once said to me that he was forty-three, been a DS for ten years, but had no desire to climb higher on the ladder. Well, perhaps the desire, but not the gumption. Whereas Summercourt was thirty-six, sharp as a Stanley blade and aiming so high she'd be needing a ladder extension before long. He laughed, but I knew it rankled. As would the work he'd have to do tonight. For the last while, I've been working on something too, apart from the dinner. I always have a sketch pad handy, and I've been compelled to use it this evening. It might be of consequence, it might not. We'll see.

I set the table and quiet calm settles over me like a caress. Sometimes I wish I could capture a perfect moment like this. On the surface it's an ordinary scene, a small thing – just me waiting for dinner to cook while I do a sketch or two in our kitchen. The low lights throw a cosy fan against the bright lemon walls, the old sash window looks out over the rooftops towards the estuary. I sit at the scrubbe

d pine farmhouse table centre stage, across which so many of mine and Charlie's conversations have taken place…where we've laughed and sometimes cried. But it's not an ordinary scene – a small thing…it's our heart, our home. Sometimes the small things aren't small at all when you look more closely. They're the big things. The foundations of everything we hold dear.

I sketch for a few more minutes until I hear the front door bang and Charlie's footsteps in the hall. He walks into the kitchen and gives me a smile. 'Hello, love. You okay?' I ask, closing the cover of the drawing pad.

'Better for seeing you.' He shrugs his coat off and hangs it on the back of a kitchen chair. I get up and take it through to the hall. Hang it on a peg. He never remembers.

'I should have done that, shouldn't I? You look tired,' he says when I come back. I smile and kiss his cold cheek. He smells of winter air and mints.

I nod at the folder on the table. It was the one I saw his boss give him. 'That work? You don't normally bring stuff home these days.'

'Yeah. I was asked to read through again. Misper. Teenager been gone for three weeks – doesn't look good. He sits down. 'This case is no nearer to being closed and quite frankly I've had enough. Twenty-two years on the Force and it never gets any easier. Becky Proctor. Blue eyes, big smile and everything to live for. Chances are, the life full of promise will have been snuffed out by now. Ground underfoot by some evil filth.'

My heart flips and a tingling sensation runs the length of me. I draw the file towards me, flick it open and gasp. My trembling fingers trace over the photo of the teenager. 'Becky...so that's your name,' I whisper.

'You've got that otherworldly, serene look,' Charlie says, sits back, folds his arms. He's got the 'I can't be doing with all this and I want my stew' look.

He sighs. 'Yeah. Becky Proctor. Heart-breaking to think she'll not see her sixteenth birthday.'

I shake my head, give him a wide smile, flick open my drawing pad and slide it next to the open folder. He does a double take. My eyes confirm what I already knew. My rough pencil drawing is more or less identical to the photo of Becky Proctor.

Charlie's eyes find mine. 'How did you…' He swallows. 'Did one of your connection thingies tell you she was dead?'

I laugh. The delight in my chest reminiscent of a child's at Christmas. 'No. One of my "connection thingies" told me she was alive!'

Chapter Two

Charlie draws his hand down his face in a mime-artist attempt to replace one expression with another. In this case, raw shock becomes relaxed nonchalance. He shoves a hand through his short-cropped dark hair, making it stick up like a clothes brush. I try to keep a smile hidden, but it wants to be found. He shakes his head, shoves his other hand through his hair and then rests it over his mouth as if trying to stop his words. 'How did you know, Nancy?' He looks at the drawing again and then back to me.

'Well, it's funny, but I haven't had this kind of connection for ages.' At this, I see a shutter go up behind his eyes. He's always been the same from day one. That's why I never tell him about my psychic experiences nowadays. Nonetheless, I continue in a business-like way. 'I usually see the spirit messengers, as you know. But on occasion I see a series of images, like old photos snapped down in quick succession. I call it the playing card effect. Or sometimes it's more like a scene from a film – it rolls, but there's no sound. These scenes or images are often – yet not always – accompanied by heat or a tingling feeling in my fingers. Well today I had the film-rolling one. About half-an-hour before you came home, I saw you in the office with Abigail – you were talking and then you picked up a folder.' I nod at the table. 'That one. I got the tingles and I knew I had to grab my pencil and paper.'

Charlie scrubs at his nose with his fist. He raises one shoulder; spreads his hands. 'You might just have been thinking of me at work…pictured me, rather than saw me?'

I can tell he's hiding something. His eyebrows are doing the jiggle dance and his Adam's apple is bobbing like a float on a lake. 'So, you *weren't* talking to Abigail Summercourt just before you left?'

'Er, not immediately before.' A crimson tide floods his cheeks, giving him away.

'And you weren't discussing *that* file?' I nod at it again.

'Look, even if we were. It's a coincidence. All the things you experience can be explained away logically.' Relaxed nonchalance is peeling from his face like damp wallpaper; raw shock is seeping back in.

Why is he in denial? Even though he's the biggest sceptic, in this instance, he's just being stubborn. I'm irritated beyond all reason. There's a spiky crawly ant feeling in my chest, but I can't show it, or he'll retreat even further. How much more evidence does he need? Taking a deep breath, I push my sketch towards him. 'How do you explain that then, love?'

Charlie looks at it, twists his mouth to the side. 'Well...you might have seen a photo of Becky on the local news and it stuck in your subconscious somehow.' There are beads of sweat threading themselves together to form a salt moustache along his top lip.

This is too much for me. I bang the heel of my hand on the table. 'You know that's rubbish! Why do you always put up barriers, Charlie? What are you scared of?'

My husband sits back, folds his arms tight round his body and does a false laugh. 'I'm not scared, just trying to make you see there is always a log—'

'Logical explanation. Yes, you always say that.' I stare at him and he stares back. How can I make him see that my connections aren't a threat? 'Look, Charlie. I think it's because you're so worried about this girl, that the case somehow came through to me. You've been quiet and a bit withdrawn over the last week or so, haven't you?'

Charlie sighs and twiddles his wedding ring round on his finger. I think I'm getting somewhere. 'Maybe. I hate it when youngsters go missing.'

13

'Of course you do…particularly given her age.' I swallow down a lump of emotion. I can't go there right now, back to my own loss…or I'll crumble. 'And it seems to me that I can help you find Becky. It will be a relief to her family, and you might get that promotion you've been talking about for years if you do.'

I see a light switch on in his brain as his hazel eyes grow round and realisation dawns bright in them. 'Do you think you could?'

'Yes. Absolutely.' I cross my fingers under the table, because I've never attempted anything like it before, and look down at the photo of Becky giving the heat in my cheeks chance to cool.

'But how?'

Yes, how, Nancy? 'Um. Objects. You'll have to bring me a few personal items of Becky's and I'll be able to get messages when I handle them.' *You hope.*

'Really?'

I raise one eyebrow and treat him to a hard stare. 'Yes, really.' The only times it's happened during my 'career' is by accident. But he doesn't need to know that.

Charlie shakes his head and picks up my pencil, fiddles with it. 'Hmm. I don't know love…'

'No. Because you still think it's illogical mumbo jumbo, don't you?'

'W-ell…'

'You know the first time you said my connection, or gift as my gran preferred, was a load of rubbish? You know the time, years ago, just before we got married?' Charlie shrugs. 'Well after you said it, your uncle Ted appeared behind you, stuck his tongue out at you and said, "Take no notice. Our Chaplin never did have much of an imagination." I didn't tell you at the time because I was so angry with you.'

There's a *crack* as the pencil snaps between Charlie's fingers and his bottom lip trembles. 'My uncle Ted's pet name for me was Chaplin... 'cos of me being called—'

'Charlie yes, I get it.' I cover his hand with mine. Give it a squeeze.

'I can't remember telling you that before?'

Oh dear. Is he still not getting it? 'You didn't. You told me you were close and that you were devastated when he died in that motorbike accident. But nothing else.'

'And Uncle Ted really stood behind me – stuck his tongue out?'

'He really did. He'd a Manchester United top on and jeans.'

Charlie grins and his eyes brim. 'He loved Man U.' Then the smile disappears. He blinks moisture from his eyes and furrows his brows.' Why didn't you tell me?'

I give him my best 'as if' look. 'Because you wouldn't have believed me. And as I said, I was angry. Later I couldn't see the problem really. I loved you as you were – no point in browbeating you about something you had no interest in. Scepticism is something I'm used to.'

'Sorry, Nance. It's just so alien to me…' He spreads his hands and sighs. 'But what you've just told me *is* making me think.'

'Good. Thinking's good.' I pat his arm and smile. 'Now shall we have that stew and flesh out a plan to find young Becky?'

TWO DAYS LATER I'm alone in the living room. Charlie's at work and the door is locked and bolted. I need absolute calm and silence for what I'm about to do. On the old knotty coffee table in front of me, there's an array of Becky's things – precious items that wouldn't mean much to anyone else. Three objects; a slice of the teenagers' world laid in front of me waiting to be tasted. Charlie managed to get the things for me. He hasn't told his boss what I'm attempting to do however, because he says psychic assistance is frowned upon by and large. Psychics been known to help the police sometimes, but overall, at best they normally bark up the wrong tree, and at worst, lead the investigation away from the target at great expense. Charlie said that these days, more than ever, time is money, and there's not much of that about given the government cuts to public services.

Draining a mug of tea, I link my fingers and crack my knuckles. I'm actually not really sure how to begin, because the only time objects have 'spoken' to me as I think of it, is when I'm not trying. The first time was once when I was about nine, I picked up a ring from Mum's jewellery box that had belonged to my great-granddad. I remember that a prickly sensation ran the length of my hands and arms and I saw a very quick 'rolling film' snippet of him digging a hole in the sand on a beach, a knotted hanky on his head. He was laughing at a little girl in a blue swimming costume who jumped up and down on the edge of the hole and then fell in. Mum had wept when I'd described what I'd seen. She'd been the girl in the costume. She said she was sad that she herself hadn't inherited the gift from her own mum, but was pleased that it had been passed down to me.

Another time, when I was a few years older, I'd picked up an old ornate hand mirror at a boot sale and was surprised not to see my own reflection, but that of an old lady wearing a red beret and a scowl. It had freaked me out a bit, but I'd known immediately that it was the previous owner and there was nothing to be scared of. That time I'd only had a slight tingle in my fingertips. Perhaps because the mirror was of no real importance to me. Over the years it's happened now and then, but mostly, there's been no real significance attached to the experience.

My gran told me that we all connect to the spirit world differently. She said the object connection was quite common amongst we 'gifted' ones. I was full of questions but she told me there aren't always answers. Ours is to do, not to question. Then I think about a conversation I had a few weeks ago about it with my friend Penny who holds evenings at the spiritualist church. She's a medium, and as such, has very different experiences to me. She likened it to radio waves getting mixed and misdirected. Perhaps the message in the object is for someone else, and gets transmitted to the wrong person instead. I found out there's an actual word for it – psychometry. It's thought the energy of the owner of the possession can stay with it. Makes sense to me.

Whatever the reason, I need to try and channel my senses, or radio waves…get them to help me work out where this young girl is. Make a connection, as I prefer to think of it. Because I've never attempted such a thing, I'm not sure it will work. But I have to have more confidence in my gift. After all, it's mine for a reason, isn't it? Gran was right. Ours is to do, not to question. I look at the items again and then taking a few calming breaths, I spread my fingers and hover my palms a few centimetres above the first item – a green teddy bear missing an eye. The doorbell rings. *Damn it all!* I consider ignoring it, but whoever it is will probably push the bell again and so jump up, stomp out and down the hall.

It's a delivery man with a parcel. I scrawl my finger across the little computer screen – the signature looks like the last journey of a dying fly. The man looks at it and says it's grand. Grand? A wiggle, squiggle and splat? Oh well, he knows best. About to tear open the package, I stop. It's just a couple of new aprons for work. If I start looking at those, I'll lose concentration and the calm mood I've tried so hard to create will be lost. Back to the task at hand.

The teddy waits there on the table, squinting at me from one shiny amber eye. A few deep breaths. My hand hovers. And…nothing. No tingles, no old images snapped down in quick succession like cards, no rolling film images. Damn the delivery man. Why did he have to turn up right then? The aura of calm's gone. I can feel it draining away like sauce through a strainer. I pick up the bear, hug it to my chest, sniff the fur. Is there something? A slight tingle in my wrist? A warmth floods my right arm, followed by pins and needles faintly traversing my forefingers.

Snap.

An image of a small child in a tartan dress whirling the teddy around a bright pink room.

Snap.

The same child, older now, picnicking on a beach, Teddy's taken for a paddle.

Snap.

Teenage Becky in a bedroom crying her heart out, the teddy clasped to her chest, it's fur damp with tears.

Then…nothing.

The dealer's put the pack away.

I hold the teddy at arm's length, see my hands are shaking so place the bear on the sofa next to me, assess what I've learnt. Becky's definitely confused, troubled… unsure of what to do. I take a minute to catch my ragged breath, look around the familiar surroundings, and listen to the sound of Seal Cottage. A hiss as flames lick the resin from a log in the burner glowing red – a nice contrast against the whitewashed stone chimney. The creak of old beams as the wind shows who's boss outside, and the heartbeat-tick of Gran's old clock on the shelf next to the window. My breathing is regular, normal. I'm calm, confident – ready.

The next object on the table is a much-worn red t-shirt, more like pink actually, from frequent washing. Across the front is emblazoned – *One Direction – World Tour 2015*. Charlie said this was the shirt used as scent for the sniffer dogs in the early days of the hunt for Becky. My hands hover, then touch the material, but this time there's nothing at all. Not even a sense of anything.

Last, but hopefully not least, is Becky's notebook. It's A4 sized, with a cover of blue and red flowers on a gold background. As soon as my hands move to the book, a tremor starts in my fingers and the air between my palms and the cover feel charged with electricity. I pick it up and quickly turn the pages. She's as fond of art as I was at her age. I had a book just like this once. There're drawings of seabirds, horses, doodles, snippets of poems and near the back, a recent photo of Becky amid of a class of teenagers in a hall. She's sitting on a bench smiling, and has her arm draped around another girl's shoulders. This girl has a blonde pigtail and a scattering of freckles across the bridge of her nose. My gut tells me they are best friends. At the end of the rows sit adults, presumably teachers.

My head jerks up from the book and my eyes are drawn to the whitewashed chimney breast behind the log burner. Across it plays a rolling film of Becky at school with her friends larking about in a hall. I'm certain it's the scene from the photo in the book. Becky smiles for the camera and then she smiles at someone else. Oh my God! A gasp escapes me and my heart thumps in my chest. Giddiness makes my head swim and I clutch the arm of the sofa to steady myself. Then the scene fades, but Becky's smile is imprinted on my brain, because it tells me everything I need to know.

Scrabbling in my handbag for my mobile, I scroll contacts and press the call button. 'Charlie, it's me.'

Charlie tuts. 'Yeah, I know that because, duh, your name comes up on my—'

'Cut the snarky bloody c-comments.' My words tumble over each other to be free but tangle themselves up in the rush. My pulse is racing and my hand's shaking so much I can hardly hold the phone.

'Hey, you alright, Nance?'

I take a deep breath, blow it out in slow release and say, 'I think I know how to find Becky.'

Chapter Three

The wind reaches icy fingers under my hood, pulls out strands of hair and uses them as a blindfold. I yank them free, tuck them back in again and tighten the cords at my chin. It's not the best day for a walk, but after the call to Charlie, I have a need to feel the salt breeze on my skin, walk the cliff paths. The sun's playing hide and seek with some charcoal clouds. I'm guessing the clouds might get tired of the game soon and bugger off. Being on the beach and by the water calms me like nothing else can – a salve for my raw emotions. Charlie said he'd meet me on the bench at St Georges Cove. I could tell he'd prefer to just talk in the house, but I told him that after my session with Becky's things, I needed to get out for walk. The walls of our cottage felt too close and confined. I get like that sometimes when I'm inside. Trapped like a snail under the weight of its shell.

Half an hour later I'm on the ridge overlooking the cove. The wind's behind me now trying to push me over the edge so I lean back into it, watch three seagulls trying their best to get across the estuary without being yanked into the water. They are calling to each other, all of them determined to have the last word. At the other side of the estuary, in the distance, I can see a few walkers on Rock Beach and towards Daymer Bay. I adore it there and plan to take a little visit soon, it's been too long. In the summer those beaches will be swarming with holiday makers, but now they are pristine, deserted and bring a touch of the tropical island to a windswept Cornish winter.

There are some little brightly coloured dots on the stretch of blue at Daymer; kite-surfers, I think. I keep promising myself to get back into surfing, but I never do. I was a keen surfer in my youth, spending endless summer days riding the waves. Then in the evenings, a group of friends and I would light a fire on the beach, talk about our dreams, share a few beers and delight in the simple pleasures of being young and free of responsibility. I tell myself off for breaking my promise to get back in the water again, and make another that I'll do just that before the end of the year.

I spot the bench a little way off and a dog walker heading towards me. I sprint down the path just in case the dog walker's heading for the same place to rest. A one-sided game of musical chairs. On the bench I catch my breath and nod as the dog walker passes. The dog shows interest in my wellingtons, but the owner just tugs on the lead, walks on, head down, expression closed. Perhaps she's not best pleased that I won the game. On the other hand, she's probably just anxious to get behind closed doors and in the warm.

My mobile phone says 14:10. Charlie should be here in a few minutes with any luck. The bench is bone cold and it won't be long before I am too. A few minutes later, a tall figure in a green hooded coat strides over the hill and down the path. It's Charlie, hunched-shouldered, hands stuffed in his pockets and even from this distance I can see he's frowning.

When he's in hailing range he says, 'Bloody hell, Nance, it's brass monkeys out here!'

'It's a bit fresh!' I grin and the cold air grabs the opportunity to kiss the warm inside of my lips, so I purse them and blow into my cupped hands.

The bench jolts as Charlie plops himself down next to me. Facing me and the wind, I see that his nose is a lovely shade of pink and his eyes are watering. 'Why can't we go home and have a nice cup of tea and some of that apple pie you brought back from the Kettle yesterday? I can't think straight out here in the Arctic.'

'A bit of an exaggeration, it's April next week. But yes, it is a quite nippy. Just five-minutes and we'll go.'

'Okay. I'm timing you,' he grumbles looking at his watch. 'Right, what have you got for me? You say you know how to find Becky.'

His tone is already verging on disbelief, before I've even said anything. My hackles go up, a growl's in my throat, but I reserve my bite until I'm sure it's needed. 'Yes. As I said on the phone, I had the rolling film connection as well as a good few snapshots from the book and bear.'

Charlie blows into cupped hands and tugs his hood further down his forehead. 'Yeah, and why you couldn't have told me the rest over the phone instead of dragging me—'

'For goodness sake, just listen! I needed to clear my head, process what I'd learnt.' Charlie looks suitably chastened, so I continue. 'The bear told me that Becky is so unhappy. She didn't want to leave home because she loves her parents, but she's under the spell of someone. And the photo in the book and the footage I saw confirm—'

'Footage?' The wind whips his hood back and nips his short hair into stiff peaks.

'Yes. The rolling film scenes I see. I told you about it the other day.' He's so slow on the uptake sometimes. 'Anyway, it confirmed that she's under the spell of who I think must be one of the teachers, and her best friend knows all about it.' I pull the photo out of my pocket and flick my finger at the face of the girl with blonde hair and freckles. 'This is the friend' Then I point to a good-looking man in his mid-twenties with dark curly hair sitting at the end of their row. 'And *this* is the teacher.' Becky's smile's directed at him. I look up just in time to see Charlies' best, 'you've got to be joking' face tuck itself under one of fake-contemplation.

'Really? Ye-s. Well…' He pulls his hood back down, twists his mouth and looks across the estuary. 'Hate to say it. But I think you're barking up the wrong tree on this, love.'

'Why's that?' My question's curt, clipped.

Charlie doesn't look back at me, just sighs and shoves his hands into his pockets. 'Dawn Owen. The blonde girl, *is* her best friend – so you're right about that.' He gives me a friendly nudge and treats me to an encouraging smile. Can he get anymore patronising? 'She's been questioned a few times and the poor girl's completely in bits about losing her friend. If she knew where she was, she'd say.'

'Not if she's promised Becky. You don't know the strength of friendship between teenage girls like I do.'

He glances at me, raises and eyebrow. 'How many teenage girls do you know?'

'None. But I *did* used to be one, Charlie.'

'Hmm.' He looks back at the scene.

'Don't hmm, me. I know what I'm on about. And I reckon she's with that teacher and feels powerless to get away.' I close my eyes and think about how Becky sobbed when she was nursing her teddy bear. 'She's conflicted, bewildered and out of her depth.'

Charlie stands up and turns to face me. 'Mr Johnathan Markham's been questioned too – as have all the staff who taught Becky, or had anything at all to do with her. One or two seemed a bit dodgy so we put them under surveillance. Nothing at all. Diddly squat.'

'And Johnathan Markham?'

Charlie bites his bottom lip. 'It's confidential, all of this is of course. But Markham's gay. Hate to say it, but you're—'

'If you say anything about barking dogs and trees, I'll lamp you one.'

He sniffs and looks at his watch. 'Time's up. Let's go back and have that cuppa.'

We walk in silence for a while. Charlie tries to start a conversation a few times about the case, but my head is so packed full of thoughts it feels like an overstuffed cushion. There's something not right here. I'm as certain as I can be that this Markham *is* who Becky's with. The smile they shared on the footage told me everything I needed to know. She was in love with him. And him with her? Perhaps. He was certainly in lust. So, logic dictates that…

I grab Charlie's elbow and he jumps in surprise. I say, 'He has to be lying, Charlie. He's straight. He and Becky are in a relationship.'

BACK IN THE cottage and full of apple pie and tea, Charlie sits in his favourite armchair and toasts his feet at the wood burner. His eyes go on a slow blink and then he yawns. He'll be asleep before I get him to agree to my plan if I'm not careful.

'So, first thing tomorrow will you get someone to question Dawn again? Tell her you know she's hiding something – put the frighteners on her. Tell her she's obstructing the course of justice. Then when she tells you where Becky is, go and arrest Markham. Becky might be safe at home with her parents by this time tomorrow, thank God.'

Charlie does a dramatic eye roll. 'Okay, Miss Marple. I'll get right on it.'

If he shuts his eyes again, I swear I'll… 'I'm not in the mood for this. Why can't you do as I ask?'

'Because it's ridiculous. You can't just go round willy-nilly threatening fifteen-year-old girls. Hauling them into the station and what-not. We have to arrange it properly, get the parents to be there, stuff like that. There's procedure. And we don't have any new evidence to warrant it.'

I'm finding it hard to keep my temper. There's a little figure of indignation stomping round my chest. 'What I found out is the new evidence. I know it's true, Charlie. I can feel it in here.' I thump my left breast.

'Oh right. I'll tell my boss that, shall I? We've got to speak to Dawn Owen and Johnathan Markham again, because my missus feels it in here?' He does the chest thump and tuts.

I sit on the edge of his armchair and take a deep breath try to slow my racing pulse. 'No, of course not. When we started all this, you said you'd keep my involvement a secret. Just tell her that you have a hunch. Say you've been reading the notes again and something's pointing you to Dawn. The way Becky's looking at Markham on the photo too. That's enough to start with, isn't it?'

Charlie rubs his eyes. 'I don't know, Nance. It all seems a bit airy fairy.'

'So just let's ignore it, hope it sorts itself out?' He toasts his feet some more, shrugs. I say, 'If I'd have ignored the ghost that told me to warn my mother about going for a walk on the cliff path, I'd have been motherless.'

30

Now he looks interested. 'Eh? When was this?'

'I was eight. The ghost of an American airman walked through our garden when I was playing with my doll's house on the patio. He said "Tell your ma not to go for her walk later. Looks like rain."'

Charlie smirks. 'And did it?'

'No.' But it had been raining for days before hand.

'And?'

'And I told her. She didn't go. Then we heard on the news that night, that part of the cliff path she always walked on had collapsed into the sea.'

I watch his face for signs of scepticism. There were none. He gives me a level stare. 'Look, Nance. I *do* think there must be something to all your…' he puts his head on one side, circles his hands in the air and then lets them slap onto his thighs like a couple of landed fish. Words of description have obviously failed him. '…More than I did before, anyhow. But I can't see what you told me being right. Let's just see what happens. If we don't find her in a week or two, we'll try your suggestion.'

I get up from the arm of his chair go to the kitchen and wash up the empty pie dish. I need to put some distance between us. There's a hollow feeling in the pit of my chest where nervous excitement had been earlier, just before I handled Becky's things.

Disappointment fills the pit and a general feeling of deflation settles over me. I feel used and discarded like an old pair of socks with too many holes. Not fit of purpose, just because can't present him with the street name and address of where to find Becky. Is that what he was expecting? Probably, or something like it. But then perhaps I'm being too hard on him. The majority of the population do find psychic ability hard to swallow. It's not your general everyday stuff, is it? Well, except for people like me.

I finish washing up and tidying the kitchen and decide to try and make Charlie see it from my point of view. The last few months I've been having more connections of various kinds. More than is normal for me anyhow. It's as if I'm being told that I need to be more productive… Actively use my abilities to help others more, rather than just let them come, or pass me by at random. The connection with the elderly couple the other day was upsetting, and yes, draining, but I could tell Graham felt a certain amount of relief when he realised he'd made the right decision about his future. And his face had shown such gratitude when I'd told him his dad had always loved him. These are the things that help us make sense of life. Sometimes satisfaction and wellbeing can't be found in material possession, or the next thing to look forward to. Acceptance, love and the absence of fear is often all we need. If my connections can help people achieve that, then their life will be so much the richer. My life too. But how will I make the change?

An idea that my time at the Whistling Kettle is coming to an end has been pulling at my sleeve for a while now. The pack of new aprons that were delivered yesterday won't be opened if I can help it. But what exactly will I do to fulfil my desire to help others in the only way people like me can? At the moment an answer escapes me in a general sense, but in the specific, I have Becky to help. Maybe she's the first of many. I dry my hands on a tea-towel and decide to make Charlie listen. But when I go back in the living room, I find he's asleep. Shall I wake him? He looks so peaceful, and he probably deserves a break from all this. God knows the things he must have seen over the years. In the early days he used to talk about some of his cases, but then he told me he wanted to try and leave all the angst and misery behind at work. That made sense, but I don't think you can in his type of job. I'm sure many a pressing problem and sad event have slipped out of the station, hitched a ride with him and found a home in the creases and wrinkles of his forehead.

I switch off the table lamp, sink into my matching armchair at the other side of the log burner, and watch the light from glowing red embers play a flickering chase with shadow across his face. No point in waking him. He obviously needs his rest.

But then so do Becky and her parents. God knows how they must be feeling. Actually, I do have an inkling…more than an inkling. Old wounds threaten to rip open, bleed out heart-wrenching memories. So I squash them – force them into the far recesses of my mind and focus on Becky. A daring idea presents itself. I glance at Charlie. No. If it all went wrong, he would be furious…but if it worked…

The daring idea waits. Won't go away. So I grab it with both hands, fold it into my heart and keep it safe for tomorrow.

Chapter Four

At least the weather's kinder this morning, which is a blessing, because standing on a street corner for nearly half-an-hour, trying to look nonchalant would be impossible with rain hammering down and a hooley blowing around my ankles. Wearing a skirt today wasn't the best idea. The high school which Dawn and Becky attends sprawls a few hundred yards away across the road. Parents are beginning to roll up now in their four by fours, evacuating their offspring by the gates like huge metal beasts giving birth. Please don't let Dawn be in one of them. Let her walk in like some of the other kids now dawdling up the street. Dragging their feet. Their hearts and minds anywhere but here.

For the fifth time I pretend to talk into my mobile phone, look up and down the street as if I'm waiting for someone. And then I see her behind a group of younger kids. She's fairly tall, and her bright blonde hair is shining in the weak morning sunlight. She's on her own. *It's now or never.* I stick my sunglasses on, shove my phone in my pocket, pull the drawstrings of my hood tight under my chin and cross the street. My pulse rate's rocketing and I'm rehearsing my lines as if I'm a shoo-in for an Oscar. I let her almost walk past me and then I tap her arm. 'Dawn, can I have a quick word?' I give her my best friendly smile.

Dawn's gaze sweeps the length of me and settles on my face. She gives a half-smile, then frowns. 'Err…who are you?'

'I'm a friend of Becky's family. I want to have a word because they're at their wit's end.'

Dawn sighs, shakes her head and her ponytail swings. 'I'm sorry, but I don't know anything. I told the police over and over.' I watch as the truth is submerged beneath her sea-grey eyes and heat floods her cheeks. She looks over my shoulder towards the school gates.

I step nearer the railings to let a trio of boys walk past and beckon her to do the same. I notice her bite the inside of her cheek and her eyes flit about like a couple of unsettled butterflies, but she side-steps. Good. Swallowing my apprehension, I fix her with a level stare and say in a low voice, 'Look. I know that you know where Becky is. I also know you promised to keep her secrets, but she's upset, confused and deep down she wants to end this.' I temper my words with a little smile. 'She just wants her mum.'

The butterflies look like they're being hunted by a sparrow and she steps round me, head down. 'I don't know nothing.' I lightly place my hand on her shoulder, but she shrugs me off. Starts to walk away.

'Stop right there, young lady,' I say in a voice that sounds like my mother's. Dawn stops, gives me a sidelong glance then directs her gaze to her feet. 'You know everything. You know about Mr Markham…everything.'

Dawn's mouth drops open and her cheeks turn pink. 'How…I mean…' She stops her words with a cupped hand.

I square my shoulders, set my jaw. 'Never mind how I know. The important thing is that if you keep Becky's whereabouts a secret, you're obstructing the course of justice. You'll get a criminal record when all this comes out, and it will come out, Dawn…eventually.' I try a raised eyebrow and fold my arms. Mainly to stop my hands trembling. 'All you need to do is tell me where she is, okay?'

Tears build behind the sea-grey eyes and her complexion pales, leaving her freckles looking like cinnamon sprinkles on cappuccino. I feel like a bully, but it has to be done. In a small voice she says, 'I-I don't know where she is. Well, I know it's a caravan in Newquay, but she hasn't said exactly where. She said the less I knew the better, in case they tried to get me to spill.'

Relief courses through my veins like a freight train. It's all I can do to stop myself not whooping for joy. 'Okay. But you're in touch still.' It's a statement not a question. She nods, bites her bottom lip. I pull out my phone, scroll to contacts. 'Give me her mobile number.'

A tear spills onto her cheeks. 'I promised her I'd never tell.'

Poor kid. 'I know, love. But this is for the best. Trust, me. She's in above her head and she'll thank you in the end.'

Dawn pulls out her phone, recites a number and brushes the back of her hand across her eyes. 'Is that all?' Her tone's defiant, angry.

'Yes…thank you. And you have done the right thing, Dawn. You'll see. And don't even think of phoning Becky and warning her, or Markham for that matter. You'll be in big trouble if you do.'

At first Dawn looks as if she's going to ask more questions, but her expression darkens. She tosses her head and snorts. 'Yeah, whatevas.' Then she pushes past and strides down the street to the school gate.

HALF-AN-HOUR LATER I'M in Newquay in Aldi's car park. My stomach's churning and I pace the car park, then stop to look at the white caps the Atlantic is wearing and wonder for the umpteenth time whether to just hand the whole thing over to Charlie and his colleagues now. They can go and pull Markham and Dawn out of school, make him take her to Becky. My gut tells me Becky will be more likely to go home willingly if I have a word first, though. Her feelings will be in turmoil, and the last thing we want is for her to resent her parents and the police – see Markham as a defeated hero.

Charlie might think I'm being a Miss Marple, but I genuinely want to let her know that people will understand. Maybe she'll listen to me. I need to make a decision. Then I think of Becky's turmoil – the chaos of her feelings that were almost palpable when I held her teddy close to me yesterday, and realise I've already made it. The weather's turning, so I set my back to the wind and walk down past the shopping trolleys, and into the public phone box on the corner. Then if the police take Becky's phone later, I can't be traced. With trembling fingers, I call her number.

'Hello, who's this?' A girl's voice asks. God. She sounds so young, so vulnerable. But then she is, isn't she? She's fifteen. Just a kid. Johnathan Markham has taken advantage of a child. Anger pushes from my depths and I picture myself slapping him. Telling him exactly what I think of him.

'Hello?' she says again, irritation has replaced curiosity.

I take a big breath. 'Hello, Becky. You don't know me, but I'm a friend. I know you are a very unhappy young lady, and that you don't know how to tell your boyfriend. I also know that right now you'd like to go home to your mum and dad. They miss you so much, Becky.'

There's a long sniff and a muffled sob. 'How do you...I mean who are you?'

'That's not important right now. I need you to tell me where you are so we can get you home, sweetheart.'

'No. I can't go back. Not...not after what I've done.' Becky stumbles over her words and begins to cry in earnest now. Huge gut-wrenching sobs that break my heart.

'Listen, Becky,' I say. But she can't hear me because she's crying so much. I raise my voice and hope my tone is more soothing than shouty. 'Listen Becky, you have done nothing wrong, do you hear me? Nothing.'

'I have. Not only have I run away from home...but I have been sleeping with my boyfriend and my parents will go mad when they know who he is...' There's a sudden break in the wailing and her voice holds a note of uncertainty. 'D-Do you know who he is?'

'I do. And I know that's why you're not to blame.'

This elicits fresh sobs which take a while to pass. 'Johnathan's not a bad person you know.'

I beg to differ. 'Of course he isn't. I think he must feel as trapped by the situation as you do. Just tell me where you are, and we can sort this whole thing out together.'

'Will he get into trouble? You know…with the police? I love him…but he hasn't let me speak to anyone. He doesn't even know I sometimes speak to Dawn. I hate it here, but if I leave, he'll get in trouble and he won't love me no more.'

Now what? I have to keep lying, because I have to get her to tell me where she is. 'I think if he says sorry, they will be lenient with him. And if he loves you, he will understand. But you're my main concern. You need to go home. Now, can you let me know where you are?'

'It's a caravan park. I can't remember the name of it. I haven't been allowed out since…you know.' More crying.

'Hey, calm yourself, Becky. Go outside now, have a look.'

There's some rustling and a door banging, the sound of footsteps as Becky walks along what sounds like gravel. 'I can see the sea. I think Johnathan said it's Crantock.'

'Okay, Becky. Well done, love. Now stay there, I'll send someone to get you.'

'No! No I only want you!' she wails. 'I'm not coming if it's not you.'

What now? I promised Charlie I'd keep well out of it. There's no way his boss can find out my involvement. 'Okay, okay. Don't worry. In a little while you'll be safe.'

'So you're coming?'

I thump the wall with the heel of my hand. This kid has been manipulated and lied to enough, but I can't risk her running off, panicking…I swallow down guilt and say, 'Yeah. I'll be there as soon as I can. Is there a number on the caravan so I can come straight there?'

I hear more crunching gravel. 'Err…yeah. Twenty-Seven and there's a metal red rose thing under it too.'

'Great. Go inside now and I'll be there very soon. You have been very brave and have done the right thing, Becky.'

'Have I though?'

Her tearful little voice reaches inside me, threatens to yank out all the pain of stolen motherhood, all my years of anguish and loss, screaming into the daylight for all to see. To reduce me to a sobbing wreck right there in the wind tunnel by the regimented shopping trolleys. It's all I can do not to break all the rules and run straight to her. Envelop her in my empty arms. But this is about Becky and her future. Not me and my past. From emergency reserves, I dredge up a voice resembling normality and say, 'Absolutely. See you soon.'

Chapter Five

I'm in the car now staring through the windscreen. It's warmer in here, yet inside I'm cold. Numb. 'You actually spoke to her?' From the car phone, Charlie's disembodied and incredulous words provide a soundtrack to the silent ocean. It's beating its fists against the harbour wall as the weather deteriorates. 'That's bloody fantastic, Nance! She's in a caravan at Crantock? There are only one or two parks there. We'll find her in no time.' Charlie gives a short bark of laughter, relief and surprise in its delivery.

'Yes. Please be quick. Take a WPC, tell Becky I'm sorry but I couldn't come. Say I really care about what happens to her and hope she'll be happy. And Charlie, be gentle. Be very gentle.'

The scene outside blurs as a raincloud overhead sprays a machine-gun fire of raindrops across the windscreen. I think about another child. A long-ago moment where a little hand slipped into mine. It's warm and tiny, and my fingers close around it like a protective glove. I hear a voice calling me mummy, see the ghost of a smile…I swallow as tears rise, threaten to copy the clouds. I feel removed from myself. So I fixate on my coat zipper, the red waterproof material…I'm wearing my oldest tan fur-lined boots because they're comfy, but judging by my wet sock, they must have developed a hole in the heel.

'You didn't tell her your name and who you were?'

Charlie's obvious concern about my involvement being revealed is timely and welcome. Anger dries my tears, brings me out of the past with a jolt. 'No. I mean we wouldn't want that, would we? DS Charlie Cornish has a psychic for a wife. All that mumbo jumbo and hocus pocus interfering with good solid police work.'

'Hey, Nance. Don't be like that…'

'Just tell Becky you have no clue who I was. Tell her and your boss that you were tipped off by a member of the public who saw a girl at the caravan park that she recognised from the newspaper. She hung up, wouldn't leave her name.'

'But what about Dawn? She saw you, talked to you.'

'I had my hood up and pulled tight round my face, had sunglasses on. Forget that now. We'll talk later. Get going!'

'Okay, Nancy. Thanks.'

'HI, HONEY, I'M home!' Charlie says to my back as I lift the apple pie from the oven and wipe the side down, while closing the freezer door with my foot.

'Great timing. It will be about ten minutes!' I turn and give him a smile. 'I made your favourites for dinner.'

'I know. I could smell the wonderful aromas of apple pie and spaghetti Bolognese as soon as I step through the front door. It's like being hugged by a childhood memory.'

'You're in a good mood!'

I am! Bolognese followed by apple pie and cream — what more could a man ask? I'm cold, tired and hungry, but I don't care, because today has been one of the best in my entire career. Charlie walks over and takes me in his arms. 'Thank you so much for today. You have no idea how happy I am. Sorry for the brief text. I wanted to ring, but the office has been in a whirlwind.'

I kiss him quickly on the lips, and look him in the eye. 'I've been on tenterhooks since that text. Tell me all about it.'

Charlie looks at his watch. 'I'll do better than that. Come on.' He leads me into the living room and grabs the remote. 'Time for the local news.' Charlie flops onto the sofa and I perch on the arm, a tea-towel over my shoulder.

The familiar face of the presenter is all smiles as he says, 'There was rejoicing in Padstow today when missing teenager, Becky Proctor was reunited with her parents. The local girl had been missing for over three weeks after she failed to return home from school on the afternoon of the fifth. Everyone had begun to fear the worst.'

There's a big picture of Becky on the screen and then a shot of her school.

'But this morning, Becky was located by police in a caravan park in Newquay. This was after a sighting of the teenager by a member of the public, who then tipped off the police. Investigating officer, DS Cornish said that the police and Becky's family would be eternally grateful to this person, who wanted to remain anonymous.'

Charlie looks at me, takes my hand, kisses the back of it. 'I can't stop thinking about the moment when the caravan door opened and Becky looked at me, her eyes wide, fearful. Her fear turned to relief when she realised who DCI Summercourt and I were. It was as if she'd been waiting to be rescued. As if some evil enchantment had been lifted and she was set free. Allowed to be a kid again.'

'We understand that a member of staff at the school has been arrested and is helping police with their enquiries.'

I look at Charlie. 'So has he admitted everything?'

'Yeah. He couldn't do much else, could he? The caravan belongs to him. Becky has told us everything. I reckon he's going to get between eight and ten years.'

I throw my hands up. 'What a bloody fool.' I go back to the kitchen and Charlie follows. 'I mean, what the hell did he think would happen? He and Becky would live happily ever after in a caravan? She'd never go out again for the rest of her life?' I stir the sauce, and slide garlic bread out of the oven.

'God knows. Abigail and Bob are questioning him at the moment.'

I raise an eyebrow at him and drain the spaghetti. 'Abigail now is it? You normally call her boss, even when we were at the Christmas party…and why Bob? Surely you should be there, given you were the one tipped off and found Becky. I was surprised when you said you'd be home for dinner to be honest.'

Charlie grins. 'I told a fib. Said I'd got a stomach bug and Abigail said I must go home. I'm her favourite person now. Her new bestie.'

I frown. Put the spaghetti down and fold my arms. 'Really? Why did you fib and why is she your bestie?'

'I fibbed because I wanted to be here with you. You're the hero of the hour, not me. If it wasn't for your…um intuition, Becky would still be in the caravan with Markham. And why's she my bestie? Just before you phoned and told me where Becky was, I'd been saying to her that I reckon we should interview Johnathan Markham again, Dawn too. It was a hunch I had. You know, like you told me to say last night?' I nod. 'I said I'd been looking through her file again and I thought Becky was still alive. It was something about her expression on the school photo. The way she was looking at Markham.'

'Blimey. That would have impressed her.'

'It did. Then when I said a woman had just phoned about the caravan park, me and her jumped in a car and off we went! Little Becky's frightened face when she opened the door, proper sent a lump to my throat, though.'

The thought of another little face brings a lump to mine. I busy myself putting the spaghetti into bowls. 'Let's eat this before it gets cold. Can you get the cutlery out and pour the wine, Charlie? And then I want to ask you more about Becky.'

Charlie has a mouthful of spaghetti when I ask what Becky said when he and the boss showed up. He swallows it, dabs his mouth with a napkin and says, 'She asked if Abigail was the lady on the phone from earlier who she'd spoken to. I didn't know where to look, Nance. It was really awkward. Obviously, Abigail...' He stops. 'Actually, Abigail feels wrong. I'm going back to calling her the boss. Anyway, she didn't have a clue what Becky was talking about, and I had to play dumb.

'That was easy for you then,' I say crunching into a piece of garlic bread, my expression deadpan.

'Oh, ha ha.' Charlie takes a sip of wine. 'The boss noted down the number you called Becky from. A public phone, clever.'

'That's me. Clever's my middle name.' I pull a face.

'Hmm. Becky was so upset, scared of what her parents would say. The boss told her not to worry about it and was really nice to her. I've never seen her so caring to be honest.'

'Good. I thought she was lovely on the few occasions we've met. At the Christmas party we discussed meeting up for a drink, as you know. But never got round to it. And Becky will have needed careful handling. Poor kid would have been in a mess – her head will be all over the place. Even now she's home, she'll be conflicted.' I stop. There's a catch in my voice and a tickle at the back of my nose.

Charlie looks up from his plate at my eyes, which are swimming in tears. I sniff and dab at them with my napkin. He asks, 'What's up, love?'

I shake my head and push a fork of spaghetti around the dish. 'It's silly really. I felt like I'd betrayed her when I said I'd come and get her, then I didn't. I know I had to do it for her sake, but I lied to her. She's only a child. A child that has been abused, taken away from her parents…then another adult lies to her too…' I drop my fork, cover my face with my hands. 'She sounded so vulnerable. So needy.'

'Hey, Nance. You did what you had to. She'll understand. And she's back with her parents now.'

I try to stop them, but my shoulders start to shake and tears escape through my fingers. Charlie comes over, gives me a squeeze. 'No. Don't do that. It'll make me worse. I'll be okay in a minute, love.' I wipe my face and pat his knee. I can't afford to give into this sadness.

Charlie looks at me. I look away, take a sip of wine. He hovers for a moment, then obviously at a loss, he goes back to his plate, picks his fork up, then sets it back down again. 'Nance. I know it's been a bit of a day for us all, but why are you so sad? Becky's been found because of you. What am I missing here?'

I can hardly get my words out. The depth of pain in me is like a punch to the gut. 'It's what *I'm* missing. I know we don't talk about him much because it's still too painful...but it's sixteen years today since Sebastian...since our little boy...' A sob breaks through and I cover my face again, talk through my fingers. 'Speaking to Becky brought all the old hopes and dreams...' I blow my nose. '...all the 'what ifs' to the surface. What if maybe nowadays medical science has answers to his heart problems. Maybe nowadays he would have lived. And the loss, Charlie. It brought the fact back that my chance to be a mother has long passed. I feel empty in here.' I clasp my hand to my stomach. 'And here.' I thump my heart.

I wipe my tears. Mostly I try to keep memories of that time submerged. The pain of losing Seb and before that, the anguish of being told because of the complications of his birth, we wouldn't be able to have more children. Now and then, and usually unexpectedly, a memory escapes and swims to the surface. And it does help when his spirit visits. But lately the past has been a frequent companion. Especially today…Sebastian's birthday…if he'd have lived beyond the three months he'd been given, he'd have been the same age as Becky.

'I've just twigged what day it is…and I'm so sorry, Nance. I don't know what to say.' Charlie rubs his chin. 'I should have realised before, but I've been really busy and…like you said, thinking about him is so painful. I don't have the words to make you feel better. Just wish I did.'

'I know you don't. Nobody does. But, Charlie, I might have some words to make you feel better. You're still hurting too, even though you don't acknowledge it. Not out loud anyhow.' I trace a finger down his cheek. 'And now that you understand what you call my mumbo jumbo a bit more because of me finding Becky, I want to tell you something.'

Charlie swallows and clears his throat. 'What is…' he begins. Then he tries for levity. 'No emotional bullets please, I've left my Kevlar vest at work.' I give him a look and he stops smiling.

'It's Sebastian. About two years after he passed, he came back to see me. I wasn't even thinking about him. I was just in the shop, wiping down the counter and I turned to see a little boy by the door. He was dressed in blue denim dungarees and yellow T-shirt, looked about five-years old. He had your dark hair, except it was curly and he had my eyes. I knew right away it was him, even though he wasn't a baby.' I stop, take a breath. 'He said…' Fresh tears chase older ones down the landscape of my face. 'He said *I love you, Mummy. Please don't be sad, because I'm happy.* Then he gave me the most beautiful smile and did the off switch.'

Charlie blinks. 'The what? Did you say the off switch?'

I give a soft laugh. 'Yeah. It's when spirits just vanish, like someone's turned a light off.'

'Oh. I see.'

Charlie's expression tells me otherwise, but I leave it. 'Since then, he's visited me about six times over the years. Sometimes when I'm missing him, other times for no apparent reason. He's sometimes about five – sometimes a little older. And once,' My words are caught in a sob and I take a moment. 'Once I was out in the garden doing a bit of weeding and I put the garden fork down, only to feel his little hand take mine. It was warm, solid and the sense of him being there, *being really alive*, took my breath away. That time he just said Mummy. Nothing, else. Then he looked up at me, shielded his eyes from the sun and kissed my hand. Next he was gone.'

Charlie's eyes fill, and his face can't decide whether to be happy or sad. So it's both at the same time. Any words of comfort for him have become trapped in my throat. I shake my head and get up from the table, take my plate to the sink.

To my back he says, 'I'm sorry for being so insensitive, Nance. And I'm glad our boy visits you.'

I release a huge sigh and turn to him. 'So am I, sweetheart.'

We are left with our own thoughts. The kitchen is silent, save for the plop, plop, plop of a dripping tap in the sink. Charlie's staring ahead, watching a droplet of water form, grow fat and fall. Then another and another. The buoyant mood we shared earlier has been crushed under the weight of not enough yesterdays with our boy, and the burden of too many tomorrows without him. An overwhelming desolation takes hold of us both. I watch Charlie's face. His usual resolve to be strong is driven to its knees, as a tear droplet forms, grows fat and falls. Then another and another.

Chapter Six

I'm back in work and it feels like the last three days haven't happened. It's as though I've been dragged through a vortex and planted back in the day before my break. We are up to our eyes in customers, and I haven't stopped rushing around for a minute since setting foot back in the place. It's so full-on. Before, I've just got on with it, told myself that others have it far worse. Now, I'm actually beginning to resent it. It swallows up my life, munching through it with great bites. My job prevents me from doing what I'm really supposed to.

Finding Becky and making a sort of breakthrough with Charlie about my connections, has given me such a boost. I was heartbroken at first, when all the memories of losing Sebastian became unexpectedly tangled up with Becky's story. But after Charlie's heartfelt comment about him being glad our boy visits, and the way he was touched by it, the future looks so much brighter. Though I knew I was fed up with waitressing, throughout the day, the unshakable conviction that my future lies in using my connection properly is lodged firmly in my head and heart. The next hurdle is, how exactly will I do it? I'm no closer to finding the answer to that than I was a few days ago.

In the kitchen, I place two bowls of minestrone soup with a plate of homemade bread on a tray and deliver them to a young couple by the window. They're sitting in the same places as the elderly couple Graham and Marge had been, when Graham's father made a connection. They both have short dark hair and wearing waterproofs, walking boots and looks of love on their fresh faces. When I took their order, the woman was twirling a shiny gold band and diamond ring around the third finger of her left hand – a silent but joyful proclamation of their recent marriage. The guy could barely tear his gaze from hers as he asked me what the soup of the day was.

They thank me and I watch them from the counter as they eat. I wonder how Graham and Marge are doing and if they will ever be back. Then I remember how much in love they still were, maybe not in the same way as the young couple are by the window right now, but no less strongly or deeply. Love for a partner's a funny thing. If you're lucky it's always present, but not the same. It changes – morphs into something else, other manifestations. Over time, the love I have for Charlie, and his for me, I think, has lost the immediacy and the intensity of longing to see each other at the end of each day. I imagine these honeymooners must still feel that way.

Nevertheless, I do miss him when he's working late and the sound of his key in the door lifts my heart, just as much as it ever did over twenty-years ago. Our love is a constant in my life. I don't have to question it. It's there, always. Like a heartbeat, keeping me alive. Safe.

'You alright, Nance? You look miles away,' Leanne asks as she breezes past.

'Yeah, just thinking about life, the universe and everything.'

'Right. Not much then. Did you take that woman in the corner's order – just come in about five-minutes back?' Leanne nods at a thirty-something, black suited woman with a blonde ponytail. She's absently picking her nails, her gaze flitting between the fishing boats in the harbour and a phone on the table.

'Oops, no I didn't see her. On it now.' I twist a few strands of hair that have come loose up into my tortoiseshell clip, dust flour from my red and green stripy apron and hurry over.

Because the woman's sitting in a corner table with her chair obstructing the walkway, I have to squeeze past. In doing so, over her shoulder, I see a text that's just come through on her phone. *Sorry I'm late. Will try and get there by 1.30 xx*

The woman replies to the text and sighs. She startles when I ask if I can get her anything. 'Goodness! I didn't hear you come over.' Her cheeks flush pink but there's a smile in her blue eyes.

'Sorry. You were lost in your phone.' I smile too, and take my order pad out of my pocket.

'Ah yes. My husband has let me down again. He said he'd be here at 12.45 and now he says he won't be here for another half hour. Marvellous.' Her tone is light, jokey even, but I can tell she's irritated. Hurt perhaps.

'Do you want to wait for him?' I hope she doesn't, because we're so busy and need the table.

'No. I'm starving and he might not make it anyway. He's so busy with his job. He's an estate agent. Well, part owner of the business actually.' Her words come out quick, and run into each other as if they're worried they'll be trapped – remain unreleased. 'And I've just got a promotion,' she sweeps her hand down the smart suit. 'I don't always dress like this.' She gives a nervous laugh as if she's just realised she's babbling on. 'And we're supposed to be celebrating with lunch and then a nice dinner this evening. Never mind.'

Those last two words hold a depth of feeling belying the matter of fact tone in which they're presented. I have a hunch that this young woman's used to being let down in all sorts of ways by her husband. 'Well, let's hope you have a nice evening instead.' I give her a big smile and hope it helps.

'Yes. Let's hope.' She looks at the menu. 'Can I have the prawn salad on ciabatta and a cup of tea please?'

I note it down and I am just about to leave, when she hands me her key fob. It has a photo of a handsome dark-haired man. 'That's Aaron. Love him to bits, even though he's a pain in the arse.' As I look at him, a series of images flash one after the other in my mind. Aaron kissing a woman with long dark hair, another with a different scantily clad woman sitting on his knee in what seems to be a club, and another with him kissing a woman who has blonde curly hair.

The woman's looking at me expectantly. She's probably wondering why I'm staring at the photo but not saying anything. 'He looks...nice,' I say and hand it back. I want to chuck it on the floor.

'You don't sound too sure?' She looks puzzled.

I think quickly. 'No, it's just that I think I might have seen him before. He has one of those faces.'

She brightens. 'He's an estate agent in town. Standish and White's, that's where you've probably seen him. He's Aaron Standish.' The pride in her voice is obvious as she says his name.

'Oh yeah! That's it.' I make a swift exit to the kitchen and prepare her lunch. Poor woman. She seems so nice and so in love with her husband. What an absolute shit of a man. His wife's waiting here to celebrate her promotion with him, and he's probably with one of those women I saw. Once again, I think how lucky I am to have Charlie. The poor girl deserves to know about his cheating, but I can't tell her, can I? How would I begin to explain what just happened when she handed me his photo?

Ten minutes later, the tea joins the prawn salad on a tray, and I'm just about to walk back into the café with it, when it hits me. I didn't actually look for this connection to a living person. The unpredictability of my gift never fails to puzzle me.

BACK HOME, MY hands are mixing together a marinade for the chicken stir-fry and chopping garlic, while my head's still puzzling over the woman's cheating husband connection this lunch time. What was I supposed to do with that information? Should I have said something? The more I think about it, the more I think I should have. Perhaps I could have said that someone told me he was often out with other women. Too late now. I stop and wash my hands and look at the clock. Charlie will be home in half-an-hour. Just enough time to talk this new development through with someone who will understand.

Fishing my mobile out of my bag, I pace the kitchen and bite my nails. Then I wish I hadn't, as the bite of raw garlic burns my tongue. 'Penny, do you have a moment?'

'Um, I'm just making dinner. Is it a quickie?'

My heart sinks. 'Not really. It's about a weird connection I had this afternoon.'

She laughs and I can hear pans rattling in the background. 'Aren't they all weird in the normal world?'

'Yep. But this was another kind of weird.'

'O-kay. You're not really making much sense, Nancy.'

No, I'm not. And I realise there's too much to say over the phone. It's Saturday tomorrow, maybe she's free. 'Can we arrange to meet tomorrow? Just for coffee somewhere?'

'I could manage an hour about eleven?'

'Perfect.' We arrange to meet in town, and I feel so much better knowing I'll be able to get it all off my chest. It's no good talking to Charlie about it. He's not ready for more revelations – his head would explode. I'm laughing at this image when he comes in.

'How's tricks?' he says and kisses me on the neck.

'Tricks are okay. Might fancy another magic show soon though.' My cheeks flare with colour and I turn back to stirring the veg in the wok. Why did I say that?

'What do you mean?' Charlie picks a bit of carrot out of the pan and blows on it.

'I mean I'm getting a bit fed up of working in the café. Fancy a change.'

He knits his brows together and chews the carrot. 'But what would you do?'

'Not sure yet. But let's face it, we don't need the money since your parents left us their house and savings.'

Charlie presses his lips together and blows down his nose. Then he grabs a tissue and dabs at it. 'Look, Nance. That's our nest egg. We said we'd not touch it until we'd retired. We can't be too careful nowadays. I could lose my job, just like that!' He clicks his fingers and then pulls a face and looks at the damp tissue stuck to them.

This again. Charlie has always been careful with money. But both his parents died close together over the last two years, and now after their house sale, we have more than enough for our old age. There's no need at all for him to worry. I take the wok off the heat and turn to him, put my hands on my hips and look him in the eye. 'Charlie, how likely is it that you're going to lose your job? I mean, really?'

Charlie's eyes slide away and he walks over to the fridge, pulls out a bottle of lager. 'Alright, at the moment it's very unlikely. But you never know.'

Something about the way he said 'very unlikely' piques my interest. I serve up dinner and take the plates over to the table. 'Get me one of those, will you?' I nod at the bottle in his hand. Grabbing two glasses I sit opposite him and say, 'When's the promotion, then?'

Charlie nearly spits out his drink. His eyes widen and he wipes his mouth on the back of his hand. 'How the hell did you know?'

I nearly choke on my own drink. 'You've got a promotion?'

'No. But I was talking to Abigail, I mean DI Summercourt yesterday, and she said it hadn't gone unnoticed how well I'd dealt with the Becky Proctor case.' Charlie stops and he's the good grace to look embarrassed.

'Right. Well you did solve that case single-handedly, with not much to go on, didn't you?' I give him a smile, but can't help feeling a bit miffed.

'You did help quite a bit.' He smiles back and stuffs a forkful of food into his mouth.

Is he for real? I "helped"? How about I solved the whole thing with my connections, found out where Becky was through her best friend, and then badgered him to do something before it was too late? 'Er, yes, you could say that.'

'You were brilliant, love.' His tone is dismissive, and he doesn't even look up from his food.

A bit miffed graduates into annoyance now, to be honest. 'Not just mumbo jumbo, eh?'

'Course not.' He swallows those words down quickly with his food and waggles his fork at me. 'Anyway, the boss says if I wanted to put in for promotion, she'd back me up. In *theory*, solving cases makes absolutely no difference to a promotion. You have to do an exam and answer questions from a panel and stuff. But I think it will count for me in practice.' He's beaming now like a child who's got an unexpected 'A' for his homework from a stingy teacher.

I smile and he talks about a new case, while I listen absently and chew my thoughts along with the stir-fry. If he gets a promotion, there's even less worry about money. But would he have to move from Truro station? That would be no good. And there's no way I'm moving out of Cornwall. Or even out of Padstow come to that. This is my home. Where I belong. I wait for a break in his ramblings and voice my concerns.

'Well, that's the beauty of it. Old Bob is retiring at the end of the year and so there'll be a vacancy where I am. I wouldn't want to move either. So, it's all perfect, really.' He pushes his plate to the side and takes a long pull of his lager.

I think he might be getting ahead of himself but don't say so. 'Yeah, but as you say, you'll have exams to do. I don't want you counting your chickens.'

'Nice that you have confidence in me.'

'I do have confidence in you! But I know what you're like. You can't afford to take anything for granted, or you might be disappointed.'

'I know. But my success over Becky, plus the years of excellent service there will stand me in good stead.'

'Abigail said this?'

'We-ll, not in so many words.' He shifts in his seat and folds his arms. 'But that's the impression I got.'

Hmm. I'll have to find a way of getting through to him it might not be that simple. Of making him less complacent about it all, but tonight is not the time for that chat. 'Well, that's brilliant news.' I lean across and give him a peck on the cheek. Then I pick up our plates and take them to the sink. 'Oh, I'm popping out for coffee with Penny tomorrow morning. You hadn't planned anything, had you?'

'I'm working until three, so it makes no odds to me.'

'Oh, I'd forgotten that. Perhaps we could do something nice on Sunday if the weather's nice, then? A picnic at Crantock beach? We've not been there for ages.'

'Yeah, could do. You can make those sausage rolls I like.' He gets up from the table and goes upstairs.

I hear him run the shower. The same routine for twenty years. He comes home, eats the food I've cooked, then goes upstairs to shower and change while I clear away. I've even been instructed to make sausage rolls for Sunday's picnic. At the sink I plunge my hands into the washing up water, and stare at the bubbles gathering around my wrists. Why am I so grouchy? Why is our routine getting to me after all these years? He works later than I do, so if he cooked, the evening would be over before we'd had chance to enjoy time together. He used to help clear away, until I shooed him off upstairs to get changed so we could relax. So the poor guy's not to blame, is he? What's wrong with me? I was only thanking my lucky stars earlier because I had a man like him and not like bloody Aaron Standish.

Through the kitchen window, the first stars are venturing out, and a sickle moon ghosts between dark wisps of high cloud. The main sweep of lawn is in shadow now, though underneath the garden lights on the little patio, clumps of daffodils nearby nod together as if they're listening to my thoughts and agreeing with me. I wish I could see the water. In the daylight, because we're on such a steep hill I can see the River Camel in the distance as it laps the shores of the town, rushing on its way to the Atlantic just around the corner. Watching the water always calms me. I close my eyes and imagine it's daylight, and soon the answer to why I'm so moody settles into place.

For the first time in a long time, Charlie's excited about new prospects. Even though he's achieved success because of my connections, it's not what annoys me. Okay, it does a little, because my role will never be known. But it's more than that. He's fulfilled. He feels useful, a valuable part of the community. In short, he's doing what he wants with his life – going for his goals.

I need to do the same before I get left behind, like so much flotsam at low tide.

Chapter Seven

Everything feels different this morning when I set out to meet Penny. My moodiness has vanished with the night. Spring is bursting from the hedgerows lining the little lanes, and daffodil fields in the distance makes it look like the sun has crashed into the hills. The sky is an impossible blue, swept of cloud, and on days like this, it's hard to be downcast. There's a bounce in my step and a lightness of heart that I hadn't even noticed was missing. Very soon I'm in town, and am tempted by the cheery displays in the shop windows. Noting my reflection, I'm not so cheered by my hurriedly thrown together ensemble of chunky white sweater, shabby jeans and too-tight quilted grey jacket. Because of the sweater I look like I've gained a couple of stone and the crow's feet under my eyes could have benefited from a dab of foundation. Perhaps I could do with a makeover? Spring sales in my favourite clothes shop beckon me in, but if I don't get a wiggle on, I'll be late. My phone tells me I am already late. Never mind. I might treat myself on the way back.

I hurry along in the shade of tiny cobbled street, and at the end, a slice of the harbour view waits. It's like a narrow painting, except it's moving. Sun on their wings, gulls sweep in and out, alighting on rigging, and various brightly painted hulls rise and fall in a vigorous Mexican wave. The clank of halyards against masts grows louder as I approach, and once out of the street and in the harbour, the whole canvas is revealed to me in all its colour, noise and vibrancy.

Padstow harbour is full of bustle this morning. It's never quiet, but this early in the season it's nice to see. I wave at Leanne as I pass The Whistling Kettle. It's odd not going in, but a nice odd. Then dodging round a clump of selfie-taking tourists, I skirt the harbour wall and head for Cherry Trees Coffee House. This café is our main competition and I must admit, the standard of their cakes is neck-and-neck with ours. Some might say better, but not me. I do make most of ours after all.

Penny's there sitting at a table by the window. She's scrolling through her phone and seems lost in thought. Unlike me, Penny always looks smart, despite always wearing causal clothes. Today she's wearing a crisp blue shirt and brown jeans with her biscuit coloured hair twisted into a messy chignon. Nothing special, really, it's just that Penny has style. It comes naturally to some. The shirt reflects her eyes, the jeans tone with her hair. At the window, I watch her for a few seconds and then I pull a daft face. She doesn't see me though. An elderly woman sitting at the table behind her does, and her face can't decide if it's amused or disapproves. I stop larking about and tap on the window. Penny's head jerks up and a half-smile lifts one side of her mouth. She then does a mock frown and jabs a finger at her watch. I nod and make for the door.

As I walk inside, I'm greeted by a waft of fresh coffee, warm bread and garlic. My stomach politely reminds me that it missed breakfast and I plan to rectify that as soon as possible. Penny stands up and gives me a warm hug. She smells of roses and cinnamon. Can't recall the name of her perfume, must remember to ask. 'It's about time,' she says, sitting down again. 'I was just about to ring you.'

I widen my eyes in mock surprise. 'I'm not late, am I?'

'Ten minutes.'

I laugh. 'Ten minutes isn't late. Not for we born and bred Cornish folk. Everything is 'dreckly' here.'

'Er, I *have* lived here twenty-five years you know.' Penny shakes her head at me and sighs.

'Then you should know better, maid,' I say in a condescending tone and grab a menu. 'Ooh, the Cornish brie and bacon croissant looks good…but then so does the full Cornish breakfast.'

'You've not had breakfast yet? It's ten past eleven.'

'I forgot. I know we said just coffee, but I'm starving.'

Penny takes the menu. 'Mm, I've had breakfast, but the magic mushrooms look delicious.'

Did I hear her correctly? 'Magic mushrooms? Have you a penchant for hallucinatory fungi?'

She giggles. 'No. Look, it says, magic mushrooms – wild mushrooms, tomato relish, poached egg, and hollandaise on grilled walnut bread.'

I laugh. 'I didn't see that. Mm, it does look good. Let's order.'

WHILE WE WAIT for our food, we catch up on the day-to-day. Penny's husband Joe is thinking of early retirement. He's fifty-five next year and he's had enough of his teaching job. His great passion is painting, and he's had a few exhibited locally. Joe now wants to have a bash at doing it full-time. Penny says that if he doesn't follow his heart now, it will be too late when he's sixty-five. She's fully behind him and even though she's coming up to fifty, plans to increase her hours at the surgery. She's a secretary, receptionist, oversees the medical records. In short, she practically runs the place.

'Anyway, enough about my life. Tell me more about this 'weird connection' you had yesterday.' Penny leans her elbows on the table and rests her chin on interlocked fingers.

I tell her. 'So what do you make of that? Weird, no?'

'It is a bit. Will you—' She stops as our tea and coffee arrive. The waitress places our cups down and our cutlery. We thank her and then Penny takes a sip of coffee and stares into space towards the harbour behind me.

'Will I what?' I prompt.

'Will you try and warn this woman somehow? I feel that's why you were shown the philandering husband.'

'Not sure how I can. I don't know how to get in touch.'

'You know where the husband works, though. Maybe you could warn him instead.'

I hadn't thought of that. 'Yeah. That's a good idea.'

Penny's doing the staring through the window at the harbour thing again. 'You know, Nance, I think you're pretty special.' Her eyes focus again. She looks at me intently.

This isn't what I expected. What exactly does she mean? 'Thanks…but in what way?'

'Compared to me. Like you, I've had the spirit view, as I call it, since I was a kid. But mine is different to yours. I sometimes saw spirits and was never afraid, but seeing them never really meant anything to me, or anyone else. Later in life, I thought I'd try to help those who were missing loved ones who'd died. So, I'm more like a medium – a half-way house for messages between those who have passed and the living. As you know, I do the spiritualist evenings, but they're not always successful. Yes, there's always one or two from the other side, but the messages are often very obscure. Sometimes they help others, sometimes they don't.' She shrugs and sips her coffee again.

'I'm sure you do help, Pen,' I say, because she looks so despondent, sad.

Her blue eyes lock onto mine and crinkle at the edges in a smile. 'Thanks. I think I do most of the time. But you. You have one hell of gift. You pick things up from handling objects, psychometry to give it its proper title, spirits visit you with straightforward messages for the living, and now you have connections as you call them to people who are still with us. You actually saw this man and what he was up to. Pretty bloody amazing I say.'

Her expression is full of wonder. God knows what she'd say if she knew about Becky Proctor. 'I suppose it is…'

'No suppose about it. I've never heard of anyone like you, let alone met someone with your talent.'

I open my mouth to say something, but can't find the words. She's right. My nan had connections – spirits passing on messages, but as far as I know, not the object thing, and certainly not the seeing what the living were up to either. The waitress brings our food and we start eating.

'So this *means* something,' Penny says through a mouthful of mushrooms and egg. She points her fork at me. 'You must do something with it. An extraordinary gift like yours is too good to waste.'

I nod and power through bacon, eggs sausage and beans as though I'm worried someone is going to snatch my plate away. This is exactly what I've been thinking for some time, but how can I do it? There's a need inside me to help people on a day-to-day basis. But I can't just wander the streets grabbing sad or worried looking people as they go past, and ask them if they have an object I could handle, can I? I'd be carted off pronto for a nice rest in a hospital. One thing I am sure of, I'm handing my notice in at the café on Monday. Charlie can moan all he likes, but I'm done.

'Earth to Nancy.' Penny taps the edge of my plate with her knife.

'Sorry, did you say something?'

'Yes. I asked what was on your mind. You're ploughing through that breakfast at the speed of light with a frown on your face as deep as a furrow in a field.'

This makes me laugh. 'I have a lot on my mind. And you have been so helpful, Pen. You've confirmed what I'd already decided really. I'm going to leave my job and try to help people with my connections. You know, every day? Not just by accident. I'm going to actively seek connections of every type. Put this 'extraordinary gift', as you called it, to proper use.'

THE RIGHT MOMENT to tell Charlie is buried under cooking, washing up and watching Netflix later. Charlie is in a buoyant mood and says there's an interesting case he's working on. For the first time in a long time, he feels confident about his abilities as a copper and that's largely down to the Proctor case. He thanks me again for my part in it. Half of me wants to tell him that my part was pretty all of it, but the other half wants him to feel he's been successful. It's nice to see. And I'll need him on side when I broach leaving my job later, too. I ask him to tell me about the new case, but he says I'll only be bored by it. It's a spate of robberies, garages around Truro.

I WAKE WITH a start at 3:03 a.m. according to the digital bedside clock. Charlie's snoring and has one arm flung across my shoulder. I gently roll him over and sit on the edge of the bed while I gather my wits, a dream fresh in my mind. I open the curtain a crack, to find that the sickle moon from a few nights ago has grown a bit fatter, and a handful of stars have gathered round to support its weight. The top window is open, and I take a lungful of salt air and damp grass, think about what has just been revealed to me in a lightning-bolt flash as I slept. Unlike most dreams, this one is still clear, tangible. I was in a summerhouse at the bottom of our rambling garden and people kept coming in and telling me their troubles. They brought me their things. Things that were very dear to them. They brought objects, or problems, or photos. And I helped them. I helped them all.

Too excited to go back to sleep, I slip my dressing gown on and go downstairs to make a cup of tea. It's all falling into place now. Okay, some details are becoming a bit hazy, but I know that this is the way forward. It will be my new business and I even know what it will be called. I smile to myself as I remember the big sign on the side of the summerhouse. *Nancy Cornish PI.* The PI stands for Psychic Investigator, not Private Investigator. Genius what your brain produces when left unattended.

NEITHER OF US wants to admit we might have been a bit ambitious to go for a picnic in early April. The sun's shining from a forget-me-not blue sky, but the north wind is making it a tad chilly. It's fun, nevertheless, huddled together in our little beach tent watching the Atlantic playing with a few brave surfers. It flings them into the air, sucks them down under its waves, then spits them out as if they're irritating apple pips. We've eaten the sausage rolls, and I must say, they were some of my finest. Now we're on the tuna sandwiches and Charlie's pouring our tea from the old flask we've had for the last five-hundred years. He looks at me and smiles over the rim of the cup as he takes a sip, and the right moment pops its head round the tent and gives me a wink.

I draw in a deep breath. Here goes. 'Charlie. I've made a big decision about the future and I'm not sure you're going to like it.'

He puts his cup down and sighs. 'What is it?'

'I'm going to hand my notice in on Monday. I'll give them up to a month to find someone else, but I don't think they'll have a problem replacing me.'

Charlie's mouth drops open and he shakes his head. 'You have got to be kidding me. Have you got another job?'

I swallow hard and wiggle my toes in the sand. 'Not exactly. I will have though, when I get my business up and running.'

'Business?' he says, in an incredulous tone. And then more forcefully. 'What business?'

'I plan to have a summerhouse built at the end of our garden. It will have central heating, a place to make tea and coffee – maybe a microwave.' I hear his intake of breath but fix my eyes on the horizon. There's a fishing boat crossing the bay and I follow its path – straight, unwavering. 'A couple of sofas and maybe a desk and a little filing cabinet. It has to have Wi-Fi of course.'

Charlie sighs. 'Oh of course. What on earth are you talking about, Nancy?'

'As I said. It's my new business.' He looks like he's about to explode. His cheeks have got two high spots of colour and he's shoving his hands through his hair. I hurry on before he can speak. 'The Proctor case has been a catalyst for me as well as you. I'm going to use my connections properly to help as many people as I can. Penny said I have a rare and extraordinary gift. And she's right. I'm going to be a PI.'

Charlie's mouth wobbles – it looks like he can't decide whether to laugh or cry. Then he presses his lip together and stares at me. His soft hazel eyes turning to hard brown conkers. 'You are going to be a private investigator? That's ridiculous. You need training, experience. You can't just set up business in a bloody shed at the bottom of our garden!'

I bite back a snippy response, smile, and put my hand on his. 'It will be a summerhouse, not a shed. And no. Pay attention, dear. Not a private investigator, a psychic investigator.'

'A what?' If his frown gets any deeper his eyes will disappear. 'How the hell is that going to work? And how will we pay the bills?'

'I've not worked through every little detail yet.' *I've worked through nothing really.* 'But I'll ask people to pay me what they think my service is worth. It's all about making a difference in people's lives. And to be frank, we don't have to worry too much about money with your parents' nest egg. If it goes horribly wrong, then in six-months I'll go back to the café.'

Charlie's silent for a few moments, just keeps shaking his head in a very irritating manner. Then he says, 'But people will think you're a weirdo. You'll have to advertise…I don't want people making a laughing-stock of you.'

Is it me he's concerned for or himself, I wonder? The soon-to-be new DI won't want a weirdo psychic wife talked about behind hands, will he? No, that wouldn't do. 'Will people be so shocked? It's not as if being psychic is totally unheard of.'

'No. But a psychic investigator is pretty out there, Nance. You have to agree.'

'I don't, actually. And once I start to solve their problems, and the word gets around, I'll be a valuable part of the community. Just like you are.' There's flaky pastry from the sausage roll on the blanket over my legs. I dust it off and avoid his eyes. 'Let's face it, without me, Becky Proctor would still be living with a paedophile in a caravan on the hill over there.' I nod up the beach towards the far cliff top.

Charlie releases a slow breath and mumbles something unintelligible. Then he says, 'Look. I can't pretend to be happy about it. But you seem pretty determined.'

'I am. It's something I need to do. Something I must do.'

'Well then, who am I to stand in your way?'

He gives me a peck on the cheek and starts to pack the picnic things into the bag. Hmm. Somehow I don't think I've heard the last of this.

Chapter Eight

My last day at The Whistling Kettle is actually here. I can hardly believe it. After twelve years, I'm hanging up my apron. It's both exhilarating and daunting, and right now as I walk through the door and see Leanne's tear-stained face, I think daunting has the edge. I give her a smile, but a lump forms in my throat and my eyes flood. She flaps a tea towel at me.

'Don't you start. I've just got myself under bloody control.' She hurries into the kitchen and I follow.

'Hey, come here and give me a hug,' I say, slipping my jacket off and hanging it on the peg at the back of the door. God, I remember gluing that peg in place all those years ago. I never thought it would stay on.

'No hugs until later, or I'll be a mess.' Leanne dabs at her eyes and gives me a wobbly smile. 'It's the end of an era, Nance.'

'It is. But we'll see each other all the time. And who knows, you might be a client of mine one day.'

She nods and points at a gaily wrapped parcel on the side. 'The boss asked me to give you that.'

I raise my eyebrows. Judith was not best pleased to say the least, when I told her I was leaving. She owns the place and used to work here with me in the early days before Leanne, and before chronic arthritis stole her mobility. She's the one who taught me to bake properly. Wheelchair-bound, Judith rarely goes out now, but sometimes her husband brings her down for a visit, and to see how her shop's doing. I perch on a stool and undo the wrapping paper. Inside is a box stuffed with tissue paper. Carefully I lift out a wine glass. It's engraved with the words:

Nancy Cornish

the

World's Best Baker

I blink a few times and press my lips together hard, but it's no good, the tears come anyway. Leanne comes over and gives me the hug she refused just now. She hands me a tissue, takes the glass and says, 'Oh that's so lovely, Nance. Didn't you once say she taught you all she knew?'

I blow my nose and sniff. 'Yeah. I used to say she was the world's best baker and she said I think I might have competition one day.' I notice a card in the box, but the words blur after the first line. I shake my head and hand it to Leanne.

She clears her throat and reads. 'I know I was a bit grumpy on the phone when you told me you were leaving, but that's only because I knew my shop was in safe hands. It nearly broke me to walk away, (or wheel away). but my mind was at rest knowing you were running the show. I could almost believe I was still part of it all, knowing you were there. Though that young Leanne is doing a grand job too.' Leanne stops, turns pink and says to me, 'Oh isn't that lovely?' I nod. She continues. 'You have been a wonderful friend and colleague, and this is just a little something to show my appreciation. Don't be a stranger and I wish you every success with your new venture. Love, Jude xxx'

I dab my eyes and turn the glass round in my fingers. It twinkles as it catches the early morning sun angling in through the window, and I remember the twinkle in Judith's eye and her ready smile. 'It is more than a little something. It's everything.'

Leanne shakes her head and puts her hand to her mouth. Through her fingers she says, 'I don't think she meant the glass. I think she meant this.'

I take the envelope which had the card in and folded inside is a cheque. A cheque made out to me for five-thousand pounds. My breath is taken, and the tears start again. 'Oh my God, Leanne. I can't accept this.'

'Of course you can! She wants you to have it. It will come in handy for your new business. That summerhouse cost three grand you told me.'

'But I could never repay her for—'

'Err hello. You've already paid her over the years. You've done long hours, come in early and finished long after you should have gone home. Take it. Judith wants you to have it, Nance.'

Leanne's earnest expression helps to settle my mind. She's right, isn't she? Jude wants me to have it. I'm overwhelmed. 'Okay. I will.' I give her another quick hug. 'Right, come on. These scones won't bake themselves. And you'll be teaching the new girl on Monday. You're the world's best baker number two now.'

Leanne's eyes swim, so I turn away before mine get a chance to copy them.

THE NEXT MORNING, I watch my spoon chase a few remaining cornflakes round my bowl. I can't remember eating the rest, but then I'm on automatic pilot today. Everything feels a bit surreal. *The First Day of the Rest of Your Life*, Leanne's card said when I'd opened it upon waking. She'd made me promise to wait until today to open it, and the gorgeous pair of jade earrings she'd given as a leaving present. She said they'd match my eyes. Though my eyes are more red than green at the moment, due to all the goodbyes and wonderful gifts I've had. As well as Judith's and Lee's, so many customers had popped by yesterday with gifts and well wishes. Leanne was over the moon with my gift for her. A painting of St George's Cove by a local artist she'd admired one evening as we'd passed the gallery on our way home. It will be very strange not seeing her and all the customers each day. I put my spoon down and trace the word on Lee's card again, and a little flutter of excitement wakes up and scampers around in my tummy.

Charlie has been a bit quiet on the subject, in fact in general recently. Half-hidden in my heart is the unwelcome idea that he thinks I'm going to fail. Even after I found Becky, I'm sure a good part of him thinks it was just due to luck. He was only saying the other day that it was a good job I had the idea of speaking to Becky's best friend, Dawn, or it might have taken much longer to track the teenager down. The fact that my connections had pointed me in her direction wasn't mentioned. He can't dismiss it out of hand anymore as mumbo-jumbo, but I'm guessing he wants to ignore it as much as he can. Well that's tough, because by the time he's home tonight, he won't be able to, because there'll be a summerhouse looking at him from the bottom of the garden with the words – *Nancy Cornish PI* – in big letters above the door.

THREE HOURS LATER and the summerhouse is half assembled. It was delivered a couple of hours ago and two workmen Bill and Ben – yes really – have been hard at it ever since. I have been making tea and cake to keep them going, and in another hour, it will be ready to fix the letters in place. I had them made at a local carpenter's in Scandinavian pine and I couldn't have wished for better. I'm just about to print off more flyers for my new venture, as the little pile I had in the cafe all went yesterday, when Bill and Ben ask me if I want to come and have a look at their work, to make sure all is as it should be.

My heart's as light as a party balloon as I walk down the path to my new office. Wow. Just wow! The wood has been painted a lovely light green which blends so well with the shrubs and trees surrounding it and the patio doors are wide open as if it's welcoming me inside. Over the doors, *Nancy Cornish PI* sits dead centre, and sets the whole thing off perfectly. Inside, the smell of new wood pervades the air and even bare of rugs and furniture, it already feels so comfortable.

'Everything okay for you, Nancy?' Ben asks.

'Everything is more than okay. It's bloody fantastic!' I turn and fling my arms out to the sides.

Young Bill looks a bit startled by this and steps back into the doorway. 'Don't worry Bill, I'm not crazy, just so thrilled with it. Now would you like more cake before you go?' Bill looks hopeful, but Ben says they have to go to another job.

Once they've gone, I get a garden chair and sit inside by the window, picturing how it will soon look. By tomorrow, the sofas will be here, and I'm picking up the rugs this afternoon. Then tomorrow afternoon, the guy's coming to connect the internet. The desk and office chair and filing cabinet will be here by the end of the week, and in the middle of all that, the plumber's coming to sort the little kitchen and radiators. It will all be perfect. I have one last look around and then decide I'll pop around Padstow with my flyers and ask in the shops if I can leave some on the counters.

On my way back up the garden path, I see a woman I'd guess to be in her early sixties, peering round the side of my house. She's wearing brightly coloured boho clothes with a long grey plait over her left shoulder. Probably selling something. 'Hi, can I help you?' I say, as I close the gap between us.

The woman's eyes dart away from mine and colour mottles her neck. She looks back and clears her throat. 'I hope so. Though I'm not sure how. Are you Nancy Cornish?'

'Yes.' I put my head on one side and wait. I can tell she's struggling to get her words out and seems very nervous.

'My name is Louisa Green, and I picked up one of these in the café the other day.' She pulls one of my flyers from her pocket and waves it at me. She tries a smile but her bottom lip wobbles.

My first customer, but a week early. She can't have read the opening date. Despite the summerhouse not being ready, my conscience won't let me turn her away, because it's obviously taken a lot for her to come here. I smile and offer my hand. 'Hello, Louisa, would you like to come and look at my new workspace? It's just finished, and you'll be the first person to see it!'

Louisa brightens and her soft grey eyes crinkle in a smile. 'I'd be delighted.'

She follows me back down the path and I sweep my hand the length of the building. 'I'm so excited by this new venture, I can't tell you.'

'It's lovely,' she says and peers through the doors. 'But is it ready?'

'Not quite, but I can get an extra garden chair and bring us a cuppa from the house. Will that be okay? Or you can come back another time…'

Her brow furrows and she pulls the flyer out again, scans it, runs her finger over the opening date at the bottom. 'Oh, what a fool I am. You're not open yet, are you?'

'That's not a problem, honestly. Please, come inside.' I step through the doors and after a moment's hesitation she follows me.

I dust the garden chair down for Louisa and grab another from the shed next door. Worrying the side of her thumb nail, she asks again if it's okay to see her today, so I take time to reassure her. Then I hurry to the house to make tea and consider my first customer. At first glance, Louisa looked a confident outgoing woman with her chunky jewellery, and long cotton turquoise and lemon dress with the handkerchief hem. But her appearance is like a flamboyant outer shell with which she camouflages her insecurity. Instinct tells me she's not had it easy. Intuition also tells me that I'll like her. My heart tells me I can help to resolve what's bothering her.

When I return with the tea, she's sitting straight backed, feet neatly together, with a few weathered envelopes on her lap and on top of those, two photographs face down. I put her cup on a large upturned plant pot next to her, and sit opposite. She thanks me for the tea and then says, 'Before we start, Nancy, how much do you charge?'

This forthright approach throws me. 'Um…I…'

'Because I like to pay my way upfront, and I'll be embarrassed if I've not enough in my purse today. I should have mind you, because I got some out of the wall yesterday and—'

'You pay what you think my service is worth,' I say, to stop her anxious ramblings.

Louisa stops mid flow. Her lips are still wrapped around a silent word, and for a moment she's a waxwork. 'Really? That's very trusting of you.'

'Is it? I think most people are decent and honest. And I'm not really in this to get rich. I'm here to help people.'

She twists her mouth to the side. 'Hmm. That's where I'm not sure if you're the right person to come to. You see, I read the leaflet and it said you're a psychic investigator. It said as well as being used to visitors from the spirit world, you can sometimes help people find lost things, or maybe even loved ones.'

I nod. 'Yes, I have been very successful where that's concerned recently. Although I can't divulge details.'

Louisa pats the things on her lap. 'Like you also said to do in your advert, I've brought along personal items which might be a useful connection to those things.'

'That's great. So why don't you think I might be the right person to come to?'

'Because the person I want you to investigate has been missing from my life for forty years.'

That is a long time missing. But Louisa's staring at me intently, so I put my best confident face on and say, 'Okay. Just tell me your story and we'll go from there.'

Louisa's story is long and sad and explains why she's wearing camouflage. She'd forsaken her childhood sweetheart for the flashy good-looking guy. When she married him, she found he had his own camouflage. Underneath his handsome exterior and outgoing cheery persona, was concealed the ugly face of a wife beater, womaniser and control freak. He was a big drinker too and as a consequence, died of it last year. A long lingering death from liver disease.

'How does that make you feel?' I ask.

'Honestly? I feel liberated. 'That might sound callous, but broken ribs and black eyes over the years and living in fear will do that to you.' She sweeps a hand across her dress. 'I was never allowed to wear colourful clothes, make-up or anything.' Poor

Louisa. I touch her arm lightly but keep silent. 'A few years into our marriage I got pregnant. It wasn't planned, but I was overjoyed. I had a new life growing inside me. An innocent life which I was going to protect. I promised myself that I'd leave once the baby was born.' Louisa stops.

There's a seed of sadness putting roots down in my heart. This story is going from bad to worse. I give her a moment, then ask, 'I'm guessing you and your child didn't leave?'

'My child died when I was six-months pregnant after my husband came in drunk and slapped me around a bit. I stumbled and fell hard with my stomach against the corner of dining room table. In the hospital after I'd lost him…I had a son. A beautiful boy…' Louisa puts a trembling hand to her mouth, then tosses her head as if she's shaking away remembered pain. 'Anyway, in the hospital, Howard, my husband, made me tell the doctor that I'd tripped up in my carpet slippers on the slippery floor. If I told the truth, Howard said he'd make sure that was the last thing I did…I made sure I never got pregnant again.'

Indignant anger on her behalf simmers in my gut, but I have to rise above it if I'm to be of use. 'What a terrible man. I can't imagine what life was like for you.'

'I bet you're wondering why I stayed.' Louisa's eyes hold an ocean of anguish.

'Well…I…' My words fade into a sigh. I have been. But she must have had her reasons. I can't judge.

'Because he'd made me feel so worthless. Insignificant. I was more scared of leaving him than I was of staying. I had no friends or family, because he'd isolated me over the years. I felt I couldn't survive in the outside world. That must sound nuts to you.'

Strangely it doesn't. I get it. 'Now you've explained it so well, no. It makes perfect sense, sadly. My heart goes out to you, Louisa.'

'Thanks, Nancy. But I've rambled on more than I needed to…though it feels good to get it all out. The reason I'm here, is that when I was in the loft sorting through some of Howard's things after he died, I came across these letters from the man I should have married.' She holds them out to me. 'He begged me to take him back and said I was making a mistake marrying Howard, but I wouldn't listen. Such a fool. Such a *bloody* fool.' Louisa shakes her head. 'My life could have been so different with Mark.'

I place the letters on my lap and nod at the photos. 'Are they of Mark?'

'Yes, one of just him and one of him and me.' She passes them over. 'I've searched for him everywhere. I wanted to tell him he was right and that I'm sorry for not listening all those years ago. But after endless sleuthing, I find he's not on social media, he's left his old house in Perranporth, and the older neighbours remember him, but nobody knew where he went. He seems to have just vanished off the face of the planet. He's not dead because I checked the records. So, Nancy. You're my only hope.'

No pressure then. I lean forward and pat her knee. 'I'll see what I can do, Louisa.' Then I release a slow breath and start with the letters. I hold them one at a time in my hands and close my eyes. Concentrate. And after a few minutes there's…nothing. I can feel Louisa's eyes on my face and it's not helping. Maybe this was a bad idea. The whole thing of having people here in front of me while I'm trying to make a connection…why didn't it occur to me before that it might not be a great idea? I've always been alone before. Damn it!

I open my eyes and muster a smile and a confident expression. Louisa looks hopeful. 'Did you find anything?'

'No. It doesn't always work straight away…and to be honest, it might not work at all. My connections can't be made to order, just so you know.' Her face falls. 'But let's try with the photos.'

I turn the first one over. It's Louisa with Mark on a harbour somewhere, their backs to the sea. I'm guessing they're about twenty, so late 1970s. They are both wearing wide flares and she has on platform shoes. Her jet-black hair is lifting on the breeze, and though still a striking woman now, she was stunning back then. Mark has shoulder length brown hair and a strong jaw line. I can't see his full face, as he's looking adoringly at her, while she's grinning at the camera. I can sense the love between them, but that's all. I concentrate so hard, but nothing comes.

After a few minutes more, Louisa says, 'That was taken at Porthleven in 1977, I think. Mark had brought up the subject of marriage. He hadn't proposed, but he was getting serious about our future. I was so happy…then the next week I met Howard. He came to work in our office.'

I don't reply, just tuck the photo under the letters. This next one is the last chance. My hands feel clammy and my throat's dry. You can do this, Nancy. Calm yourself. and relax. I turn the photo over. It's one of Mark on his own, sitting at a wooden table outside a pub, a pint in front of him. Judging by his clothes, it was taken the same day as the previous photo. He's wearing a navy tank top and underneath, a white shirt with a big round collar. This time he's looking straight at the camera. He has an open face and incredible blue eyes. I feel he's a really nice guy. I look into his eyes and silently ask him where he is. He doesn't answer. That's it then.

I look up from his face into Louisa's. 'Nothing again?' she asks.

I'm just about to say I'm sorry, when the fingers holding the photo start to tingle, and on the wood panelled wall behind her, a series of images are slapped down one after the other in quick succession – the playing card effect. Mark wandering a cliff path hands in pockets, head down. He looks about ten years older than in the photo in my hand. Mark on a cliff edge looking into the waves. In his heart, a tumult of confusion, a desire to end it all fights with a fear of dying. He's in his forties, or maybe fifties. Then there's an image of an old Cornish stone church, stark against a blue sky and ocean. Mark's not in that image. Then there's nothing…just the summerhouse wall again.

I smile at Louisa's puzzled expression. I say, 'Well, don't get your hopes up. But I have seen a few images. One is of a church. And I know where that church is.'

Her hands fly to her cheeks and excitement shines from her eyes. 'Does that mean you know where Mark is?'

'Not for certain, but it's a start.' I feel more confident than my words sound, but I don't want to let her down.

'Where's the church?' Louisa says as if she's worried someone will overhear.

Unable to keep a big smile from my face I say, 'Tintagel. Just up the road!'

CHARLIE GETS BACK just as I've rearranged the rugs again for the fiftieth time. He appears in the doorway with a look on his face of what I can only describe as grudging respect.

'This is nice,' He says, as he comes in. 'Nice rugs too – Moroccan-ish.' He rises on the balls of his feet then lowers himself again, folds his arms, sniffs.

'Yeah, I like the greens reds and yellows.' I push a strand of hair from my forehead and smile at him. 'What do you think of the lettering above the door?'

'Yeah, nice.' Charlie runs his hand along the windowsill and asks, 'What's for tea?'

That's it? That's the extent of his interest shown in my new venture? 'You don't want to ask about my day? What's happening tomorrow, that kind of thing?'

He shrugs, turns his bottom lip down. 'Okay, what happened today? I didn't ask, because you're not up and running until next week, are you? You said you wanted a few days to get organised.'

I hold my finger up and sit on one of the garden chairs. 'That's the thing, Charlie. I wasn't supposed to be, but my first customer had other ideas.' I wave him to sit down opposite.

He sits. 'Right. Were you successful?' I tell him all about Louisa and that I'm off to Tintagel in the morning. 'I thought you said the sofas were coming and the internet was being connected?'

'Yes, but Jenny from next door said she'd be here for them. Isn't it exciting, Charlie? My first real Psychic Investigator job!' I throw my hands up and laugh.

He crosses his legs and strokes his chin. 'Ah, but what you're going to do tomorrow isn't exactly psychic is it? It's good old-fashioned detective work.'

Is he for real? Yes, but I wouldn't know where he was, unless I'd done the psychic part this afternoon, would I?'

'No… guess not.' But you haven't found him yet. He waggles a finger and gives me his earnest, I-know-better-than-you look. 'The first rule of police work is not to count your chickens.'

Why is he being so obstructive? Then it hits me. All this sniping and underplaying my part in finding Becky, the reluctance to accept my change of career, all of it. It's because he feels threatened. Does he *actually* think I'm some kind of competition? That I'm trying to muscle in on his job? Is his self-confidence so low that he's, what? Jealous of my abilities?

I sigh. 'Charlie, let's get one thing straight. You're the detective. I have no wish to be a policewoman. I have no wish to be in the police. The problems I hope to be dealing with are not crime related. I aim to help my community in whatever way they need – be it large or small. However, having said that, what might seem small to some, might be a huge thing to the person needing help. Okay?' He gives me a nod. 'So, police work and crime is your bit and psychic stuff and helping people solve their problems is my bit. I only call myself PI because it might grab people's attention on the flyers. A play on words…or initials in this case.'

A far away stare make his thoughts unreadable. Then he says, 'Look, Nance, I just don't want you to be disappointed. Not everyone believes in psychic stuff and you might not get many people wanting help. I only worry because I love you.'

'Charlie. I do know that. But I feel like I have to try. This feels right. Can't you be happy for me, give me some credit?' My voice carries a wobble of emotion which annoys me. I clear my throat.

'Course I am, love. Well done.' He gets up and walks over to me, pulls me into his arms. I snuggle my head against his chest and listen to the rhythm of his heart. Steady and constant like our love. I wish he believed in himself as much as I do. Because if he did, he'd be much happier. And though he would never admit it, I'm sure he feels relieved now I've spelt out my position. He's the detective, not me. I pull away and give him a kiss before he walks away. At the door he says over his shoulder, 'Off for a shower now.'

I say, 'It's cottage pie.'

Charlie turns to face me. 'Eh?'

'For tea.'

'Lovely. I don't deserve you.' He gives me a little smile and walks away up the garden path.

Chapter Nine

The next morning, I pull up into the car park opposite the visitor's centre in Tintagel and check for the third time that I have my notebook and pen. All good PI's have those. A wiggle of excitement in my belly brings a smile to my face as I get out of the car and head into the town. I thought the local shops and pubs might be a good place to start. If he's local, and I'm assuming he is, or this is all about to fall flat on its face, shopkeepers might know him or recognise his photo. I pull it out of my bag and wish it wasn't forty years out of date. But that's all I've got, and I'm hoping it's enough.

It's been quite a few years since I came here but it's changed little. The confectionary shop still looks exactly the same with its bold pink exterior, and in the window, the delicious array of 'handmade crumbly fudge made daily', cakes, pastries and ice-cream. I'm tempted to sample some, but I'm not a tourist, I'm working and need to keep focused.

I set off through the town and each step takes me past more pubs, shops, and across the road, an ancient Post Office run by the National Trust. It's not in operation as a post office of course, that would have been an ideal place to ask about Mark. I come to a newsagent. As good a place to start as any. Five-minutes later I'm back on the pavement. The lady behind the counter didn't recognise the name, or the photo. It's the same story in five other shops and two pubs. By the time I get back to the confectionary shop, the buoyant mood that carried me here this morning has slipped its rope and is floating away on the tide. Maybe I'll grab a bit of chocolate fudge to sustain me, and ask about Mark at the same time.

As the shop assistant is boxing up my fudge, I slip the photo out of my bag, put it on the counter and ask, 'I was wondering if you recognise this man. He's supposed to live in Tintagel, but so far I've had no luck. The photo's not recent, unfortunately – it's forty-odd years ago. He's called Mark Davies.'

The round-faced woman pushes her glasses up her nose, glances at the image and nods once. 'Yeah, he's a gardener and tends the graves up at St Materiana's as well. Keeps himself to himself. That's why you've had no joy so far. He tidied my dad's garden last month. He's getting on a bit now.'

At last someone's heard of him! My spirits rise again. I say, 'Yeah, I suppose he must be. Early sixties.'

The woman rubs her chin, sniffs, hands me the box of fudge. 'No. He's eighty-four next March.'

Shit. We're obviously talking about the wrong person. 'Oh…that's a shame. The man I'm looking for is definitely not in his eighties.'

The woman's plump cheeks puff over a wide smile. 'No. I was talking about my dad. He needs help with his garden as he's getting on.' She chuckles. I thought you were flattering me, 'cos I'm in my fifties. But Mark, yes, he must be about what you said.'

I chuckle too. 'I see. So do you think Mark might be at this church now?'

'Couldn't tell you, my dear. But why not go up and have a look?'

'Where is it?'

'It's the one on the hill overlooking the sea. You can walk to it. Just go down the road and it's signposted.'

I thank her and leave feeling a bit like a failure. What kind of a PI gets a clear vision of the church on the hill, identifies it as Tintagel, but then spends forty-minutes asking questions round town? The connection couldn't have been much clearer. *Go to the church, you dopey mare.* On the way back through town, I stuff myself stupid with the fudge. I only intended to have one or two pieces, but as I turn down the hill at the signpost, I see only two bits in the corner of the little box. Oh well, I need energy to walk up the steep hill to the church. That's my story and I'm sticking to it.

Spring is threading herself through the hedgerows and bursting from the grass that lines the little lane. Hawthorn flowers, bluebells, wild garlic and daffodils provide a riot of colour, and pungent aromas rise from damp earth and crushed garlic flowers underfoot. It's only just gone ten-thirty in the morning, but May is proving to be a hot month. I slip my jacket off, toss it over my shoulder, and feel the sun's rays immediately sheathe the bare skin on my arms. The sky's a cornflower blue, there's salt in the breeze and jackdaws chase each other over the fields calling out across the land. How lucky I am to be here and now, walking the Cornish lanes, doing a job that will hopefully bring two hearts together once more.

Rounding the bend, I see the ancient grey church sitting squat against the sky and hillside. Before I set off, I googled it to see if it was open, and the information told me it's probably eleventh century. How many people must have passed through its doors over the years? What was in their hearts? Were there prayers on their tongue? Had they knelt and pleaded for the help of ailing loved ones, asked for mercy? Had they made wishes, asked for love?

At the entrance to the graveyard there's a prominent sign reading – *Adders. Please Keep Your Dog on a Lead!!!!* Four exclamation marks. Blimey, must be a veritable vipers pit in there. Unless they just don't want dogs rampaging about digging up the graves. I hope it's the latter, but nevertheless I walk quickly up the path to the church keeping my eyes peeled for wiggly shapes ready to launch themselves at me. Lining the path there's some large crumbling gravestones, some dating from the 18th century. Newer stones shelter in the long shadow of their grief and then as I pass a tiny one, I get a clear image of a woman wrapped in a tattered brown shawl, anguish lining her face, holding the still form of a new-born. A lump in my throat, I lift my eyes to the sky. I can't be distracted from my mission today by the dead.

Outside the church, I shield my eyes from the sun and scan the graveyard and the surrounding grounds. No sign of Mark. No sign of anyone. To my left, the ocean sings its endless lullaby, as if shushing restless sleepers. In the sun's haze, the horizon's just a suggestion blending the sky and water, and a deep sense of peace calms my mind. I fill my lungs with a deep breath of salt air and exhale. If Mark's not here today, I'll just come back tomorrow.

Before I leave, I decide to have a look inside the church. There's an ancient arched door and I put the flat of my hand against the rough sun-warmed wood. I feel its age, see a glimpse of the past as a procession of worshippers slip through like tendrils of mist. I lower my hand to the black metal latch handle and lift. I step inside and immediately in front of me is a tall vase of beautiful white lilies, their heady scent lifting the must of old stone and pews. I run my hand over the ancient stone font and walk through the empty church towards the aisle and the stunning stained-glass window.

I watch the dust motes dance in the blue red and yellow shafts of light filtering through the glass and close my eyes, immerse myself in the peace and silence. Then from behind, I hear a shuffle and quiet footsteps. Looking round, from behind a pillar I see the back of a grey-haired man who's clearly trying to tiptoe out. Something prompts me to say, 'Hello? Don't leave on my account.' My voice sounds big and intrusive in the silence.

He raises a hand. 'It's okay. Time to get back to work anyway.'

I hurry after him and tap him on the shoulder just as he's about to go through the door. He turns and I'm looking into a pair of incredibly blue eyes. There are more wrinkles and creases around them now than in the photo, but I'm certain I've found my man. 'You're Mark Davies, aren't you?'

His eyebrows dip. 'Yes…I'm not sure I know you though.'

I take his elbow. 'You don't. Let's go outside and I'll tell you why I'm here.'

TEN MINUTES LATER we're sitting on the graveyard wall in the sunshine while Mark's trying to come to terms with what I've told him. 'I know this must be a shock. Particularly the bit about how I found you,' I say and offer a smile.

Mark shakes his head. 'You could say that. And Louisa wanting to find me after all this time. She's all I ever wanted and dreamed about. I left Cornwall for a bit after she married. Worked up in Scotland.' He draws his hand down his face. 'I wanted to be far away in case I bumped into them both. I didn't know she'd moved to Padstow. I came back, but not to Perranporth where we met. I lived down in Sennen for a quite some time. Then I moved here about three years ago. I felt closer to Louisa, but not too close in case I saw her with him. Cornwall's a small place.' His voice drifts and I can tell his thoughts are in the past.

'I know you've not been happy, Mark.' I put my hand on his arm, remember the bleak image of him walking the cliff paths and staring out to sea, despair in his heart.

He gives me a sidelong glance. 'No, I haven't. I had a few relationships over the years, but they never lasted. I'm the kind of idiot who only falls truly in love the one time.'

'You're not an idiot.'

Mark heaves a sigh. 'Maybe not. But it's not made me happy to say the least. Well, apart from when I was with her…Louisa.'

'You could be again. Shall I take you to her?' I hop down from the wall.

Clouds of doubt settle in Mark's eyes and he strokes his chin a few times. 'What if it's too late? She might just be harking back to happier times before she met him. Now he's dead she wishes she'd stayed with me, but it might just all be fantasy. Fond remembered ideals of youth. The reality might be something else.' I'm about to say something when his expression hardens and his eyes flash. 'I wish I'd have known what he was doing to her all that time. I'd have bloody killed him.'

There's silence for a few seconds and into it I offer, 'Louisa realised she made a terrible mistake not long after she married him. She told me she wished she'd stayed with you. And now she wants to put that right. Just see what happens, Mark. There are no guarantees of a happy ending. But surely it's worth trying…and what do you have to lose?'

Mark gives a hollow laugh. 'My sanity. My self-respect. What's left of my heart?'

'I get that. But you'd never forgive yourself if you didn't at least meet her. She's been looking for you for some time.'

More silence while Mark stares at the ground between his boots. Then he shoves his sleeve up and dusts a fly off a suntanned arm. 'The day she finished with me I was going to propose. I'd got the ring in my pocket and booked a nice restaurant. Then she came round early to tell me it wasn't working.' He shrugs and stares at a huge Celtic cross listing to one side of an ancient gravestone nearby.

There are no words, so I keep my mouth shut. After a while I say, 'Come on, Mark. Let me take you to her.'

'But I'm in my work gear.' He dusts his jeans off and examines the dirt under his nails.

'I'm happy to take you home so you can shower and change. I expect Louisa would appreciate a bit of time to prepare too. I'll give her a ring while I wait for you to get ready.'

Mark looks as if he's going to protest, but then his mouth relaxes, and he gives me a lovely smile. 'Why not? Faint heart and all that.'

A WHILE LATER, I'm sitting in my car watching a dapper Mark walk up the path of Louisa's house. He doesn't get chance to ring the bell, because the door's flung wide and Louisa strides out to meet him. She throws her arms around him and after a moment's hesitation, his arms leave his sides and envelop her in a bear hug. There must be something in my eye because the scene blurs temporarily. I dab at it with a tissue and see that they are laughing and crying at the same time, then Louisa takes his hand and leads him inside. At the door he stops and raises his hand to me. The look on his face confirms that I've absolutely made the right decision in leaving the café and starting *Nancy Cornish PI*. My heart swells with joy as I wave back and drive away.

Chapter Ten

The sofas look wonderful in the summerhouse, the green leather compliments the walls, and the red scatter cushions I bought in a sale last week add contrast. I sink down into one of the sofas and switch my laptop on. Louisa's messaged to say thank you and that she'd be in touch later. I've also got an email from someone called Alison. She's got my email address from one of my flyers and wants to book an appointment as soon as possible. There's a phone number. My goodness. Who'd have thought I'd have two clients before I'm properly open for business? I grab my mobile and key in the number.

'Alison? Yes, it's Nancy Cornish. I got your email – I'm not officially open yet, but I guess I'm functionally up and running. How can I help?'

'I'm not sure you can…but your leaflet said you might help find things that are lost? Well it's not a thing, it's a cat. My cat Rufus went missing five-days ago, and it's not like him…Do you think you can help?'

A missing cat? All sorts of scenarios rush through my head, particularly the squashed cat at the side of the road one. How do you tell a distraught owner that kind of thing? 'I'm not sure. I can try…'

'Oh, thank you!' The relief in Alison's voice doesn't help my worries. 'And if he's…gone, I'd rather know. It's the uncertainty I can't stand.'

I arrange a time for tomorrow morning and end the call. *Please be alive, Rufus.*

CHARLIE SEEMS MORE animated and interested in my day than he was yesterday. He actually said well done and commented how rewarding it must be for me to help people 'put their lives back together'. I was tempted to ask who he was and what he'd done with my husband, but thought better of it. After dinner we're cuddled up on the sofa watching TV. I have my head on Charlie's lap and he's stroking my hair. I'm starting to drop off when he says, casually, 'Oh yeah. You know I said you'd be bored the other day listening to me going on about the new case we're working on – the garage robberies?'

'Yeah.' I yawn and stretch but I'm wide awake. Charlie's casual voice is pretend casual. It's the voice he uses when he's after something important to him, but he pretends it isn't.

'I was wondering if you could perhaps give us a few pointers. I have one or two photos of the suspects. Maybe you could have a look and see if anything comes to you.'

A wave of irritation sweeps through me. Cheeky sod! One minute he's pooh-poohing my connections, next he's expecting me to use them for petty crime. No wonder he was being so nice earlier. I take a deep breath and try to keep my voice level. 'I don't think so, Charlie. I'm not using my connections for trivial stuff.'

He shifts under me and I sit up, face him. He's frowning. 'It's hardly trivial, love. They hold up cashier's at gunpoint and get them to empty the tills.'

'They're insured, surely?'

'Ye-s but…'

'Has anyone got hurt?'

'No. But they might.'

'And they might not. No. Sorry, I'll only help out in serious cases.'

Charlie's quiet for a moment. 'It might help with the promotion if I nailed another case so soon after Becky Proctor.' The tone of his words is wheedling, like a child's bargaining for a treat.

'That's not fair, Charlie. You can't put that on me.' His huff and eye-roll fire a response I can't keep in. 'Besides, I'll remind you that it was me who nailed the Proctor case, not you.'

I receive a wounded look as he jumps up from the sofa. 'I'm making a cup of coffee. Do you want one?' he tosses this disdainfully over his shoulder like a theatrical feather boa. I'll give him that. Charlie plays the injured and indignant party down to a tee.

Following him to the kitchen, I get the mugs out of the cupboard while he fills the kettle. 'Look. I know how important this promotion has become, but as I said, I won't use what I do like some side-show. Yesterday, I told you that you were the detective. I don't do police work and have no wish to start. My connections are strictly for people who need help. Proper help.

'Like a woman who's lost her cat? That's *so* important compared to armed robbery isn't it.'

He doesn't get it. Not at all. 'Charlie. Sometimes animals are people's only source of love. I don't know Alison's story, but Rufus is her world. I can tell, even over the phone.' He plunges at the cafetière as if it's about to leap up and bite him. 'No point in talking to you when you're like this. You stick to your 'career', I'll stick to mine.'

The disparaging way he said 'career' gets my hackles up, but I agree. Isn't that what he wants? There's no point discussing it further. We return to the sofa, opposite ends this time, and sip our coffee in a frosty silence.

ALISON'S A SLIM fifty-something brunette with a nervous smile and shy brown eyes. She's dressed in a green T-shirt and black jeans. My razor-sharp detective abilities tell me immediately that she's of a nervous disposition, because her fingernails are bitten down to the quick and she keeps tucking them under her armpits, as if she's ashamed of having them on show. Or it could be that she's just worried to death about her cat, and normally isn't nervous at all.

We sit on facing sofas in the summerhouse and sip cloudy lemonade. She's asking all about my connections and seems fascinated by it all. I must admit this is such fun. Who'd have thought at the beginning of the year that I'd have such a wonderful new job? Certainly not me. This morning I'd found another email from Louisa saying how well she and Mark had got on yesterday. It was as if the last forty years hadn't happened, and they were talking about a short break somewhere together to really relax and catch up. She'd also said she'd transferred two-hundred pounds into my account. She wished it could have been more, and she hoped it was okay. I was overwhelmed. Two-hundred pounds for a morning's work. Well, not work really, and the rewards of that morning are immeasurable.

'Okay, Alison. Can you tell me about your life and Rufus, just so I can get an outline before I look at any items you've brought with you?'

She nods. 'I'm a widow. My husband died four-years ago in an accident at work. I don't work now because the life insurance policy has left me comfortably off.' She takes a breath and her cheeks turn pink. 'Well, also I left my job so I could pursue my dream of becoming a writer.' There's a mix of embarrassment and pride in her voice.

'Really? That's brilliant. You should always go for your dreams, I say.'

Her smile is wide now and she forgets to shove her hands under her armpits. 'Thanks. A few weeks ago, an agent showed interest in my first novel. She asked for the whole thing and says she'll get back in a few weeks. I was thrilled. Mind you, my friend Kate said I shouldn't just go with the first one who offers. She said my novel needs more work too. I expect she's right.'

'Oh? This Kate is an editor or something?'

'No. She's just my very best friend who's looked after me since Jack died. I don't know where I'd be without her. I always listen to her advice, she's so wise. She read all of my book for me too.'

I smile, but already I'm getting an uncomfortable feeling about Kate. Surely getting an agent's attention is a good thing. I say, 'Okay, that's nice. Can you tell me now about Rufus?'

Alison's eyes water and she pulls a tissue out of her pocket. 'Rufus is like a baby to me. Jack and I couldn't have them, you see. We got him when he was a kitten and he's almost eight now. He's black with a white bib and three white socks. He never stays out for long. Just out in the garden and over the fence to do his business and then back again in half-an-hour or so. Rufus is…was, by my side night and day…and…' Alison flaps her hand in front of her face and blows her nose. 'Kate's mentioned that we should get a place together, which would be great. Especially on long winter evenings. But I'm not sure Rufus would like it. He's used to just me.'

'I see. You must be devastated he's gone,' I say and hand her a clean tissue. I could do with one too. Her mention of not being able to have children strikes a deep melancholy chord inside me. Sebastian feels close today.

'I am. I let him out as usual five-days ago in the morning for a pee before breakfast and he never came back.'

'Right. I think I have enough to build a picture. Let's see what you've brought me.'

She hands me a photo of a handsome cat and a much-chewed catnip toy. I hold both in my hands and look into Rufus's big green eyes. Immediately the rolling film connection starts, and I see him playing with the catnip toy. Then I see him in what looks to be a dark garage. There's a bowl of water on the floor and the remnants of dried cat food on an old saucer. There's a cat litter tray which is in desperate need of emptying, and he's sitting hunched in a corner, looking thoroughly miserable. There's a little silver car parked in the garage, but I can't see what type it is. Then the connection stops and I'm staring at the photo again.

I sigh and Alison says, 'Did you see anything?'

I look at her hopeful face and though it wasn't a pleasant image, I'm pleased I have something to tell her. At least it's not the squashed cat scenario. 'I did see something. I'm happy to tell you that Rufus's still alive.'

Her face crumples but she smiles through her tears. 'Thank God! Where is he?'

'Well, that's the bad news. I think someone has taken him deliberately.'

I tell her about the garage. 'Do you know anyone who has a silver car?'

'What kind?'

'I couldn't see, just a small one.'

'I know quite a few people who have silver cars…there's my niece, my brother…Robert the next-door neighbour.' She puts her hand over her mouth. 'Robert hates cats. Do you think it's him?'

'Anything's possible. But why would he want to keep Rufus, if he hates cats?'

Alison shrugs. 'I don't know. To teach me a lesson? He said last year that I should keep Rufus off his plants. He has been known to spray on them.'

'Robert or Rufus?' My attempt at humour leaves her cold. 'Okay. Well, that's a start. I'll pop round to yours later and do a bit of investigation. Just jot down your address on this pad.'

She gets up and clasps my hand in hers. 'Thank you so much. I know I haven't got him back yet. But I'm sure we will eventually.' She jots down her address. 'Should I ask Robert outright, save you coming over?'

'No. Leave it to me. If you ask, he might move him…or…' I don't know how to end the sentence without alarming Alison.

'Oh…yes. Okay. Well, I'll see you later then.'

AFTER LUNCH, I'M sitting outside Alison's semi in the car. She lives on a hill in Wadebridge and I can see for miles across the rolling green hills dotted with sheep. The yellow rape fields sweep down into a deep V as the Camel cuts a sparkling path through on its way to the sea. I frame the scene with my forefingers and thumbs. Maybe I should take up painting again.

I'm interrupted in my musings by the door next to Alison's opening and an elderly man, presumably Robert, steps out. He has a shopping bag and a walking stick and looks very unsteady on his feet. He shuffles a few steps and stops outside his garage. I wonder how he's going to manage walking to the shops in his condition. He can't take his car, or Rufus will escape. Then he points a gadget at his garage door and it slowly buzzes open. I get ready to race across the road to grab the cat, but I soon realise it's not the same garage. It has white walls and very organised, compared to the dark dank one I saw. Then Robert gets in his little silver car and drives away.

Now what? Alison waves to me from the window, so I get out and hurry up her path. Once inside she offers me a cuppa, and while I wait, I wander round her living room looking at photos, touching ornaments, running my hand along the windowsill. As I do this, I get a few images of Alison laughing with people, holding Rufus, typing at her desk – a look of determination on her face. I'm about to pick up a photo of Alison on her wedding day when she comes back in. 'That was taken twenty-five years ago. Jack looks so young without his beard. And look at me, I can hardly believe that I was once twenty-eight. Feel about a hundred, lately.'

I pick it up and look at the couple. Alison's fresh-faced and staring adoringly at Jack. He has blond wavy hair and his new wife's love is reflected back in his calm blue eyes. About to put it back, a bolt of electricity races through my fingers and up my arm. I have to grab the frame with my other hand in case I drop it. Alison's talking about how time flies by as she pours the tea, but all I can hear is a man's voice calling me over and over. Then on the white wall above the TV, Jack's bearded face appears and he beckons me. I walk over to the TV and he looks down at another photo of a group of people on holiday. They are all arm in arm on the beach, their backs against a vibrant sunset, the sea lapping over their feet. Alison is there with two men and three other women. It's quite recent.

I look back up at Jack, but he's gone. 'Who's in this photo?' I ask her, picking it up and putting the wedding photo down.

'Oh, that's me with Kate and our friends. We went on a short break to Mallorca last year. Me and Kate paired up as we're both single. It was such a lot of fun.'

I'm keeping Jack's brief connection a secret for now. Just until I'm more certain of my hunch. 'Have any of the ones you've just mentioned got a silver car?'

Alison frowns. 'None of my friends would dream of taking Rufus.'

'Maybe not. I just need to eliminate them from my investigations.' Goodness. I sound like Charlie.

A deep sigh. 'Okay. Well, Helen and Greg do…and Kate.'

I say nothing. We drink our tea and Alison tells me despite the fact we hadn't found Rufus, she's glad it wasn't Robert. 'I wouldn't be able to live next door to him after that and I can't be doing with moving house now.'

'No. I don't blame you. Can you give me the addresses of your friends?'

'I can, though as I said, Rufus won't be with them.' She gets up to fetch paper and as soon as she's out of the room, I hurry over to the wedding photo again and snatch it up. This time there's nothing. Not even the suggestion of a tingle in my fingers.

I take our mugs out to the kitchen and she hands me the slip of paper. She sighs and shakes her head. 'I feel like a traitor doing this,' she says shoving her hands under her armpits.

'I know. But we need to check. Hopefully Rufus will be somewhere else, and we'll have to start again.' Then I ask Alison to give me Rufus's carrier, cat treats and catnip toy, just in case.

FOLLOWING MY HUNCH, I park outside Kate's house and wait. Alison told me she works every day part-time until just after lunch, as a secretary in the local primary school. It's coming up for one-thirty, so I expect she'll be here anytime. She too lives in Wadebridge, but nearer the centre. I'm just wondering if I've time to pop into the grocers' afterwards, as I think we need more potatoes when a little red car swings round the corner and pulls up on Kate's drive.

Red? It's red? Damn it. Has she got a new car without Alison's knowledge? It might not be Kate of course. I watch as a woman gets out of the driver's side. She's tall, mid-fifties with shoulder-length brown hair and a full figure. Yes, she's the woman in the photo. She's wearing a two-piece lilac suit, kitten heels and a matching handbag. A little over the top for a job as a school secretary. A wedding maybe. I get the impression of a woman who's trying to be something she's not. A showy, bright façade to hide a darker interior. Kate puts her key in the door and goes inside. Great. This case isn't as straightforward as yesterday's. But then I imagine yesterday was a fluke. Charlie says all good detectives have to work for their reward.

I lean down to the footwell of the passenger side to grab the paper with the other addresses on it from my bag, and when I straighten back up again, there's Jack sitting in the passenger seat next to me. I give a little yelp because his appearance is so totally unexpected, and he smiles. 'My goodness you gave me a start, Jack.'

He stares straight ahead. 'Kate is the one.'

This connection is one of the strongest I've ever had. Jack seems so …so real. Well, they all are real, but he looks and feels like he's still alive. He's wearing navy overalls and dusty work boots. His blond hair is now threaded with silver and he rubs his beard as if he's pondering something. He's looking across the road at Kate's house. I gather my wits and say, 'But she has a red car.'

'Isn't hers.'

'Who's is it?'

'Not shown to me.' Jack's voice is slow, confused.

I can tell my questions are taxing him, and the last one has no relevance really, so I get to the point. 'Is it shown why Kate has Rufus?'

Jack seems more certain now. 'Punishing Alison. She wants Alison to do what she says.'

We sit in silence and I sense he's waiting for my lead. 'Okay, I have a plan. I'll ring Alison and tell her to ring Kate – say she needs her immediately, as she's feeling upset about something. Then I'll open the garage door and grab Rufus...hopefully. Unless it's locked.'

'I'll come. Rufus won't run from me.'

I MAKE THE call to Alison. Predictably, she's sceptical that Kate has Rufus, but agrees to do as I ask. FIVE-MINUTES LATER, Kate rushes from the house, jumps in her car and drives away. I grab the cat carrier, catnip and treats from the back seat and walk up the path. Jack's already standing outside the garage. I have a quick look up and down the street and pull the garage door up. It's a bit stiff, but it opens, and I hurry in. There's a silver car in the middle and Rufus's cowering in a corner, so I make myself as small as possible, tip some treats into my hand and make encouraging noises. Rufus's not having any of it, until I feel Jack beside me. He kneels down and holds his hand out, says, 'Hello, my lovely boy.'

If a cat can look overjoyed, Rufus does. He trots over to Jack and rubs his head on his knee purring like a well-tuned engine.

Jack strokes him and Rufus climbs up onto his chest. Jack cradles him and whispers words of love into his cat's ear and kisses the top of his head while Rufus pads at his overalls. I can hardly believe they've made proper contact. I once went to hug my gran and it was if my arms had hit an immovable force. There are aspects of my ability that I'll never fathom. When I notice tears dripping from Jack's chin, I have to look away. A spirit can cry? This is heart-breaking. The joy of their reunion will be short lived. Parting will be devastating for both, but for now they are together again, and it's beautiful to witness.

Jack heaves a deep sigh and smiles, though his eyes are still moist. 'Time to go back to Mummy.' He kisses the top of Rufus's head again and puts him in the carrier while I quickly secure the door. Jack puts his hand on the top and pats it. 'I'll see you again one day, boy. Until then, look after Mummy. I love you.'

Jack stands up and I scoop up the cat treats and toy, quickly brushing my tears away. 'Thanks, Jack. I don't think I could have done this without you.'

From behind me he says, 'Please tell my wife I love her.

I turn to tell him how much that will mean to her. But he's gone.

Chapter Eleven

By the time I pull up outside Alison's I feel emotionally punch drunk. Jack was such a lovely man. Why can't he still be alive to spend his days happily with the woman he loves? It seems so unfair. So many vile people, dictators and the like live into old age, and yet Jack... I sigh and wish I had the answers. Nevertheless, a pitiful yowl from the back seat reminds me that there is a happy ending to this particular case. I pick up the carrier and walk up to the front door, only it's ajar and I can hear voices coming from the living room, obviously Alison and Kate. I push the door open, close it behind me and walk along the hall. Outside the living room, I pause to gather my wits and ready myself to explain about Kate. It isn't going to be pretty. About to go in, I hear,

'As I've said, Alison, there's no need to get yourself in a state about your book and the agent's decision. Even if she wants to sign you, I think you should say no. I reckon she's untrustworthy. Because let's face it, that book isn't ready. There's plenty more agents out there and we need to get it perfect. I'll help you. Then you can pick and choose.'

'Really? I don't know if—'

'Well I do. You know I always sort you out, get you through?'

'Yeah, you do, Kate…I'll do as you say when she gets back to me.'

'That's my girl. Now, do you want me to make more tea?'

I push the door open, look at the two women sitting on the sofa and say, 'The front door was open, so I came through. And look who I have with me.' I walk in and set the carrier down by Alison's feet.

'Oh my God! You found him. You found my baby!' Alison drops to her knees and releases the door catch. Rufus comes out slowly, sniffing at his familiar surroundings as if he can't believe he's back. Then when he sees Kate he hisses and spits. Kate's staring at him and me open-mouthed, reminiscent of a geisha as her skin blanches under her rouged cheeks and bright red lipstick. Alison scoops Rufus up in a flurry of kisses and hugs and he settles his head under her chin. 'My poor, poor, darling. You've lost such a lot of weight. If I could get my hands on who did this to you…' She sniffs as tears roll down her cheeks.

I sit on the chair opposite and nod at Kate. 'There's your culprit.'

Alison shakes her head and looks at Kate in bewilderment. 'No. No…I thought there must be some mistake when you called.'

'No mistake is there, Kate?'

'Who the hell are you?' Kate's regained a little composure, but her eyes have become dark as coals.

'I'm someone who Alison asked to help find her cat. With a little help, I tracked him down to your house. Or I should say, garage. Imagine that?'

'That's preposterous!' Kate flushes scarlet. Then she gets so her feet and squares her shoulders.

I stand too. 'If only it was.' I sigh. 'I've been told you took him to punish Alison for being successful with her writing and ignoring your advice. You're jealous. You want her to be submissive and dependent on you. And from what I overhead at the door just now, I think that theory is right.' Kate opens her mouth, but I hold up my finger. 'I did puzzle over why you didn't do away with Rufus though. But then as I drove here, I decided it was because you were going to hand him back, eventually. You'd be the heroine in Alison's story and from then on, she'd be even more grateful to you. Am I right?'

Kate throws her hands up. 'I've never heard such a pile of bullshit in my entire life! I never took Rufus, Alison. Don't believe this…' She flaps a hand at me and turns her mouth down at the corners. '…This person.'

Alison glares at her and takes Rufus to the kitchen, closes the door on him. Then she comes over to Kate. 'Why would you do such an evil thing, Kate. I thought you were my dearest friend.' Her voice is shaky, but I can tell it's from barely controlled anger rather than tears.

'I didn't!'

'Why would she lie?'

'I have no idea.'

'Of course I'm not lying,' I say. 'The fact that you had a red car foxed me a bit, because I was shown a silver car in a garage. Then Jack put me straight.'

Alison put her hand to her mouth. 'Jack?' she whispered. 'My Jack?'

I smile and slip my arm around her. She's trembling all over and I lead her over to the sofa. As we sit, I say. 'Yes, your Jack. He's got the measure of this one.' I sweep my eyes over Kate. 'He also helped me get Rufus into the carrier.' I swallow and try to control the catch in my voice. 'It was an emotional reunion.'

A sob escapes her and she grabs my hand. 'Oh I so wish I could see him too.'

I nod. 'Me too. He was a lovely man and it's so unfair that he's no longer with us. But the last thing he said to me was – "Please tell my wife I love her." I hope that brings you some comfort.' I glare at Kate. 'And the courage to do what you know you must.'

'My Jack. My wonderful Jack.' Alison takes a moment and wipes her eyes. 'Then she stands up and brings her face close to Kate's. 'Get. Out. Of. My. House. I never want to see you again.' Her words are spoken quietly, but there's no mistaking the fury bubbling under the surface of each.

Kate snorts, 'You're bloody mad! How the hell can your dead husband come back? If you believe this woman, then you're more stupid than you look!'

This time Alison's hand does the talking and Kate rubs her cheek in disbelief. 'How dare you!'

'Get out now or God help me I won't be responsible for my actions.' Alison shoves two fingers hard into Kate's shoulder. I stand up in case Kate shoves back, but she just glares at us both and stomps out. At the front door she shouts over her shoulder, 'After all I've done for you! You'll come to your senses soon, but it'll take me a long time to forgive you!'

Alison hurries up the hallway, her face a mask of anger. 'Get out NOW!'

Kate shoots out of the door but turns at the gate. 'And that bloody cat. I should have killed the filthy animal when I had chance!'

Alison's about to give chase, but I put my hand on her arm. 'Let her go, Alison. Don't upset yourself more than necessary.'

As we watch Kate disappear around the corner, Alison slumps against me. She's ashen and trembling and I'm worried it's all been too much. I guide her back inside and sit her down. I make tea and feed Rufus who wolfs it down at light-speed while Alison recovers her composure. 'How could I be so wrong about somebody? She's been my rock,' she says as she takes the tea.

'It happens. And sometimes rocks can crush people. But you're stronger than you think. You proved it just now.'

Then with a loud meow, Rufus runs in and leaps onto Alison's lap. He's ecstatic, doing the traction engine purr and kneading her legs. 'Ow, Rufus.' She laughs and puts a cushion under his claws. 'I have missed you so much, little one. There were times I thought I'd never see you again.'

I watch them for a few minutes while I drink my tea and then decide my work here is done. I smile to myself as I picture myself as a comic book heroine in a Wonder Woman type outfit spinning around like a top, the reds and blues of the outfit blurring into one. Nancy Cornish, Psychic Investigator – specialising in happy endings. 'Okay, Alison. I'll be off now.'

Alison puts Rufus down and follows me to the door. 'Thank you so much, Nancy, for everything.' She gives me a big hug. Then she reaches into her handbag hanging on the newel post at the bottom of the stairs. 'And I got this out the other day. You know, just in case you performed a miracle.' She smiles and hands me an envelope. 'And you did.'

Inside the envelope is three hundred pounds. Two-hundred from Louisa and three today. That's crazy money. I'm touched, but this is too much and I tell her so.

'You said pay what I think your service is worth. And this is what I can afford at the moment. It should be much more for what you've done.'

I take the envelope because I'm guessing some cases I solve won't be as well paid. Not everyone will be as generous, mainly because they won't have the money. But I'd do it for nothing, though Charlie wouldn't like that. I smile at Alison. 'I don't know what to say.'

'There's nothing to say. But are you sure I can ring you if I need to talk things through?'

'I'm more than sure. And you can pop round for a cuppa any time if you feel lonely. I did think you might join a writing group so you could meet like-minded people and make new friends too.'

'I wanted to do that ages ago but…' She blushes and looks embarrassed.

'Kate thought it wasn't a good idea?'

'Yep.'

'All that's behind you now, Alison. Go with your gut and your heart. Now go back inside and give that little cat a big cuddle.'

'I will. Thank you, Nancy. I'll be sure to spread the word about you to anyone who will listen, too.'

Driving home, I wish I'd done this years ago, because I feel I'm making a real difference in people's lives. Hopefully Charlie will be more pleased for me when I tell him. Particularly when the old skinflint sees how much people think my service is worth.

Chapter Twelve

I'm having second thoughts. Okay, if truth be known, I'm having third and fourth thoughts. What seemed like a fire-cracker of an idea when I set out for the high street twenty minutes ago has shrunk, shrivelled up, turned into a damp squib. Suspended from chains, *Standish & White Estate Agents'* sign swings in the breeze as I approach along the pavement. This morning, buoyed by the recent success of my new venture, I thought about the young woman who'd been stood up by her husband in the Whistling Kettle a few weeks back. She'd been the catalyst for my departure, or at least, seeing her husband up to no good had been. The connection I'd experienced while holding the woman's key fob with the photo of Aaron Standish was extraordinary. Penny had said so. Yes, I'd had connections when handling objects before, but to the dead, or as in Becky's case, because I was actively trying to find a connection. The Aaron Standish connection was a new thing entirely. I'd forgotten to deal with it all until last night.

But as I stare up at the sign swinging in the fresh breeze a few feet above my head, I wonder what to do next. What I should do is go in and warn him off, just as the firecracker had intended. But now I'm here, it feels quite daunting. I take a breath and gather my wits. I owe it to Mrs Standish, so I'm going in. I had that connection for a reason and it's to help the poor woman. That's what my life's mission is nowadays, helping people. So I need to get a pile of gunpowder lit under that damp squib. As I push open the door, I hope that some kind spirit will cover me, because I don't think Mr Standish is going to be very pleased with what I have to say.

Aaron Standish is sitting behind a desk tapping away at his keyboard. His dark hair is expertly styled, green eyes, lightly tanned skin and a five o'clock shadow that I'm guessing is painstakingly maintained every morning with various grooming tools. He's very handsome, and nobody knows that more than him. He's got that confident self-assured air about him that would be very attractive to most people. Most people who don't know what a shit he is. There's a woman with dark curly hair sitting with an elderly female customer at another desk nearby, and as I step in and close the door, Aaron looks up at me and says with a winning smile. 'Hello, madam. Can I help you at all?'

'Yes. I'd like a quick word about a personal matter.'

136

The smile falters. Slips to one side. 'Oh yes?' He waves to the chair in front of him. 'Take a seat.'

Once seated, I lean my elbows on the desk and lower my voice. 'It's about your wife. She's a lovely lady – thinks the world of you, and I'd like you to stop cheating on her.' His smile vanishes completely, his bushy black brows become one and he starts to say something, but I hold up a finger. 'I haven't finished yet. Actually, what I said wasn't quite right. I'd like you to either stop cheating, or let her go. She deserves better.'

'What the hell are you talking about?' He hisses, and his colleague gives him a sharp glance. 'I'm not cheating on her. I have never cheated on her.'

I don't bother to lower my voice this time. 'You're a liar, Aaron, and a cheat. The whole town will know soon if you carry on denying it to my face.'

This time the elderly customer looks over too. She's more interested in our conversation than looking at the houses in the brochure. Aaron's colleague sends him daggers. I'm thrilled at the way I'm dealing with this. The fire-cracker spirit is back and raring to go. Aaron whispers, 'Can we go into the back please?'

I follow him into a little kitchen and lean against a sink full of dirty mugs. One on the side says *Aaron* on it and I pick it up.

Concentrate for a few moments. 'Lucy's a lovely girl, Aaron. You really don't know how lucky you are.'

He shakes his head. 'Who the hell are you, and how do you know my wife?

'Both those questions are irrelevant. Are you going to stop cheating on her?'

'I've told you I...'

I cut him off and describe the girls I saw him with and in what situations. His tan pales and he leans heavily against the wall. 'So, your choices are stop it, or leave Lucy. I'll check on you from time to time. And so will your granny Alice. You were her favourite as you know. She's appalled at your behaviour. She thought the world of Lucy too, as you also know.'

'What the hell? Granny Alice?' Aaron's Adam's apple bobs as he swallows hard and draws his hand down his stubble. 'But she's been dead three years.'

'Yeah, I know.' *I only know because I got her coming through when I picked up his mug. Lucy's name too. Lucky that.* 'But she's watching over you. I see dead people quite often.' I smile at his bewildered expression and try not to chuckle when I realise I sound a bit like the boy in *The Sixth Sense*. Then I remind myself not to get too carried away. I have a job to do here.

'You see dead people?'

'Yep, their spirits. Anyway, I can't stay here chatting all day. Must get on.'

Aaron suddenly squares his shoulders and thrusts out his chin. 'You're just a bloody loony. You might have known my Gran before and have come here making all this shit up.'

I go up to him, put my face close to his and say, 'She's standing next to you right now.' I look at the kindly grey-haired old lady gazing at her grandson with a mixture of bewilderment and sadness. She hovers a trembling hand over his shoulder and begins to talk. 'She asking you to remember the day you got on your knees at her bedside and begged God not to let her die, but it was already too late. You were devastated and before you left, you whispered in her ear that you loved her and would never forget her. She's always loved you and knows you're a good boy at heart. Her 'little soldier'.'

Aaron lets out a strangled sob and bites on a knuckle. 'I...I...' Tears well in his eyes and pour down his face. He's obviously taking me seriously now. Granny Alice nods her affirmation and pixilates.

I look at him for a few moments. Then I pat him on the shoulder and leave.

I CAN'T REMEMBER when I last skipped. But this afternoon I can't stop my feet doing just that, all the way down the garden path to my wonderful office. It's all finished now. It has the desk, filing-cabinet, electricity, heating – everything. Inside I add a twirl to my skipping and a little dance to a tune only I can hear. It's loud, joyful and inspiring. Three cases taken on and solved already, and who knows what next week will bring?

Thinking about cases, I remember my big brand-new appointment book's still in its cellophane and get it down from the shelf. Binning the cellophane, I flick it open and inhale the brand new inky, fresh stationery smell. Nothing like a virgin notebook to put a smile on your face. Lists on a computer are very useful, but I've decided this book is where the appointments will go. It feels more formal somehow – a physical reminder of my new career. I might make a few notes in it too. I'll have dates and names to look back on when I'm old and grey, so I can reminisce and say things like – *Ooh, look. Louisa and Mark's case was thirty years ago! My word, doesn't time fly?*

I sit at my desk, take a pen and write in the appointments I've had so far. Then I think about what the book will look like in years to come. It won't smell fresh and new by then. It will be dog-eared and might have cake crumbs or chocolate stuck to the page, or a ring impression from the bottom of a coffee cup. The pages might have yellowed, because the book's been left open by a window in summer. Or they might have a water mark or smudges. I'll be able to pick it up, run my fingers across its pages and be reminded of how I was feeling on specific days and times. Dog ears, cake crumbs, coffee rings and the smell of long-ago summers will document my life. You can't get those on a computer list, can you?

MY SURPRISE PICNIC idea is a good one, but I notice Charlie pat his belly with an expression of dismay. The material of his new purple T-shirt is straining over it. But what does he expect? He's full of chicken salad, home-made bread rolls and cheesecake with fresh strawberries. Might be time to hit the gym. He's not getting any younger… and the butter knife is already dipping into the middle-age spread. But right now, I decide against raising that subject. We're relaxing in beach chairs watching the surfers bounce over the waves while sipping a cool beer. This is certainly the life. Charlie said how thrilled he was with the picnic idea, bless him. He hates being inside the office this weather, and he deserves a treat. He seems a bit more relaxed at the moment and not as huffy about my work.

I pack away the empty containers and sit down next to him. I take his hand as we watch the fingers of red yellow and purple stroke across the navy sky. 'A beer on our local beach at sunset with a full belly,' I say with a smile. 'What could be better?'

He kisses the back of my hand and looks across at me. 'Just one thing, my emerald- eyed, flame-haired beauty.'

'What thing?'

Charlie gives me a wink and wiggles his eyebrows. 'Do I have to spell it out?'

I laugh. 'I think that would cause a bit of a stir, here on the beach in front of everyone!'

'Indeed. So let's go home soon, eh?'

'Okay.' I lean across and give him a lingering kiss.

'Forget later. How about now?'

Laughing again I say, 'In a bit. I need to let my food settle and finish my beer. And Charlie, I had another good day at the office. Well, morning really, I haven't had much to do this afternoon. Remember the woman in the café I told you about who'd been stood up by her philandering husband? The estate agent?'

Charlie says he does and listens while I tell him my story. 'These days, Nance, our conversations make me feel like I'm in some surreal dream. I hope he's going to do as you suggest. Because I don't think you should go back. He could report you to the police – say you keep harassing him. Say you have a screw loose. That won't look good for your new business will it?'

'Oh please, Charlie.' I do an eye roll and twist my curls up into a ponytail. 'He's guilty as sin. No, mark my words. He'll stop his shagging around now. His grandma meant the world to him and he was mortified that she knew about the way he'd treated Lucy.'

Peace descends as we stare out at the ocean watching the deepening sunset and listening to the shush of the waves. Occasionally the shriek of a child and the bark of a dog disturb the quiet, but there's not many on the beach now and it will be dark soon. Charlie wiggles his toes in the sand and I give him a smile. It's ages since we've been this close. So happy and easy in each other's company. I stand and dust sand from my feet. 'Come on then, Romeo. Let's get you home.'

He tells me I look incredibly beautiful silhouetted against the darkening sky, tendrils of hair lifting on the breeze. He stands and takes me in his arms, kisses my throat and jawline. He says my skin tastes of salt air and strawberries. Then I put my lips on his, and I'm lost to everything but him.

THE NEXT MORNING, I get up to find Charlie's made an early breakfast judging by the delicious smell as I stand stretching and yawning at the kitchen door. He sees me and looks disappointed. 'Why are you up? I was gonna surprise you with breakfast in bed and perhaps a little re-run of last night.'

I rub my eyes and give him a smile. 'Easy tiger. I have a pile of laundry as tall as you to do and the weekly shop. Maybe later, if you're good.' I pick up the tray of scrambled egg on toast, tea and orange juice and peck him on the cheek. 'Let's have our breakfast in the summerhouse. It's a lovely morning.'

Grudgingly he follows. Then he said he's just remembered something and dashes back up the path to get it. I look up, my mouth full of toast as he enters the summerhouse a few minutes later. He's frowning, looks unsure of himself.

'I was going to talk to you about something that happened at work yesterday, but we went to the beach and…we had such a nice time I didn't want to land this on you.' He unfolds a piece of paper, hesitates. 'Well, I don't know if you'd want to help with work stuff, as you said no to the robberies. I think this is different though. It's kind of a community thing, because the boss is a friend of yours really, isn't she?' He hands me the paper. 'This is a letter sent to Abigail. There's two more like it, apparently.'

I put my toast down, take it from him.

DI Summercourt,

You're still not taking my threats seriously. If you don't resign your post by the end of the month, I will expose your dirty little secret. Everyone will know what a disgusting dyke you are. I'm sure your colleagues will be shocked and appalled that someone like you is in a position of power. It's unnatural…you're a freak. Just think of the hardworking officers who have normal relationships -wives and children to support. One of these would be much better placed to step into your shoes. You're a disgrace to the Force. Leave. Leave before I expose you.

I can't believe it. Poor Abigail. 'But that's awful! Who'd write such vile stuff?'

'That's what I want to find out, but the boss is having none of it. She says she's leaving because she can't bear to be outed. She won't come out herself, even though I said she should, as she seems to believe that the letter's right. That being gay is unnatural somehow.'

'Unnatural? What a weird thing to say. And I know there's prejudice and sexism in the police, like any other institution, but surely there's other gay people at work?'

'One or two. I was wondering if you might try to get one of your connection thingies by holding the letter? Try to see if we can find out who sent it?'

'Did Abigail give you the letter?'

Charlie looks away, puts jam on a bit of toast. 'Not exactly.'

'Charlie,' I say, giving him a hard stare. It's my best no-nonsense voice and by his face I can tell he knows he's busted.

'Okay. I took the letter when she wasn't in the office because she needs someone to help her. She's upset and not thinking straight.'

'Sounds like she'll have your balls if she finds out.'

'I don't give a bugger. I want to find out who's behind it.' Charlie gesticulates with his toast and a blob of raspberry jam plops onto his clean white shirt. 'Fuck!'

I tear off a bit of kitchen roll and dab at it. 'Never mind. It'll come out, but take it off now. I need to soak it.'

Charlie gives me a jammy kiss as I undo his buttons. 'Are you sure you don't just want my body?'

'Yes.' I tap him on the end of his nose. 'Now get inside and put a new shirt on while I put this to soak. I'll look at the letter for you when you've gone to work and I'll give you a call if anything happens, okay?'

I TRY MY best with the letter, but I need more. Just before lunch I ring Charlie to let him know what I found. 'Hello, sweetheart. Any news?'

'I've had a bit of something, but it's all really sketchy. I haven't seen a person, just images of a church, a bible and wooden cross. I really need the other letters, or even some personal items from Abigail to try and make sense of it.'

There's a long pause. 'Might be tricky. In fact, bloody impossible. How will I get things like that without telling her about your abilities?'

Dear God, he makes it sound like a dirty secret. 'No idea, Charlie. You might have to *actually* tell the truth about what I do.' There's another pause on the line and its charged with resentment.

'Hey, I would. But some people don't believe in all that…'

'Mumbo jumbo?'

'No. I wasn't going to say that…'

'Hmm. Look, Charlie, she'll probably find out about me as word gets around anyway. Jenny next door said one of her friends asked about me the other day. She'd heard from a friend of a friend about Alison's case. So just tell the boss and see what she says. Nothing to lose is there?'

'I suppose not. I'll see. Thanks, Nance. See you tonight.'

After we end our conversation I wonder if I've been too harsh. It won't be easy explaining to Abigail about what I do. She might be a total sceptic and then Charlie will feel like a fool. He might get in trouble too for taking the letter, worse still, showing it to me. I'm worried all day, and am just about to call Charlie and apologise for being so insensitive, when the phone rings in my hand.

'Hey, you. I was just going to—'

His excited voice cuts me off. 'Nance, you'll never guess who your new client is…'

Chapter Thirteen

Why am I so nervous? I keep telling myself that Abigail is just another person coming to me for help and not to worry. Then nerves keep taking over and forcing me to admit the reason why I'm nervous is that Abigail is Charlie's boss. If I bugger this up, it might make things awkward for him. Then I remember what a lovely person she is and tell myself off. And in addition, when Charlie told Abigail what he'd done and about me, she surprised him by saying she was used to psychic people because her great aunt was one. What a stroke of luck! I take a tray of homemade ginger biscuits out of the oven and put them on the rack on the worktop next to the sultana scones I made earlier. They smell delicious. A nice pot of tea or coffee and some of those should make the meeting go more smoothly. *Stop worrying, Nancy.*

It's only as I'm carrying the biscuits and scones to the summerhouse half-an-hour later that another thought strikes. What if Abigail's gluten intolerant or diabetic? Why didn't I ask Charlie? I heave a heavy sigh and stand in the middle of the garden path like some Egyptian hieroglyphic, a large plate balanced in each hand ready to offer up delicacies to the gods. A jackdaw alights on the apple tree above my head and cocks a beady eye. 'What are you staring at?' I ask it.

The bird squawks briefly and hops away along the branch.

Not surprised it's backing off. I need to get a grip – go into the summerhouse and wait for Abigail like the confident and caring person I am. I should compose myself and be ready for whatever comes my way. From the summerhouse, ten minutes later I watch the slightly built tallish woman with blonde hair and elfin features hurry down the garden path towards me. She's wearing black trousers and a smart red shirt, and a large black leather bag hooked over her shoulder. I stand and blot my sweaty palms on my jeans, go to the door and give her a big smile.

Because I've only met her a few times I'm unsure whether to go in for a hug. I decide I'll try for a peck on the cheek and a pat on the shoulder. Abigail tries for that too at the same time and we bump noses which makes us laugh, breaks the ice. I say, 'Hi, Abigail, welcome to my office.'

'Nice to see you again, Nancy.' Her turquoise-blue eyes hold mine, but then she glances away and clears her throat. I can tell she's nervous too which makes me relax. 'Wish it could have been under better circumstances.'

'Never mind. Come in and take a seat on one of the sofas. I'm sure we'll get to the bottom of all this soon. Would you like tea or coffee?'

'Got any gin?' she says deadpan. Then she laughs and I know we'll be just fine.

After I bring the coffee down, we talk of nothing to do with why Abigail's here for a while. Thankfully, she's neither gluten intolerant nor diabetic. She eats a scone and at least three biscuits and tells me about how great Charlie is to work with and how much she loves her job, and that both her parents were in the Force which inspired her career choice. Then she tells me a bit about her great aunt Wendy, the one who was psychic. When the conversation comes to a natural end, I decide to take the lead.

'Okay, Abigail. Let's see what you've brought me to look at.'

She pulls a little flat folder from her bag, opens it and places a few photos on the coffee table between us. Then she takes a blue and white beaded bracelet off and puts that to the side of them. Finally, she takes a little silver crucifix out of a side pocket and puts that next to everything else. 'From what Charlie said about your reading of the letter, I think the author's someone I know. Someone close. There are only a handful of people who know I'm gay, and they're all represented here.'

I pick up the photos. One is of a teenage Abigail arm in arm with a teenage boy who looks like her. He's slightly taller, but he has her eyes and hair colour. In the background is a hotel and lots of other teenagers milling around. They are at a school prom judging by their clothes. Abigail's wearing a long shimmering blue dress with a white corsage pinned to her shoulder. My heart thuds in my ears and I try to focus. It's so quiet in the summerhouse save a few creaks in the wood and the tap of Abigail's nail on her teeth. I wish she'd stop doing that. I can't concentrate. I take a deep breath and close my eyes. Nothing.

'What have you seen. Anything?' Abigail asks after a few moments, her eyes wide, expectant.

'Not so far. And would you mind not tapping your nail on your front teeth? It's a bit distracting?' I add a smile to temper my words as I know she's nervous.

'God, I'm sorry. I had no idea I was doing it.'

I take the next photo. It's Abigail around about seven years old. She's dressed in white outside a church and a young priest is standing by, his hand on her shoulder. In the photo, Abigail looks nervous and shy. Once again, nothing comes to me after handling the image. I hold the blue and white beads in the palm of my hand until the cool round spheres grow warm, but still nothing. Abigail's looking at her nails as if she wants to tap them, but she

152

just flexes her fingers instead. She's got a determined expression on her face and that makes me not ready to give up yet.

'Can you tell me anything about these things? I'm getting nothing so far.'

She nods. 'That one is me and my brother Anthony at the sixth form prom. That one is me with our local priest on my first Holy Communion. The cross was given to me by the priest also. The beads were given to me by my first love, Jane. Unrequited, unfortunately. We met in the church choir and were inseparable growing up. But once I'd told her how I felt when we were sixteen, we drifted apart. The bracelet was one of her gifts to me for my sixteenth birthday.'

Abigail pauses and pours more coffee for us both. Then she says, 'By the way I'll just explain how important the Catholic religion is to my family. All my extended family, parents and sister are devout. My sister Karen is presently at a convent as a novice. Though I think it won't be long before she takes her vows. My brother and I were devout too, growing up.' She laughs. 'In a family like that, it's hard not to be. But now we're lapsed, much to the rest of the family's chagrin.'

Okay. This is good. I'm hoping a little knowledge about the items will help me focus. I rearrange them all on the table in front of me and put my hands on them. After a few seconds I feel warmth spread across my palms and my forefinger starts to tingle at the end and then flows to the rest of the fingers on my right hand. I think I need to try the beaded bracelet again. In moving pictures, it shows me a tall dark-haired girl with big green eyes as I pull each bead gently through my fingers. This must be Abigail's first love. She looks away and fades. No…No, she's not the one who wrote the letter. I'm sure of it.

Abigail gives me a questioning look. I shake my head and move on to the crucifix and the communion photo. Immediately I see a flash of the priest as if he's been caught in torchlight. Just the side of his face and the front. He looks angry, disapproving. Then he's gone. But I don't think it's him either…I can't really say why. Just a gut feeling.

Finally, I handle the photo of Abigail and Anthony at the prom. A few shots of him in quick succession pass before my eyes. Some are with Abigail. They are smiling and the depth of love he has for his sister is almost tangible. He looks towards me and the smile vanishes. His eyes cast down to the left and his cheeks colour. I feel his shame. He's guilty. But is he the culprit? It feels wrong…but he knows something. Then there's the wooden cross I saw when I handled the letter… and then it's over. My fingers lose their tingle and I put the photo down.

'You okay?' Abigail asks and I'm aware I'm staring at her, or through her to be exact, lost in my own thoughts.

'Yeah, I'm just trying to piece everything together.' I tell her what I've seen and ask how each of the people related to the objects reacted when she told them about being gay.

Jane just shrugged and said she'd guessed, but she was straight. She said it wouldn't affect our friendship. Though it did, eventually. The priest, Father Andrew said I was probably mistaken, and feelings change. I'd gone to him in despair as going to church felt increasingly awkward as I was a sinner. I was eighteen at the time and said I knew that my feelings wouldn't change. He said he was very disappointed in me. Knowledge of this would break my parents and I must pray for guidance and strength. He made me feel like I was the lowest of the low.' Abigail stops and draws a long slow breath, holds it and releases. I can tell she's reliving the shame of that day and it makes me furious that a man in such a position could behave so appallingly to a young woman baring her soul.

She smiles. 'Anthony was a bit surprised, but he was really lovely about it. He's so calming. Teaches Philosophy of Religion and Ethics at Truro College – Mum and Dad were so proud. Anyway, he suggested he came with me to tell Mum and Dad, but it wasn't long after Father Andrew had said all that, so I said no. They wouldn't understand. As I said they are devout Catholics and I was so scared they'd reject me…not love me anymore. My siblings always joked that I was the favourite growing up. As I said earlier, I joined the police because I wanted to follow in my parent's footsteps. They were so proud when I did…' Abigail sniffs and pulls a tissue from her pocket.

'But aren't some in the Catholic church coming round to more liberal ideas now?' I ask.

'Not so you'd notice. And I know I said I was lapsed…but because of the way I was brought up…I do feel like it's wrong too. They say it's a sin…Unnatural. I know deep down it isn't, if God made us, then he made me. But nevertheless, I can't shake off the shame of it.'

I'm beginning to understand why she's hiding her sexuality. 'Hmm. That's not surprising when mentors like Father Andrew behave disgracefully.'

'No. I suppose not.'

I look at Anthony's photo again and tell her my thoughts on all three people. 'So my strongest suspicion is of your brother…but I don't think he's behind the letter. Though he does know… something. Could he have told anyone about you?'

Abigail shakes her head. 'I don't think so. I did swear him to secrecy, and if he'd told my parents, they would have confronted me. They certainly wouldn't have resorted to sending malicious letters.'

We sit in silence and I feel like I've failed her. My connections aren't an exact science, in fact they aren't a science at all. But why did it have to be Charlie's boss? My other cases have been straightforward and crazily successful. The table in between us and her serious set of her mouth makes me feel as if I'm her suspect at interview. *For the purposes of the tape, despite the wealth of evidence on the table before us, the suspect has shown no relevant knowledge of who wrote the letter and we are about to end the interview. Mrs Cornish is about to be arrested for incompetence and is a disgrace to the psychic community…*Come on, Nancy. This isn't helping.

Abigail shifts in her seat gathers the photos and jewellery and looks like she's preparing to leave. I try to clear my mind of nonsense and I rack my brains, her story tumbling round in my mind. Then a thought occurs. The wooden cross must be more than just a symbol of Christianity. It must be specific somehow – it was what I first saw when I handled the letters. A hunch becomes a flash of clarity.

'You say you have a sister, Karen, who's about to become a nun?'

'Yes. Why?'

'Does she know?'

'God, no. She'd be mortified.'

I pick up the photo of Anthony again and close my eyes. I say in my head. *Who did you tell, Anthony? Who?* There's the wooden cross once more…and a quick flash of a woman's face. She looks like Abigail, but she's a little older and her eyes are brown. This is important. She's important. As if on autopilot I open my drawer and pull out my sketch pad and pencils. Abigail asks me something, but I block her out, allow my hand free reign. Ten minutes later, there's a rough likeness of the woman with brown eyes on the paper in front of me, the wooden cross hangs around her neck. I spin it around and show Abigail. 'Do you recognise this woman, this cross?'

Abigail puts a shaking hand to her mouth and her eyes swim in unshed tears. When she nods, the tears spill over and run down her face. 'It looks like…it's Karen,' she says in wonder. 'She does wear a simple wooden cross.'

'Your sister?'

'Yes…please tell me it's not her.'

I look at the sketch and trace the contour of her jawline with my finger tip, smooth the rough pencil marks. It's clear to me now. Anthony told her and she's the culprit. 'I'm sorry, Abigail. But yes, it's her. She wrote the letters.'

Chapter Fourteen

Charlie looks like one of those shocked emojis. He's just come out of the shower and his hair's plastered to his skull which accentuates his round face and his mouth is as round as his eyes. His face isn't bright yellow though, but apart from that, he's an emoji. He's a shocked emoji because I've just finished telling him about Abigail's visit and what I found out.

'So that's where she's been all day...' he says almost to himself. Then he starts scrubbing at his hair with a towel.

'Yes. After I told her what I'd seen, she said she was going to see her brother immediately. She didn't phone work or anything to say where she was?'

Charlie pulls his boxers on. 'Well, I knew she was coming to see you this morning. But not where she was this afternoon. Yes, she phoned to say she was feeling unwell and that she'd be in tomorrow.' He combs his hair and then stops, turns to me. 'I thought it was weird as she's never ill. Then I thought – hang on, she's been to see Nancy. God knows what must have happened.'

A little laugh follows, but I don't like the sneery tone hiding behind the words.

'What's that supposed to mean?' I hand him his freshly ironed blue and white checked shirt and sit on the bed.

He turns his mouth down at the corners and furrows his brow. 'Eh? Nothing. It's just that you see stuff that sometimes people might not want to know. Like today for instance.'

'She wanted to know who was sending the letters. I told her. It's a shame that it's her sister but—'

'Yeah, can we stop talking about it now? I'm looking forward to going out for a nice meal and just talking about normal stuff for a bit.' He buttons up his shirt and looks at me through the cheval mirror. 'It's been a long day.'

Oh, poor Charlie. My day has been just peachy. I've had to tell a vulnerable young woman that her sister has been sending her malicious hate mail and then try to pick up the pieces for half-an-hour after as she tried and failed to fight back the tears. She wanted answers and hopefully her brother has given them to her by now. I don't see the point in saying all this to Charlie, because he's in one of those moods. Will he ever completely accept my connections?

My phone rings, just as I'm putting my lipstick on in the hall mirror. It's Abigail. 'I'm so sorry to bother you again, Nancy. But are you free to meet me for a quick drink? I've spoken to Anthony and I could use a friendly ear.'

Charlie's looking at me, head on one side mouthing *who is it?*

'Hang on a mo, Abigail,' I say, and hold the phone to my chest.

'Why's she phoned you? Is she okay?' Charlie asks.

'She wants to meet for a chat. Shall I say no?'

He sighs. 'No. We can go out for a meal another time. I'll make myself some scrambled eggs and you can get something out.'

I arrange a meeting place and end the call. Charlie gives me a big hug and tells me how wonderful I am. Hmm. I'm only wonderful when he thinks what I do might work in his favour.

WE MEET IN the Golden Lion and luckily Abigail's not eaten either, so we order their fish pie which is legendary. As we wait, we sip our cyder and Abigail does the tapping her teeth thing while staring out of the window. Instinctively I reach for her hand and still the tapping. Her cheeks glow pink and she laughs. 'I really must stop doing that.'

'You're upset. It's allowed. Now tell me what happened today.'

She tucks her blonde bob behind her ears and sighs. 'Okay, Anthony told my sister about me because he's an idiot. His heart's in the right place, but sometimes he just doesn't think. Karen, as you know, was almost ready to become a fully-fledged nun, but for some reason she couldn't do it. Her heart wasn't in it, apparently.' An eye roll. 'She felt she wasn't being true to God. She left the convent last week and went to stay with Anthony. She couldn't face telling Mum and Dad. She felt she'd failed and was so ashamed.'

I'm beginning to wonder just what kind of people her mum and dad are. All the siblings are desperate to please them, even if it means burying their own happiness under some impossible ideal held aloft by the perfect parents. All three wanted above all else to make them proud. They must have been under so much pressure growing up. I'm not sure I'd like them. In fact, I'm sure I wouldn't. I say, 'I'm guessing he told her about you to make her feel better. She was jealous to death of your success, and that you're the favourite. Anthony told her you weren't as perfect as everyone thought.'

It's Abigail's turn to be the shocked emoji. 'How the hell did you know? That's more or less what Anthony said!'

I smile. 'It's just logical thinking. Detective work if you like. I'm a psychic investigator – the psychic bit is done, now the follow up investigation just involves a bit of thought.'

'Sure you don't want to join the Force?' Abigail chuckles.

I chuckle too. 'Nope. That's the last thing I'd want. Charlie wouldn't be at all pleased. Especially after I solved...' Damn it. My mouth is running away with me and I can see a light of suspicion flick on in Abigail's eyes.

'Solved what?'

'Solved the mystery of the letter writer,' I say. My voice sounds like I've borrowed it from Minnie Mouse, and I don't think she's fooled.

'R-ight...' She pauses while the waitress puts our food down front of us. 'This looks delicious.'

'It is. It's got two different types of fish and prawns too.' I dig my fork into the cheesy mash and ask, 'What will you do now you know about Karen?'

'That's what I want to talk to you about.' She blows on a forkful of mash and looks me in the eye. 'I've a good mind to go round and threaten her with arrest.'

'Arrest? Really?'

'Yeah. Haul her up in court – then she'd be really fucking ashamed.'

This is so unexpected, a prawn slips down my throat whole. I cough but it's too late and I wash it down with a mouthful of cyder. Blimey. I wouldn't like to get on the wrong side of Abigail.

She's much tougher than she looks. 'Would you do that? I know she's behaved inexcusably, but…'

'No. I don't suppose so. But I want her to know she can't get away with what she's done. She has to know that I will never forgive her.'

'Okay. There's a chance she might go more on the defensive and tell your parents about you though.'

Abigail says through a mouthful of peas, 'You're good at this people reading, even if you've never met the person. That is *exactly* what she might do. But then I can tell Mum and Dad that she'd written those vile letters.'

'They might side with her if they think homosexuality is sinful.'

'Hmm.' She points a fork at me. 'You're not wrong there either.' For a few moments. there's a thoughtful silence between us, apart from the scraping of utensils in ceramic dishes. Then she says, 'Which brings me onto my next question. Do you think I should come clean to my work colleagues and my parents? Then her thunder will be stolen, and I'd be out in the open once and for all. Scares the shit out of me to contemplate it, even so. Thing is, I can no more resign from the job I love, than fly to the moon.'

I'm so relieved I want to hug her, but not sure she'd appreciate it in the middle of a pub. 'Yes. Yes, I think that would be a fantastic thing to do. You'd show everyone who you really are. Put two fingers up to all the bigots, including your parents and sister. You are so concerned about making them proud, but to do that you have to be somebody you're not. You have to go through life pretending. Be you, Abigail. Be proud to be you too. You're a lovely, bright and caring woman who is a damn fine copper according to my Charlie. I've only just got to know you really, and I can see what a lovely, strong and decent person you are too. If you were a daughter of mine, I'd be proud. I'd be bloody proud.' I swallow down another lump in my throat. But this time it's not a prawn.

Abigail's cheeks are pink, and her eyes shine. 'Thank you so much, Nancy. I don't know what I would have done without you today.'

'It was a pleasure. And I hope we can be proper friends after this too.'

'I'd love that. We have to meet again soon so I can tell you how things go with my wonderful family.'

'Definitely. Charlie will be thrilled you're not resigning.'

'Hope so. And how much do I owe you? I almost forgot with everything going on.' I tell her not to worry about it. She is Charlie's boss after all. 'I wouldn't hear of it, Nancy Cornish PI.

You're a bloody fine investigator and you'll get something from me to show my appreciation in the next few days.'

THE NEXT EVENING, a curry's in the oven when Charlie comes in. 'Nancy, you make the best curry in the world and I'm starving!' he calls, as I come through from the living room with my pencil and book. 'Doing some drawings, love?'

'No, just making some case notes while I wait for the curry to cook.' I go over and kiss his cheek.

'Case notes. Ooh, get you,' He pulls a face and does a daft little dance.

I shake my head at him. 'You seem in high spirits.' Then I get the casserole dish out of the oven and take the lid off, releasing a pungent coriander and cardamom infused steam into the air.

'I am in high spirits, my beautiful wife,' he says, trying to dip a spoon into the sauce but receives a slap on the hand for his efforts. 'We have the culprits for the garage robberies by the short and curlies, or we will have when it's gone to court. And it was down to me!'

I smile and hold a spoon to his lips with a bit of chicken in sauce on it. 'See. You didn't need my connections help at all, did you? You need to have more confidence in your abilities, my dear husband.'

Charlie blows on the spoon, eats the chicken and moans in appreciation. 'God, that's good.' He chucks the spoon in the sink and slips his jacket off. 'And not only that. Guess what the boss did today?' I shrug. 'She only went and came out at the bloody briefing! I was so pleased for her!'

I punch the air. 'Yes! I hoped she'd do it. There was a little part of me that worried she wouldn't, but seems like I needn't have. Brilliant news!

'You knew?'

He sounds a bit off, but I choose to ignore it. I need to sort dinner before it goes cold. I drain the rice at the sink, speak to the colander. 'Yes. We talked about it last night. I advised her to go for it, said it was the only way forward really. I didn't mention it to you just in case she backed out of it. Besides, it would have been a breach of client confidentiality too.'

'Client confidentiality? But she's my boss.'

I spoon the rice into a dish and pop it in the oven to keep warm. 'I know, that. But she's still my client,' I say with a sigh. I don't want an argument tonight, I'm too tired.

'Right. I'll go and get changed before we eat.'

Charlie's tone is so churlish I can't keep quiet. 'For goodness sake, Charlie, do you tell me all your confidential stuff from work? No. Of course you don't.'

'Okay, keep your hair on.' He gives a wistful smile. 'It'll take a while to get used to being married to Nancy Cornish PI.' As he leaves the room, under his breath he adds, *Wonder Woman and saviour of the world extraordinaire.*

Chapter Fifteen

Contentment hasn't been much of a companion for the last year or so. It was present from time to time when someone appreciated my ginger and walnut cake, or took the time to tell me how much they'd enjoyed their lunch, but day-in-day-out, it usually left me alone. However, over the past few weeks since I started my business, contentment has been a regular visitor. In fact, I think it's moved in permanently. Every morning I get up excited about the day and how I will help the people who need me. I love to be needed – to be useful. Perhaps it's because I haven't brought up a brood of children, and helping people fills a hole left by the loss of Sebastian. If he'd have lived, maybe I wouldn't feel the same. But then I like to think being useful is something we all enjoy.

I'm in the summerhouse thinking of dusting. It doesn't need dusting really, but I noticed a long strand of cobweb in the top corner that had sticky drips of wood varnish beaded across it like a row of tiny sausages. I will need to stand on the desk-chair and get the feather duster from the house as it's up high. Maybe I'll even need the small step ladder. As I go through the French doors, a gust of wind hurls a spatter of raindrops in my face. Nice. I prop the doors open with a rock. It might be wet, but it's too warm to have the fresh air banished. I stand in the garden a few moments and let the gentle rain fall on my face. There's salt kisses from the ocean in the breeze, and I'm torn between the dusting and going for a walk on the beach. My practical head wins.

Up the ladder a few minutes later, I stick one leg out behind me and reach up high with the feather duster like some wannabe fairy with a fluffy wand. With a swish of my wrist, I wrap the web around the duster like I'm making candyfloss. Gotcha. The stepladders squeak as I move, so I put my foot back on the top step and prepare to come back down. The ladder squeaks again…but it's not the ladder this time. I look down and sitting by the door is a little ginger cat. It has huge green eyes and a little pink nose, and it opens its mouth and squeaks at me. 'Hello, little one. Where did you come from?'

It cocks an ear and does the squeaky meow again, comes inside a few steps. Then it sits down and fixes me with its emerald stare. It is adorable. Talking in a high-pitched voice all the while, I get off the ladder and crouch down in front of it. The cat takes a tentative step forward and I reach my hand out. It sniffs then rubs its head along my hand and arm. I'm smitten. It has no collar, a few matts in its coat, and as I stroke my hand along its flank, I can feel every bone and bump. Poor little thing must be starving. Tuna. We have tuna in spring-water in the cupboard. 'Come on then, my beautiful…' I look at its rear end, '…boy. Let's get you something to eat.'

He follows me up the path and in my mind's ear, Charlie's voice is saying, "why did you feed the damn thing? We'll never get rid of it now." We've had two cats and a dog during our time together and each time they have passed away, my world's fallen apart. Charlie said it was because they were my child substitutes, which was a ridiculous thing to say, as no creature large or small could ever be a substitute for Sebastian. Because that's what I think he really meant. I remember blowing up at him and he apologised. After we buried our last cat, Morris, we agreed we'd have no more. It's was for the best, and after all, they *are* tying when you go away, blah, blah. But this little scrap…he's probably homeless, or at least very neglected.

In the kitchen I watch 'Scrappy' attack a saucer of tuna as if it's going to be snatched away from him any second. Poor little sod. Must be ages since he's eaten, and maybe he's never had tuna at all. I set a dish of water next to him and when he's finished the tuna, he takes a long drink. I sit on the floor with my back against the table leg and watch him lick the saucer clean for the third time and look at me expectantly. There's half a tin left, but I will save the rest in case he's sick. I'll get some proper cat food later and some dried biscuits…that thought pulls me up short. Am I really thinking of keeping him? *You know you are, Nancy.* He comes over and climbs up onto my chest, thrusts his head under my chin and begins to purr. Charlie's lost the argument already.

Half-an-hour later I'm back in the summerhouse. Scrappy has made himself at home on the sofa and is taking a cat nap in between biting at his fur now and then. I make a mental note to buy some flea treatment when I get the food. In fact, I'll ask Penny to get both, then I can keep my eye on him. I don't want him running off. I'm supposed to be writing Abigail's case notes up, but I can't stop starring at Scrappy. He opens one eye and purrs at me, so I go over and sit by him, give him a cuddle. I wonder how Rufus is now. Hope he's settled back down with Alison after his ordeal.

Back at my desk, I'm adding a phone number to Louisa's notes which I found on a bit of paper under the computer. I'm just wondering how she and Mark are doing, when I see her walking down the path followed by Mark. Her long steely hair is lifting on the breeze and she's smiling. Her skin is radiant, and her soft grey eyes lit like translucent clouds as the sun breaks through. I jump up and run to the door. 'Louisa! I was just thinking about you, and here you both are!'

'Were you? How lovely,' Louisa says stopping at the door as Mark comes to stand beside her. He looks just as radiant as her, and the look of love that passes between them is so powerful it takes my breath away.

I usher them in and put the kettle on. They make a fuss of Scrappy and say that Charlie can't fail to agree to keep him he's so adorable. I don't say anything to that. Then they tell me that they have been inseparable since the first day I reunited them. Mark gives me two-hundred pounds as his contribution for what I did to bring them together, and I say it's not needed, but he insists. Then I tell them all about my new cases. Not the detail as it's confidential, but I paint a broad brushstroke account of the success of my business. When we're sitting on the sofas eating my date and walnut cake with lemon icing, Louisa nudges Mark and gives him the sweetest shy smile. It's as if they're teenagers again – beautiful to watch. 'Shall we tell her?' Louisa asks him.

Mark's bright blue eyes flash with humour. 'Yes! That's what we came for, isn't it?'

Louisa holds her left hand out to him and he pulls a diamond ring from his shirt pocket and slips it on her third finger. 'Look!'

She says splaying her hand and shoving it under my nose. 'We're engaged!'

'Wow! That's fantastic,' I say.

'It is,' Louisa says, fanning her face with a cushion. 'I can hardly believe it some days. And guess what. This ring is the one Mark bought me all those years ago, but he never got the chance to propose, because of my foolishness.'

'No point in raking over the past,' Mark says, dropping a kiss on her lips. 'The future is what matters. We're back together now and nobody will ever come between us again.'

They look at me for a response, but I can barely speak because of the big stretchy smile across my face. 'I am so thrilled for you both. And talking of the future. When's the big day?'

Louisa says, 'The sooner the better. We aren't getting any younger. We had July pencilled in. It will probably be by the sea or somewhere close to nature. Mark thought of Tintagel, as that's where you tracked him to. He thinks the church there on the hill overlooking the ocean would be perfect.'

'Yeah, more than perfect. July's only about six weeks off, and that still seems too long to me,' Mark sighs and gazes longingly at his fiancée.

'And we were wondering if you'd do the honour of giving me away?' Louisa says, clasping her hands and steepling her forefingers to her lips, as if half in prayer, half in doubt her words will be rejected. 'If it weren't for you, we'd never be together.'

Overwhelmed, I say, 'I'd be extremely proud to give you away, Louisa. Honoured and proud.'

I'VE JUST PUT the phone down with Penny. She's going to pop the stuff for Scrappy round later and we chatted about the day. It's great talking to her, because being psychic herself means I can speak freely about my cases, though I do keep names secret, because of client confidentiality. She's thrilled that I sorted out the amorous estate agent, aided by his granny Alice. I did wonder if she'd work out who I was talking about though – we only have two estate agents. So much for client confidentiality. Later on, any worries concerning my slip-up, is dwarfed by a towering mountain of apprehension. The reason for the mountain is because I have to tell Charlie I want to keep Scrappy. The last thing I want is another argument after having such a good day overall. Scrappy adopted me and Louisa and Mark are getting married. Wonderful! I can still feel the warmth of love surrounding them and see the unfettered joy on both their faces. I can imagine what Charlie's face will look like when he sees Scrappy, and it won't be pretty.

Luckily, he's in a good mood when he comes in and tells me that Abigail is so much happier now her sexuality is out in the open. She's apparently going round to her brother's in the next few days to have it all out with her sister. She's telling her parents before that too, to make sure the sister can't get there first. Apparently, she's going to ring me afterwards to let me know how it went. I didn't pick him up over his muttered sarcastic comment about me being saviour of the world the other night. No point. He was just pissed off because he'd advised Abigail to tell her colleagues she was gay, but she'd not listened to him — she'd listened to me.

Charlie's stretched out on the sofa, tie off, glass of wine at his elbow on the little side table. He's flicking through the TV channels and gives me a lovely smile. God, why do I have to ruin the evening? I must though. And on second thought, it's no use trying to slide Scrappy under the radar disguised as chat about my day or his, and then have him parachute into the conversation at the last minute. Charlie would have a rifle at the ready to shoot him out of the sky, and be very annoyed I'd tried to pull the wool over his eyes. No. I have to tackle it head on.

'Sweetheart...' I begin, and then the rest of my sentence cuts out, just like that. All the words are there, but not in the right order, each one has seemingly lost the power to join up and pop from my mouth into the open.

'What?' Charlie says absently, taking his socks off and chucking them on the rug.

Any other time I'd ask him to pick them back up and go and get changed. But not tonight for obvious reasons. 'Erm…I might have done something you might not approve of.'

Now I have his attention. He props himself up on the cushions and frowns at me. 'What?'

'I…the thing is…'

'Just spit it out. You're making me nervous.' Charlie takes a big gulp of wine and fixes his hazel eyes on my face. Normally warm and welcoming, they look like the glassy button eyes of a grumpy teddy bear. I feel like one of his suspects and my words won't behave.

'I think it's best to just show you. Wait there.'

Scrappy's asleep on the bed when I go in, but when he sees me, he stretches languidly and gives me the squeaky meow. He's definitely made himself at home. I scoop him up and take him downstairs and he rubs his head under my chin purring all the while. I draw in a big breath before I go into the living room. Charlie's jaw drops when he sees Scrappy.

'No…no, no. Absolutely not, Nancy.' He thrusts both palms at me to emphasise his words.

'Listen, love. Scrappy's a stray. He just came into the summerhouse this morning when I was dusting and he's so thin as you can see. Though he looks a bit better already after a good meal and I've de-fleaed and combed him—'

'Scrappy? You've named him already. Fed him? For goodness sake, Nancy, he might have an owner! They might be looking for him right now.' Charlie swings his legs from the sofa, folds his arms and glares at me.

'They won't be. Look at the state of him. I can feel every bone.' I stroke Scrappy's head and he looks at Charlie with interest. He twists his ears back and forth, sniffs the air and stretches a paw out towards him.

At this, I notice a softening in Charlie's glass buttons, but he blinks it away and says, 'But they might be. How would you feel if we had a cat and it went walkabout and someone kept it?'

'If I neglected it the way Scrappy's owners clearly did, then I'd deserve it.'

'Nancy.' Charlie heaves a sigh. 'He might have got lost and not been able to find his way back. And most important, didn't we say we'd never have another cat after Morris? Can't you remember the state you were in when he died? I was devastated too.'

'Yes, but Scrappy really needs a home. He adopted us, not the other way around.' Charlie shakes his head and opens his mouth to say something, but I hurry on. 'Look, how about I put some adverts in the shops round town with his photo, saying we found him and our contact number?' Scrappy struggles in my arms so I put him down. He makes a beeline for Charlie and leaps up onto his lap.

Scrappy sits down and gives him the hard stare, purring all the while. He lifts a front paw and places it on Charlie's chest and then does the same with the other one. My husband tries to keep a serious face in place, but it slides off into the cushions. He lifts a hand, gently strokes the cat and looks up at me. 'You're not kidding about the bones.'

'No. We'll soon fix that though.' I smile and he smiles back. Scrappy is winning the argument for me. 'It looks like you've got a friend there,' I say, praying that my next question is answered in the affirmative. 'So…can he stay?'

Charlie twists his mouth to the side and tries to look grumpy. He fails. 'I'm not happy about it, Nancy. But I suppose so. And you promise to put those ads in the shops?'

'Of course. I'll do it tomorrow.' My heart's as light as a balloon and it floats me over to Charlie and Scrappy. I sit next to them on the sofa and Scrappy walks from one lap to the other purring like a generator. I lean over and kiss my husband on the cheek. 'Thanks, love. You won't regret it.'

Charlie tickles our cat behind his ears. 'Hmm. Well, it's too late if I do. This boy looks like he's here to stay.'

Chapter Sixteen

I'm shopping for cat food the next day in our local supermarket. Charlie's informed me that Scrappy much prefers the more expensive brand, which I only bought a few sachets of. Naughty me. I'm not complaining though, because he and Scrappy are already inseparable. The cat follows him around like a little dog. In the line for the checkout I feel a tug on my jacket. I turn to see an elderly lady smiling at me. She's tucking her grey curls under a floppy yellow sun hat and fanning her face. 'Phew, it's hot in here.' She pats her pink face with a tissue. 'Sorry to pull your coat, but can I have a word with you please?'

She steps to one side out of the line. I'm reluctant to lose my place, but it would be rude to do otherwise. 'What can I help you with?' I say, hoping my smile doesn't look too fixed.

'It is Nancy, isn't it? Only I don't want to be telling my story to the wrong lady. I'm Dorothy by the way. Friends call me Dot.'

We shake hands. Hers is tiny, fragile – her skin stretched paper-thin over blue veins. 'Yes, I'm Nancy, Dot.'

'Good. Louisa showed me a photo of you. She's my next-door neighbour. Next door but two, actually. We got talking a few years ago when we had snow. Unusual, for round here. But she knocked on the door and asked if I needed anything. Wasn't that nice of her?' Dot takes her hat off and wafts it. Her curls clump in peaks and some are compressed to her scalp where the hat band has been.

'Yes, Louisa's a kind woman.' I offer a smile again and flick a surreptitious eye to the checkout queue. It's looking like the Great Wall of China and I have loads to do this morning.

'Sorry if I'm holding up your shopping. I'll get to the point.' Dot looks anxious and I can tell this isn't easy for her. 'Louisa was telling me how you brought her and Mark together after all these years. She gave me a leaflet thingy of yours because of what I told her. So here I am. I just happened to see you across the road earlier and I've been hurrying to catch up with you ever since. You do walk fast, don't you? That's why I'm so hot. Well, and because of this daft sun hat. They are supposed to make you cooler, but they don't, do they?'

'No, perhaps not. And what can I help you with?'

Dot's bushy brows knit together over her keen brown eyes. 'I just said, didn't I? Oh...' She flaps the hat again and stares past my shoulder. 'No...maybe I didn't. I'm all of a dither. You must

182

think I'm a silly old woman who shouldn't be let out on her own.' There's humour in her voice but it doesn't reach her eyes. She's obviously embarrassed and confused. The cat food will wait.

'Dot, would you like to go for a cuppa? The café where I used to work is just around the corner. You can have a rest and tell me all about your problem there.'

'Really?' Her beaming smile tells me I've done the right thing. 'I don't want to put you out.'

'No trouble at all.'

LEANNE ACTS AS if she's not seen me for years instead of a few weeks or so. 'Nancy! I was only thinking about you the other day. This place isn't the same without you!' She flings herself into my arms and clings there, limpet-like.

'Great to see you too!' I kiss her cheek and disentangle myself.

A new face looks on behind the counter. She looks about twelve with a dusting of freckles and blonde bunches. She's obviously not twelve, but I don't think she's more than eighteen. Melody I think Leanne said she was called. I wave. 'Hi, Melody, isn't it? How are you settling into the new job?'

I love it. Thanks, Mrs Cornish.' Melody goes bright red because everyone's looking at her.

'Call me Nancy, please. You make me feel like your granny with Mrs Cornish. And can we get two coffees over here when you've a mo?'

Leanne and I chat about how everything's going for a few minutes and then Dot and I make ourselves comfortable at a table by the window. It's just been vacated by a man and a woman, the café and harbour are busy today, so we're lucky to get a seat. As I stand up to take my jacket off and hang it over the chairback, I catch the eye of the man who left our table. He's standing by the door to the toilets, obviously waiting for his wife or girlfriend. It's then I realise who he is. Aaron Standish's face flares red as he looks away from me out of the window. I wonder if he's heeded my warning and his gran's? Lucy Standish comes out of the loo and I decide to try and find out.

As she walks past, fiddling with her blonde ponytail, I say, 'Lucy, isn't it?'

She stops, puts her head on one side. 'Yes?' I'm about to tell her who I am when she adds, 'Didn't you used to work here?'

'I did! Last time we got chatting about a promotion and you were waiting for your husband to celebrate.'

There's a twinkle of mischief in her blue eyes. 'Yes, I remember! Scallywag Aaron here never did turn up, did you?' She stretches out her hand to him and he takes it. He gives me a

184

bashful smile and shifts his weight from one foot to the other, clearly wishing he was anywhere but here.

'A scallywag, is he?' I smile at her and look at Aaron. He looks at his feet.

'Used to be. But just lately he's been the sweetest husband I could wish for. He's home on time, cooks, takes me out. He even cleaned the toilet last week. Didn't you, sweetheart?'

Aaron rolls his eyes and shoves his hands into his jeans. Relief floods through me. The guy must have really loved his gran to have stooped to toilet cleaning. I make the next bit up to let Aaron know I approve. 'I'm so pleased. I do like a happy ending...my gran used to say if a man cleans a toilet, he must really love you. A bit old fashioned, but she knew a thing or two.'

'Aaron worshipped his gran, didn't you, love?'

'Yes. Can we go now?'

'She'll be watching over you, Aaron,' I say with a smile.

He looks at his phone and sighs.

'Such a grump.' His wife says. 'Okay, nice to see you again, er?'

'Nancy.'

'Right. See you, Nancy.' Lucy takes Aaron's hand and off they go.

'They seem like a nice couple,' Dot says watching them walk across the road to the harbour hand-in-hand. Lucy laughs at something Aaron says and they kiss.

'They do. In fact, they are, *now*.' I make a mental note to write up this new discovery in my case notes book later.

Melody comes over with coffee and chocolate cake. Apparently, Leanne insists it's on the house, but she does want an honest opinion of the cake from the 'best baker in the world'. She made it herself. 'Okay, Dot. When you're ready, I'm listening.' I stick a forkful of cake in my mouth and give Lee the thumbs up sign as she scuttles past with a tray of food.

'Well, it all started three weeks ago. I was clearing out some stuff from the attic as there's so much clutter up there. My grandson Matt was helping me of course. I can't get up the loft ladder. Not with my knees. I'm eighty-nine, you know.' She pauses, a question in her twinkly eyes, presumably waiting for a response.

I say the obligatory, 'Really? You don't look it.' She does though. And a bit more.

'That's kind of you.' Dot smiles and eats some cake. 'This is delicious!' She shuts her eyes and chews. Then she takes a sip of coffee and sighs in contentment.

My patience is starting to fray at the edges just a little. At this rate we'll be here until Christmas. 'Did you find something interesting?'

'Where?'

'In the loft.'

'No. I can't get in there, not with my knees.'

Stifling a sigh, I say, 'Did Matt find anything?'

'He did. But now it's lost again…or should I say stolen.' Dot lifts her finger and fixes me with an intense stare. 'And that's what I want you for. To solve the mystery. The mystery of my husband's stolen medals.'

I find out the whole story over what seems like about three hours, because of Dot's meanderings, but in reality, is about an hour. It transpires that Matt found his granddad's medals in a little velvet box and put them on the side in the kitchen. Dot was overjoyed because she couldn't remember where she'd put them, and her husband Frank had been so proud of them. As were the rest of the family. He got them after his return from D Day. He'd been five-years older than her, and had passed away nearly ten years ago. The strange thing was, the box had disappeared and Matt hadn't put them anywhere else. She'd asked her daughter, Matt's mother if she'd put them somewhere after she'd cleaned the kitchen. Kathy hadn't. So, Dot has come to the conclusion that someone has stolen them. This seems about as likely as her running up the loft-ladder in stilettos, but I have to be sensitive to her beliefs.

'Was anything else taken, Dot?'

'No. That's the daft thing. Because I have a biscuit tin with three twenty-pound notes which was right next to the shoe-box, and a jam-jar half-full of pound coins too. I don't like to be without, in case there's an emergency.'

What kind of emergency she imagines I have no idea, and I'm not about to ask either or we *will* be here until Christmas and Easter. 'Hmm. You'd think they would have taken the money, Dot. Let's have another think. Maybe you put the medals somewhere else for safe keeping and then forgot where?'

She sits back in her seat and folds her arms tight across her chest, and her mouth twists into a tight pout as if someone's pulled the drawstrings. 'You sound like our Kathy and Matt. They think I've lost my marbles.'

'Not at all. A bit forgetful, maybe? I forget things and I'm only in my forties.'

'I didn't forget anything. Why won't you believe me?'

Dot's tone is a little strained and I don't want her getting upset. 'How about I have a chat to your daughter and grandson? See if they can help us?'

Dot pushes a cake crumb around her plate with a fingernail and then flicks it on the floor. I try not to laugh. 'Wouldn't hurt, I suppose.'

'Okay. I'll arrange it for later in the week. What day is bes…?'

She looks at me aghast. 'Not today? I thought it would be today. Kathy's picking me up in town at 12 o'clock. Can't you come home with us?'

Great. I have washing to put out, cat food to buy, case notes to write up, cooking to do, phone calls to make…But this is obviously really important to her. So I agree. I decide to go in my own car though so I can get away when I want to. She gives me her address and I promise to be at hers for 2 p.m. This will give me time to do at least some of my chores.

MATT AND KATHY are lovely people and not in the least angry or put out that Dot's enlisted my help. Neither of them has any experience of psychic powers, but they have an open mind because I helped Dot's neighbour, Louisa. Kathy is plump with dark curly hair and chocolate brown eyes. I imagine Dot looked very much like her thirty odd years ago. And Matt's in his early thirties with longish dark hair and the same eyes as the rest of his family. He makes us all tea and I'm forced to eat more cake and take a tour of Dot's garden, which she keeps immaculate with a little help from Matt. She grows some of her own veg too and I get a box of potatoes to take home.

Back in the kitchen, we sit round the table and I go over Dot's story again. We all draw a blank. Kathy asks if I might get a connection from some of her dad's things. She thinks there's some of his books in the loft and a walking stick in the hallway. Something in my gut tells me that's not the way forward though and I think about Dot's story some more.

'You know you cleared stuff some from the loft, Matt?' He nods. 'Where did it go afterwards?'

'I took some to the tip, some to the charity shop and some to the library. Granddad was a hoarder of books.'

I'm getting a sinking feeling and it has nothing to do with the heavy fruit cake I've just eaten. 'Is there any way the little velvet box could have been put into the wrong pile?'

Dot waggles a finger. 'No. Because I've got a system to stop that happening. I got some cardboard boxes and marker pens and made a big red dot on the boxes for the tip, a big green circle for those things I want to keep, a blue cross for the charity shop, and a big yellow star for the library.'

Matt shakes his head. 'No, Gran. You said the cross was the tip because it was useless, a cross meant rubbish, you know, crossed-out? And the red dot was the charity shop. The yellow was the library like you said, and the green was to keep.'

'Did I? Yes…I think you're right. It doesn't matter though, because I didn't put your Grandad's medals in any of them. I put them in my old puzzle bag by my chair where I sit at night, because I was going to clean them while I was watching Corrie…' Dot's words fade to silence and we all look at her stricken expression. 'Or did I?'

'You told me to put that old puzzle bag in the charity shop box, Gran. I remember it as clear as day. You said you never do jigsaws anymore and someone else might as well have the pleasure.' Matt sighs.

'Well at least you didn't put it in the blue cross box, Mum!' Kathy says, patting Dot's hand.

Dot's chin wobbles. 'But someone might have bought them by now? It was ages ago.'

'No, it wasn't. I only took them last week, Gran.'

'Was it?' Dot asks, bewildered. 'I'll never forgive myself it we don't find them…all my Frank's medals. I'm such a stupid old fool.' Tears brim and spill down her cheeks.

'You aren't, Dot,' I say. 'And like Kathy said, at least they didn't go to the tip. They are at the charity shop. We'll go there tomorrow and see what we can find, yes?'

Dot sniffs. 'Not much point in you coming, Nancy. I thought you'd be able to use some of Frank's things to lead you to the person who stole them somehow. Seems like I've wasted your time.'

'You never know. Sometimes I get feelings about things, about people when I least expect it. I'll come with you tomorrow. Matt will tell me where and when. Don't trouble yourself anymore. Have a rest.' I pat her shoulder and Kathy and Matt walk me to my car.

We talk for a while and it's clear Kathy's worried about her mum's state of mind and general health. On the drive back, I think of my own mum. While only in her late sixties, I do worry about who will look after her when she gets to Dot's age. She decided to go and live in Aberdeen once my dad died three years back. They went there on holiday once years ago and really loved the place. A crazy thing to do, but she wouldn't listen. I miss her so much and wish she'd come back to Cornwall. She has suffered on and off with depression since she's been away too. I'll phone her later and have a chat. Maybe I'll ask her to come home for good. She's got loads of friends including both Charlie's aunties. They grew up with her and so it's not as if she won't know anyone. There's social events and voluntary work she could get involved with too. I do worry that she's lonely, up there, but she would never admit it. Stubborn and determined – she's passed that on to me.

CHARLIE'S LATE. I turn the oven down for the third time and decide to give him a ring. Scrappy's climbing on my shoulder purring in my ear making it very difficult and I'm just about to sort him out when Charlie comes in the door. 'Sorry I'm late, but we've had a right old day. I'll have my dinner, change my clothes and then I'm back out on the job again. Won't be home until the morning – or even at all.' He sounds weary, but there's a spark of excitement in his eyes.

I pass him Scrappy who's been struggling to jump on him for the past few minutes. 'What's going on?'

'It's the thirteen-year-old daughter of the chief constable of the Devon and Cornwall police. She's gone missing, so it's all hands to the deck.'

That's why he's excited. He's full of adrenaline because the pressure must be on his department. 'Blimey. This is a big misper case, then.'

He cradles Scrappy and strokes him under the chin. 'Not had bigger.'

I can picture the incident room, people running around like headless chickens, all doing their best because one of their own is suffering. Abigail will be up to her eyes. There'll be no time for her to process what's happened with her sister. I nearly offer my help, but then think again. Let's see what good police work can achieve first. With any luck, my connections won't be needed this time.

Chapter Seventeen

Leisurely starts, breakfasts with my husband, and making plans for the evening have disappeared over the past three mornings. I haven't actually *seen* Charlie, apart from a few minutes when he's come home for a change of clothes and maybe a meal. Once or twice I've woken in the middle of the night and found him by my side, snoring loud enough to rattle the roof. He only does this when he's completely exhausted, and by the time the alarm went off at 7.30 a.m., his side of the bed was cold. Poor love. Charlie must be having such a tough time.

I miss him, and the over-thinking bit of my brain delights in painting garish pictures of the future. It drags a big canvas out of some dark forsaken place covered with spiders and daubs scenarios of me, as a widow, trying to get through the long lonely days without Charlie. My heart is swollen with a futile longing for the past and my eyes are as red as the summer sunsets we get here. I wonder how many more times we'll watch the sun go down as we walk barefoot on the beach. The kettle clicks off and I realise I've been staring out of the window at yet another canvas, instead of buttering my toast. I need to think of the present and positive things. I've written up all my case notes and today I'm meeting Dot at the charity shop. The charity shop's closed part of the week, so the case has had to be postponed. It's open again now though, and I can't wait to solve the 'mystery of the missing medals'.

As I HURRY up the high street towards the charity shop, I see Dot's already there. She's cupping her hands to the shop window and peering in. Her black and white checked trouser bottom, thrusts out suddenly as she bends to look at something low down in the corner, and people have to step into the road to pass her on the narrow pavement. I chuckle to myself. She's such a character. 'Hi, Dot!' I call, as I approach. 'Hope you haven't been waiting long.'

She puts her hand in the small of her back and straightens up. 'Eee gads. Did you hear the bones in my spine clicking, then?'

'Not as you'd notice.'

'Every. Single. One. Like a row of tumbling dominoes.' Dot's lips stretch into a smile. Well, I think it's a smile. It might be a grimace due to the domino effect.

'Shall we go in?' I push the door, which has a delightful tinkly old bell on it, and stand to one side.

196

She rubs her back and groans as she hobbles past.

MOST OF THE shop smells like the inside of an old drawer. An old drawer used for all those things that will 'come in handy one day'. The overall bouquet is hard to define, but there's hints of brown paper, clean, but very old linen, lavender and mothballs. Other parts of the shop smells of furniture polish, cheap perfume and potpourri. These are presumably attempts to mask the inside of the old drawer. Behind the counter is a middle-aged man with a dyed black comb-over. Two undyed salt and pepper eyebrows furrow together as his squinty dark eyes peer at an old book through Harry Potter spectacles.

Before I have time to suggest I do the talking, Dot marches up to the counter, bangs her shopping basket on the counter in front of him and says, 'The thing is. I've lost my husband's medals. They were in a puzzle bag which you've got here. Have you found them?'

The man's eyebrows shoot up to his hairline and the squinty dark eyes widen. 'Um…I'm not sure. When did you bring them in?'

'Eh? I didn't bring them in. It was my grandson. Don't you remember?' Dot rolls her eyes and tuts.

The man puts his book down, sticks his chin out and folds his arms. Oh dear

'Hello, my name's Nancy and this here is Dot.' I begin, offering a bright smile. 'Matt, her grandson, brought the puzzle bag in about ten days ago now, I think. Dot mistakenly put the medals in and would love to get them back. They are so important to her and her family.'

The man's expression softens. 'Right. Hello, I'm Stephen. Can you tell me what the bag looked like, Dot? Did it have puzzles in boxes inside?'

'Yes. Of course. I wouldn't have just tipped a load of mixed jigsaws pieces into a bag without their boxes, would I? It would be impossible to put them back together.' Dot's belligerent tone is not going to help. I know she's anxious, but Stephen's hackles are rising along with his eyebrows. His jaw's set and his lips are drawing into a tight pout.

I jump in quickly. 'I believe the bag was yellow and red…but did you sell any medals in the last while, Stephen? Maybe we can start from that angle?'

Stephen blows down his nose at Dot and shifts his gaze to me. 'Um…Yes. I suppose it must have been about four to five days ago. I didn't look too closely in the box, but one was pretty nice looking – gold, round, with white bits of ribbon and lettering. The others were just ordinary looking.'

Dot's face flushes crimson and she thrusts her neck forward. 'Ordinary looking? My husband went through hell for those. And the nice looking one was for D-Day! Frank always said he never deserved medals, because of the carnage he saw all around him. Though he was proud to have done his duty, he used to say the heroes were the ones who didn't come home. You youngsters have no clue what he and his mates went through.'

This is too much for Stephen. 'Youngsters? I'm forty-nine!'

'That's young in my eyes.' Dot harrumphs and opens her mouth to say more.

I hold my hands up. 'Okay, let's calm down. Dot's overwrought, Stephen. She's not normally like this, she's just upset that the medals have been sold and—'

'I don't need you to speak for me, Nancy, thank you.' Her hard stare could freeze an inferno. Then she turns to the shopkeeper, does a sweet smile and pats her hair. 'Now, Stephen, I'm sorry I got,' she glares at me. "Overwrought" …But can you please tell me who bought them?'

He sighs and looks up to the left. 'Um…It was a man, an elderly man. But I couldn't tell you much more than that. Sorry.'

He shrugs and wipes a finger across the dusty surface of the old book.

Dot's face is a picture. A terrifying one. So I leap in. 'Did he buy the bag of puzzles too?'

'No. He brought the bag over and pulled a velvet box out with the medals. Said he'd found them in there, and he hoped it wasn't a mistake. I said I'd no idea they were there. The bag of puzzles were priced at a fiver, but no idea about the worth of the medals.' He scratches the side of his nose and looks at Dot with apprehension and says in a low voice. 'I charged him twenty-quid.'

Predictably, Dot goes off like a firecracker. 'Twenty-quid for my Frank's medals! They're priceless!'

I think Stephen had been expecting this outburst and says, 'To be fair, the old gentleman did say he thought they might be worth more. He'd been in the war himself. He got another twenty out of his wallet I remember. But he didn't look like a millionaire, so twenties' what we agreed on.'

Dot makes a sound in her throat which could either pass for grudging respect or derision. I wouldn't like to call it. 'You don't know anything else about him. His name would be a start,' she snaps, yanking her basket from the counter as if it needs teaching a lesson.

'No. I'm afraid not,' Stephen says stepping back from the counter in a manner that suggests he's done with Dot. Just then the bell tinkles as the door opens and a young couple come in. Stephen brightens, obviously seeing his escape route. 'If you don't mind, I need to attend to other customers, now.'

Thinking fast, I stop him in his tracks. 'One more thing, Stephen. Did you sell the bag of puzzles?'

A quick shake of his head. 'No. The old gentlemen put the bag back on the shelf on his way out as it was near the door. Nobody else has shown interest yet.'

'I don't want the old puzzles, back, Nancy,' Dot says as Stephen scuttles over to the young couple.

'I know. But if the old gentleman was the last to touch it, I might be able to get a connection from it.'

Dot's face lights up and we hurry over to the shelf near the door. The old patchwork yellow and red drawstring bag's balancing on top of a little tower of ring binders, and wedged against a watercolour painting of Padstow Harbour that's seen better days. I pick the bag up and hold it to my chest. Then I take a deep breath and try to concentrate. Difficult with Stephen's babble in the background, and Dot's heavy sighing.

I feel a tug on my sleeve a few minutes later, and Dot says, 'Have you seen anything yet?'

I open my eyes. 'No, Dot. And it's really hard to concentrate in this environment.' While I didn't quite snap at her, she's in no doubt how I feel. She looks suitably abashed and stares out of the window at the passers-by. Then I feel awful because the way she behaved with Stephen and her impatience with me, is understandable. It's not about the medals. The medals are objects. Just bits of metal in the end. It's about the memories. If she could clean them as she'd intended while watching Corrie, she'd feel close to Frank. He'd worn them, handled them, treasured them. The medals are a bond with the past, a precious link to her husband.

Bearing this in mind, I stroke the worn fabric and under my breath, ask Frank for help. Slowly a familiar tingle begins in my fingers and a warmth spreads through my palms. My eyes flick open onto a battle-scene playing out like a film on the street outside. There's a flotilla of landing craft, men leaping into water weighted down with ammunition, a cacophony of whining bullets and shell bursts, men screaming, calling for their mothers...sweethearts...and then falling. Falling, broken and silent in their hundreds, on red sand washed by a crimson tide. It's almost more than I can stand. The grief and horror punches raw and violent into my core and I have to grab the shelf to steady myself.

From a distance, I hear Dot asking, 'Are you okay, Nancy. You've gone ashen.'

I raise a hand and flap her away, as the battle scene fades and a row of houses replace the carnage. I know these houses. They are the colourful 'fisherman's' cottages up the hill from where I live. They're no longer inhabited by fishermen, but they are all occupied. The row of four terraced dwellings are painted in pastel blue, yellow, pink and white and help to maintain the 'quaintness' of the town. Why the sudden switch from war to this? Does the old gentleman who has the medals live in one of these houses? A handsome man in a Second World War army uniform appears and points at the houses with a smile. Then he and the houses fade until there's nothing but the street scene, and Dot's anxious face peering up into mine.

I put the bag back on the shelf and take a moment. Then I say, 'Don't worry, Dot. I'm okay. But it was a bit harrowing.' I tell her the rough outline, not the detail. I don't want to upset her any more than she is already. I describe the soldier who pointed at the houses at the end though.

'My God. I bet it was Frank. I'll show you a photo of him later, but I bet it was, don't you?' I say I think it probably was and pinch the bridge of my nose with finger and thumb. I still feel a bit woozy after that battle scene. 'You poor maid,' Dot says taking my arm. Let's go and have a cuppa. You can recover your wits before we go up to the fishermen's cottages.'

'If it's all the same to you, Dot, I'd rather strike while the iron's hot.' I know that if I go for a cuppa with her, the whole day will be gone and I want to make something nice for Charlie's dinner. He said he should be home at some point.

'Okay. You might have to offer me your arm to get up that hill. What with my knees being like they are.'

'How about I pop back and get my car, Dot? It's a hell of a hill.'

ON THE SHORT drive up to the cottages, Dot talks about her knees, her husband, her daughter and wider family. Her words run into each other, and at one point she's garbling. I think it's because she's nervous and out of her comfort zone. It's not every day she enlists the help of a psychic investigator after all. Dot tells me she's very lucky to have so many people to care for her and she's no complaints. Well, apart from her knees. But that's to be expected at nearly ninety, isn't it?

I park up outside the first house. It's the yellow one and has a colourful hanging basket by the front door. Purple petunias and pink fuchsia. We comment on it and then Dot asks, 'Are we going to knock on every door until we find the man?'

'Can't see what else we'd do.'

'Okay. Let's start here then. I'll do the knocking and asking.' Dot fights with the door handle and the door handle wins.

I nip out and open the door, help her out too. 'It's no bother for me to knock and ask, Dot.'

She cocks her head birdlike at me. 'If you're worried that I'm going to be rude to people like I was that Stephen, you needn't. I'm on my best behaviour from now on. It's very exciting doing PI work.' She grins and despite her back and knees, hurries up to the front door of the yellow house.

The yellow house is home to a young mum with two small children. They've not been here long, so don't know the rest of the neighbours yet. She thinks there might be an elderly man amongst them, but she can't swear to it. The pink house is next, but there's nobody in. And then we move to the blue house. Dot knocks. I knock. Nothing. Great. Okay, last chance now. We start towards the white house when the front door of the blue house opens, and an elderly man pops his head out. He's got wispy white hair, a ruddy complexion and twinkly blue eyes. I'm reminded of Father Christmas, but older...and without the beard.

'Sorry, ladies. It takes me a while to get to the door these days with my knees,' he says.

Dot chuckles and goes back across. 'You don't have to tell me about knees. How the heck do you get back up this hill when you've been out?'

The man taps the side of his nose. 'I've got a magic transportation machine, otherwise known as a mobility scooter.'

'Really? Do you know, I've been thinking about one of those for a while. I'm just a bit worried that I'll knock people over with it and squash them in our crowded alleyways.'

The man does a wheezy laugh. 'You'll be fine. Best thing I ever did. It gives you back your independence.'

'I bet. It's a real nuisance having to ask relations to ferry you to the newsagents for a quarter of strawberry bon bons.' Dot's beaming and surreptitiously tidying her fringe while pretending to look back down the hill into town.

Must be nice for her to chat to someone with things in common, it's lovely to see. But we really ought to get to the point of our visit. 'We're sorry to bother you, but did you happen to buy some medals from the charity shop on the high street recently?'

'Because if you did, they were put there by mistake.' Dot takes over the conversation and puts her hand on the man's shoulder. 'They have huge sentimental value to me because they were my late husband's. He was at D-Day you know.'

'He was? So was I!' Come in, come in. I'll put the kettle on.'
The man steps back inside his house and ushers us through.

Dot goes straight in, but I say, 'You did buy some medals, then?'

He puts his hand to his cheek. 'I did, yes! Forgot to mention it when this young lady here said about D-Day!'

Dot shrieks with laughter and puts her hand to her chest. 'That's fantastic! And young lady, he says! I'll have you know I'm nearly ninety.'

'Nothing but a spring lamb. I'll be ninety-two in December!'

Inside, we find his name's Ken and he's only just returned to Cornwall after sixty-odd-years living in Wales. He went there not long after the war to find work, as his cousins live there and helped him out. He was married, but his wife sadly died seven years ago. His children live in various places around the UK and so he's come back to his homeland 'to die', as he put it. He's not ill, just old. 'Now, let me go and get those medals for you, Dot,' Ken says putting a plate of Ginger Nuts on the table in front of us. 'I'm so glad you tracked me down. You must have been beside yourself.'

When Ken's out of the room, Dot turns to me with a faraway look in her eye. 'I'm sure I know him from somewhere. Maybe we went to school together…he seems *very* familiar.'

Ken comes in and puts the medals on the table in their velvet box and pushes them towards Dot. 'Back to their rightful owner.' He sits opposite and dunks a biscuit.

Dot's eyes are bright with unshed tears as she strokes the medals before putting them in her basket. 'I can't tell you how grateful I am.' She takes out her purse and pulls out two ten-pound notes.' Here you are, Ken. This is yours.' Ken holds his hand up and protests, but she insists. 'You have to take it. It's only fair. I'm just so happy we tracked you down.'

Ken furrows his brows. Yes, that's what's been puzzling me. How on earth did you track me down, exactly?'

I tell the story while Ken listens, clearly astonished. I can tell he has a barrage of questions, but Dot doesn't give him chance. 'Ken, what's your last name? You seem really familiar to me and we are nearly the same age. So we could have been at the same school, or you might have known my Frank if you were in the war together.'

'Do you know, Dot I've been thinking the same thing! You remind me of someone I went to school with called Dot. She had a keen sense of humour like you and looked a bit similar. But time does change a person, doesn't it? I mean, we're going back seventy-odd or even eighty years. Can't remember her last name.'

Dot smiles. 'At school I was Dot Trevethan. My married name is Simmons.'

'My God, it is you! My last name's Rosevear.'

Dot's hand trembles as she puts her tea cup down. 'Ken Rosevear whose dad had Polruan farm?' He nods enthusiastically. 'I used to come up there for eggs after school!'

'So you did!' Ken thumps the table. 'I'd forgotten that.'

'I had a crush on you back then!' Dot laughs.

'Same here!' Ken chuckles. And they do stretchy smiles at each other for ages.

'Well what a coincidence!' I say, just because I think they might stay like that forever if I don't break the spell.

'Isn't it just!' Ken says. 'I can't tell you how glad I am to see you again. We have a lot of catching up to do.'

'We do! And did you know my Frank?'

Ken chews his lip for a moment. 'I can't say as I remember the name, but I might know him by sight if I saw a photo from the war days. We both came from the same town, so chances are.'

'Yes. I bet you did. He'd have left school a few years ahead of us, so that's why you don't remember the name. Oh Ken. I'm so happy you were the one that bought the medals.'

Ken clears his throat and looks bashful. And just for a moment I can see the young farm lad Dot had that crush on. I take a swallow of tea to shift a lump, and he says 'And I'm so happy you were barmy enough to make the mistake of shoving them in the wrong box, Dotty Dot…'

'Dotty Dot! Yes! That's what you teased me with back then.' She gives him a playful shove. Then they both laugh and fall into a conversation about school days and I begin to feel like a gooseberry. A very happy and satisfied gooseberry.

'Hey you two. Do you want me to leave you to reminisce and pick you up in an hour or so, Dot?'

Dot looks at Ken. 'That would be lovely, if you don't mind me imposing, Ken.'

'You're not imposing, woman! I've got a bottle of sherry in the cupboard and some fruit cake. We'll make an occasion of it.'

I arrange to come back in an-hour-and-a-half and say my goodbyes. I do the food shop and when I eventually walk up the path to my house, despite being emotionally drained, my feet have wings. What a wonderful, heart-warming case that was. Now to prepare the casserole for later and pop back for Dot. When I go through to the kitchen, I nearly drop the bags. Charlie's sitting hunched over at the kitchen table with a pot of coffee in front of him. He's got such a thick five o'clock shadow it's almost a beard, and his eyes are red-rimmed and bloodshot through lack of sleep. 'Hello, love.' he says rubbing his eyes and yawning.

'Bloody hell, Charlie. You look terrible…and how did you get back? The car's not on the drive.'

'No. I got a lift back as I was too knackered to drive. I'm going to have a shower and a kip before I go back this evening. Abigail ordered me to.' He looks at me and gives a weary smile.

'I should damned well think so. You can't carry on like this, Charlie. You'll be ill.' He flaps a dismissive hand at me and drinks his coffee. 'Any news on the missing girl?'

'Not so far. We're all working flat out.'

I massage his shoulders and kiss the top of his head. 'You'll get there, don't worry. Now eat something and then bed. Okay?'

Charlie sighs. 'Okay. I suppose you're right. You always are.'

I glance at him now and then as I abandon plans for the casserole and make a quick omelette. His expression says he's present, but the look in his eyes tell me he's far, far away. Probably puzzling over the case, worrying if he's missed something. Is it time I stepped up? Could he use my help at all? I'm about to offer it, toss him a line, but remind myself he had very mixed feelings about my input with Becky. Of course he was happy on the one hand, but jealous on the other, because I solved the case and he didn't. Do we want all that again? I wind up my rescue rope and stow it for emergencies.

I put the omelette down in front of him and he begins to eat. His expression looks a bit more positive now. Maybe he's had an idea about what to do when he gets back to the station. I've made the right decision about not getting involved. I'll certainly give it a bit longer. Besides, I have enough to keep me busy at the moment.

Chapter Eighteen

Lilly Bradley has been missing for four days. The Chief Constable's thirteen-year-old daughter went to school as usual on Monday and never returned. None of her clothes or possessions are missing, which implies she hasn't run away. The last time her friends saw her, she was eating lunch in the dining hall, but she didn't attend afternoon school. She normally takes her phone to school, but her mum found it on her bed under a textbook. The police think this was an oversight, rather than a desire on Lilly's part to remain untraceable. Maybe she was just late for school and didn't have time to look for it. This is the story so far after extensive interviews with all her friends, family, and teachers. No leads. No ideas. Nothing.

I'm pondering on the information I have about Lilly on the way back from dropping Dot home. She went to visit Ken again and seems less curmudgeonly at the moment. She told me the other day, that life is a story with unexpected chapters and twist. And who'd have thought she'd meet an old friend because of some lost medals near the end of her book? Lilly's and Dot's stories weave in and out of my mind as do worries about my husband. His thread is the most dominant right now, and I can't wait to get back and make sure he has a good meal. He's on the point of collapse. If it was up to me, he'd stay home tonight and start fresh in the morning. What he's been told about the promotion not depending on performance is obviously not sinking in, because I'm sure that's what's driving him. Of course he's concerned for Lilly, but I've never seen him this fixated. He needs rest.

My thoughts shift as I pull up at the traffic lights. I smile to myself as I think about Dot's face alive with excitement when she got in the car. She'd had a wonderful time talking to Ken about the old days again, but she was suddenly silent as we neared her house. I teased out of her that she felt guilty for enjoying herself so much in another man's company. She worried that she was betraying Frank, and was unsure if she should meet up again like they'd arranged. I told her Frank would be happy that she'd found an old friend to share memories and companionship with, and not to worry. Why shouldn't she try and grab a bit of happiness before it's too late?

CHARLIE EATS HIS casserole like an automaton. His mouth chews, his hand lifts the fork, deposits more food and returns to the plate. Lifts. Returns. Lifts. Returns. At one point I think his batteries have died. The fork hovers mid-way between mouth and plate while his eyes flutter open and close themselves, as if he's testing his lids for the first time and can't get the hang of it. Eventually he finishes and burps his thanks. I clear his plate and put apple crumble and ice-cream in front of him. I doubt he's got the energy to eat it, but he did ask for it earlier. He's obviously trying to re-fuel for his return to work. He's had two hours' sleep and is planning to leave again in half-an-hour.

'You know, I'm sure Abigail would understand if you had a good night's sleep. You'd be much more use to the case fresh.'

'Yeah. That would go down really well, wouldn't it?' He puts his hand to his ear and pretends to talk into a phone. 'Sorry, I'm not coming back in tonight because I'm a bit tired. I'm sure you'll be okay without me.'

Obviously the wrong thing to say. I pull up a chair and reach my hand to his across the table. He doesn't shake it off but doesn't offer any response. My fingers curl round, give it an encouraging squeeze, but it remains inanimate. A heavy lump of clay. He continues to eat the crumble with robotic precision. 'Nobody can say you haven't been working your arse off on this case, Charlie—'

His spoon falls with a clatter. 'I have. But it's only been recently hasn't it? I've never really done much above and beyond what's been necessary for years, have I? This girl is out there lost and alone. Or maybe somebody has her. I'm sick to my stomach with worry for her. Why are there so many evil bastards in the world, Nance?'

The anguish in his voice breaks my heart and I don't know what to say. What can I say? I have no answers.

'And you know what else? Part of me thinks if I can help get Lilly back, it will boost my promotion. How shallow is that?' Shame and bewilderment cloud his eyes. 'I need to prove I can do it. Okay, I got DS, but that was ten years ago. And I reckon that was a fluke.' Charlie scrubs at his nose with a fist, shakes his head. 'This promotion would mean everything to me. It would say to everyone that I'm good enough.'

This is so out of character, so out of the blue that I'm lost for words. Charlie hardly ever opens up like this, shares his innermost feelings. In the end I offer, 'You *are* good enough, my love. You are one of the most caring people I know.'

'What kind of a caring person worries about promotion while a girl is missing? It's all about me. Just like me dad used to say – but he should know, he was exactly the same. Worse. Made my life a misery growing up.'

'Your dad? Your dad was horrible to you?' Charlie's dad never struck me as being unkind. He was normally very quiet. So much so, he was hard to fathom.

'Oh yes. You don't know the half of it.' Charlie's eyes flash and his mouth draws into a tight pucker. 'My dad has a *lot* to answer for.'

What to do now? He's obviously distraught, over-tired, at his wit's end. Do I push him to explain, or just leave it? I pick up his heavy lump of clay and kiss it. He squeezes my hand in return and gives the most shuddering sigh. His eyes fix somewhere beyond the kitchen window, the tree tops waving in the breeze I think, but I can only guess at the scenes playing behind his haunted expression. Something tells me he needs to get it out. 'Charlie. You've never told me your dad was mean to you before. What happened when you were a kid?'

'I've never told you because we don't share our troubles. Men don't, you see. Men are the ones who protect, who 'man up' and keep it all in. Men make sure they never cry, let their guard down. Because if they do, they'll be vulnerable. Weak. Nobody's allowed to see your heart, your true feelings, because if they do, they'll use it to their advantage. Humiliate you. Expose you. Real men might feel like chucking in the towel, but they don't, they keep going no matter what.' Charlie lets go of my hand and covers his mouth as if he's trying to keep his words in. But they escape through the gaps between his fingers. 'Men are successful, ambitious, get things done.'

His fingers start to tap on his lips and then tremble, then all of sudden he slaps his hand down hard on the table making me jump. I think he's going to carry on speaking, because he opens his mouth, but nothing comes out. Then he presses his lips together and stares out of the window again, there's a twitch in his jaw as his teeth grind together. It's as if he's fighting with himself. The feelings need to come out, but his father's words are stronger. 'Charlie. You *are* successful…you do get things done,' I say softly.

'Yeah. I'm not doing too bad lately. But for years I just went with the flow because Dad told me I was rubbish at everything. School, college, policing. I was too sensitive, he said I needed to push myself, toughen up. He would laugh at me if I cried for any reason. Eventually I vowed I'd never give him the satisfaction again. I'd get a clip round the ear'ole when I was little if I ever had a go back at him. Once, when I was in my late teens, I stood up to him and said he never saw it from my point of view. That's when he said everything was all about me. I did try to make him happy, Nance. But no matter what I did, it was never good enough. Never in my whole life did he ever say he was proud of me. In the end, I suppose I just stopped trying.'

Fury's bubbling in my gut. How dare Vernon Cornish do that to my lovely husband, to his son…his only child. 'I'm so sorry, Charlie. Now I understand though. Your dad's the reason why you find it hard to show your feelings. Especially about Sebastian. To talk about him?'

Charlie puts his head to one side, looks at me. 'Yes…I suppose it is. And, Nance.' He stops, takes a minute. 'I want to say how sorry I am for being such a grumpy bastard where your connections are concerned. If I'm honest, while you were working at the Whistling Kettle, I was okay. Because of my dad's shitty influence, I'm ashamed to say I thought my job was more important. It made me feel I was worth something because I was a copper and you worked in a café. But then you ditched it and took on a whole new direction. And you are bloody good at it too. The Proctor case made me proud of you on the one hand, but I was worried on the other. My dad was whispering in my ear that I was being made a fool of by you. That I was too crap a copper to solve the crime by myself.' He lifts his hands and lets them fall to his thighs. 'Such a bloody idiot to allow him to still get to me *even* when he's dead.'

I take Charlie in my arms and we sit in silence for a while. Everything makes so much more sense now. All Charlie's resentment about the success of my work, the jealousy over Abigail and snide remarks. Also, the little questions I had about my in-laws but never dreamt of asking are all clear now. The answers are obvious, stretching back into the past like stepping-stones over a troubled river. Paving the way for truth. His mum's deference to her husband, the way she always bigged him up. Said what a wonderful father and husband he was, so proud of his work. He was a car mechanic. A good honest job, but hardly a rocket scientist. She was probably as browbeaten as her son.

'My love, you're not an idiot. If you had to put up with all that since you were little, there's no wonder you reacted in the way you did. I'm no expert, but it'll take some time to shake off, and I'm afraid you might never be totally free. These things run deep. But the main thing is, you've made a start. You've told me, opened up – shown your feelings, which is a completely human reaction, contrary to your dad's beliefs…and for that, I'm very grateful. But tell me. Why now?'

Charlie takes a sip of water. Frowns. 'I'm not entirely sure. If I wasn't so exhausted and frustrated at the moment, I might not have said anything. But I guess it's a number of things. What really matters in life has been in my thoughts since we've been working on this new case. I've been thinking about poor Lilly, about how much her parents are hurting right now. Thinking about the anguish and despair in her mum's eyes that day when we went round to collect some things from Lilly's bedroom. Remembering how much I loved our boy, how much I love you and how lucky I am to have you…' He takes more water, gives a shrug. 'And there was a poster at work in the canteen. It said it was good for men to talk, and listed the statistics on male suicide in the police and other professions.'

Fear grabs my heart and squeezes. 'Charlie…have you—'

'No.' He kisses my cheek. 'No, I've not been having suicidal thoughts, but I have been down quite a bit. But you know what?' He stands and pulls me to my feet. 'I feel much better for telling you about Dad.'

We embrace and put my head on his chest, listen to the beat of his heart, tell him I'm glad he told me and that I love him. I ask him to stay home, but predictably he won't hear of it and pops upstairs to have a shower and change his clothes. And even though I promised myself I wouldn't get involved in Charlie's work; I have a phone call to Abigail to make. I trust her implicitly, and so I know Charlie will be none the wiser.

Chapter Nineteen

The conversation in the hallway I'm earwigging into ends with a deep sigh. Charlie comes into the kitchen where I'm putting the remains of casserole and crumble into plastic containers. 'That was the boss,' he says tossing his mobile onto the table with a clatter.

I try to make my voice natural. Difficult, as I know exactly what Abigail said. 'Oh yeah? Any leads?'

'No. But she told me not to come back in tonight. She reckons the whole team is having one off. There's no point in flogging ourselves to the point of exhaustion, because it'll be counterproductive. Best come at it early tomorrow morning with fresh eyes and brains…sounds exactly like you.'

'Great minds, eh?' The little laugh I've rehearsed comes out like a guffaw, so I put my head in the fridge to cool my cheeks while ostensibly looking for a lost lid.

'Hope she's not just taking pity on me 'cos I'm old and knackered.'

'You're knackered, but not old.' I shut the fridge door and link arms with him. 'Come on. Time for bed.' I walk him towards the door. 'I'll make a milky drink and bring it up to you. Then I might pop out to Penny's. She's having a candle party or is it, jewellery? Can't remember.'

'Okay. I'll go to bed. I can see I've no choice with two bossy women running my life.'

Ten minutes later I hurry upstairs with the Horlicks, but Charlie's already out for the count. Thank goodness. Tomorrow will look so much brighter for him after a good eight hours. Tricking him doesn't sit easy, but it had to be done. Now for my side of the bargain. Something else which doesn't sit easy, yet no less necessary.

ABIGAIL'S PLACE IS not what I expected. This three bedroomed 1930s semi-detached on the outskirts of Newquay would more suit a family, not a young single woman. Wouldn't a smart apartment overlooking the river in Truro be more her style? But then Abigail isn't the type to conform. She's a strong woman, her own woman. So I shouldn't be surprised at all. Abigail opens the front door and a square of light floods the path. She's wearing a baggy green jumper and black leggings which makes her so much younger than in her smart work clothes. 'Hello and welcome. Did you bring the food?' Her eyes sweep the big carrier in my hand.

I laugh. 'Yes, of course. I would never hear the end of it if I hadn't.'

We talk about her house choice while I transfer the casserole into a pot and put it on the hob. She's a keen surfer and the location is therefore logical. Why the big house? She hates feeling confined, restricted. I don't share that it might be something to do with her stifling Catholic upbringing. No point in bringing the mood down. We talk about surfing and my desire to take it up again one day. By the time the casserole's on the table, I appear to have made her a promise that we'll go surfing at Daymer Bay before summer's out. This woman can be very persuasive.

'Charlie wasn't at all suspicious, then?' she asks, digging in.

'No. He doesn't know which way is up. It was a sneaky thing to do – waiting while he was in the shower to phone you, but he really needed the rest.'

'Sneaky is sometimes necessary. And so do I. Once we've finished here, I'm going to bed too. I'll set the alarm for four, so I should get at least seven hours. Bob and Harry are perfectly capable of running the team while me and Charlie get some shut-eye.'

'Good on you. It's hard to delegate sometimes, I expect. Especially in such a high priority case.'

'It is. But right now, I'm thinking about pudding.' She speaks to the crumble dish on the side, longing in her eyes.

I NOD AT her nearly empty plate. 'My god, you were hungry.'

'Hey. It's chicken casserole and you *are* one of the best cooks round these parts.' She gets up and goes into the hallway.

'It's apple crumble for pudding,' I call, getting up from the table. 'Would you like some?'

'Thought you'd never ask.' She comes back in laughing and sits down. She has a large canvas bag which she puts on the chair next to her. 'I have some of Lilly's things in this bag, Nancy. Thanks so much for agreeing to try and make a connection with them. I know you were uncomfortable with it. But Charlie…don't worry, Charlie need never know. Though I really can't see why he wouldn't want you to help.

There's no way I could divulge all Charlie's insecurities and also that I helped in the Proctor case. But I have to give her something. 'As I said, he likes to finish stuff he started. Like tonight after you phoned, he was still frustrated that he had to go to bed, even though he was dead on his feet and shuffled heavy-legged upstairs.'

'Talk about stubborn,' Abigail mutters through a mouthful of crumble.

'He's one of the stubbornest people I know.'

'Good copper though.'

'Yeah. Good husband too.'

'This is *so* delicious. Thanks, Nancy.' Abigail yawns and chops her spoon through a crunchy bit of crumble in her dish. Then she says, 'That evening when we met in the pub for dinner, you nearly let something slip about solving something. You covered it up by saying that you solved the case of who wrote those malicious letters to me. I wasn't convinced though.'

This is so out of the blue, I don't know what to say. 'Err...not sure I remember.'

'Yeah you do. Did you solve one of Charlie's cases?'

I bet she's a good detective, just switching a whole conversation unexpectedly – putting suspects on the back foot. I'm tempted to try and fib, but what's the point. She'd see through me. 'Okay, I did help on the Becky Proctor case.'

She jabs her spoon through the air at me. 'I knew it! One day we had zilch, the next we had Becky. Charlie's a good copper, but the 'I had a hunch' didn't ring true with me. Well done, Nancy.'

This is a pat on the back for me, but a cow pat on the head for Charlie. I put my forefinger to my lips. 'Charlie would be mortified if he knew.'

'Mum's the word.' Abigail scrapes the last of her pudding round the dish and finishes it off with a satisfied sigh. 'Talking of mums. I told my parents I was gay last week before my bitch of a sister had chance. I went round to hers after and turned the air blue. I'm sure Karen had never heard some of those words. I don't think I had either.' She laughs and leans back in her chair.'

'Blimey. What did she say?'

'That she wasn't sorry she wrote the letters, and I needed to ask God for forgiveness. She said anyone could change their ways if they tried hard enough and had Jesus to guide them. I said I was happy how I was, thank you very much. And if she loved Jesus so much, why didn't she take her vows, instead of running out on him at the last moment? I said it was all to do with being jealous of me and my success, and the only way she could feel like she was getting one up on me, was to resort to low-life despicable tactics. I left her in tears.' Abigail stares at the memory over my left shoulder. 'And you know what? I couldn't give a shit. I hope she suffers. I need to get tougher when it comes to my family and tiptoeing around their medieval ideas about sexuality...and loads of other things come to think.'

I give her a moment and ask, 'What did your parents say?'

'They were shocked, disappointed and um...saddened, I think was the word.' She looks up to the left. 'Yes, saddened, that

227

was it. They had high hopes for me, and didn't I know I could jeopardise my illustrious and meteoric rise up the ranks of the thin blue line? I said I doubt people would care very much, and if they did, so what? My happiness is what matters. Being *me* is what bloody matters.'

There's a catch in her voice on the last sentence and she takes a sip of water. I smile. 'Good for you. It must hurt, but you did the right thing. How did you leave it with them?'

'They said I should think very carefully about the way forward, and they'd be here if I needed to talk. They condemned Karen's actions, but said they understood why she did it. Can you believe that? I can't see us ever going back to how things were before. But there we are. In a way that's a good thing. Catholic guilt be damned.' She thumps her chest. 'In here I know I've done the right thing and I feel so much stronger for it. And God knows what you must think of me. I've been wanting to give you some money for what you did for ages, but as you know, I've been run off my feet!' She hands me an envelope. 'Better later than never.'

'Three-hundred pounds? You really shouldn't—'

'I really should. Now let's get on with this case.'

She makes coffee, and we take the bag of Lilly's things into the living room where a wood burner's throwing a cosy glow up the walls. Its late May, but the evenings are still a bit nippy in north Cornwall. She puts the little reading lamp on and closes the curtains. 'Okay,' I say as I plop down on one of her comfy sofas. 'What have you got for me?'

Abigail takes four items from the bag and puts them on the coffee table in front of me. They are all in clear plastic bags and have been tagged. 'The toothbrush and hairbrush have had DNA taken from them and been examined so all clear. The photo is what we used to give the media, and the rosette I took from her room the other day, along with some other stuff. I thought these might be useful to you, because she's mad on horses and so maybe there is some clue in it? No idea. I'm not the psychic.'

First, I pick up the green and white toothbrush and twiddle it round in my fingers. It smells faintly of mint and the bristles are splayed out at the edges, evidence of enthusiastic brushing. It's time Lilly had a new one. A slight buzz in the tips of my fingers starts up, but doesn't go anywhere, so after a few moments I put it back down. The hairbrush has fine strands of long conker-brown hair wrapped around its barrel. I hold it up to the light and the scent of hairspray follows the arc of my hand. The buzz comes back stronger this time, and a light electric pulse flows across my skin like liquid. My breath is taken by some light-speed rolling images on the wall next to the log burner. A pair of hazel eyes flecked with green stare at a mirror in a dimly lit bedroom –

fingers with nails bitten to the quick drag a hairbrush through the long conker hair – in the mirror, the eyes watch a thin strip of light under a bedroom door. Terror widens them. Then the brush falls from my grasp to the table with a clatter. The images are gone.

'You okay?' Abigail asks, leaning forward on the opposite settee, elbows resting on her knees.

'Yeah…I think Lilly was scared of something, or someone…possibly at home. Least, I think it was Lilly I saw.' I pull the photo closer and pick it up. 'Yes. Same eyes.' The photo is of a pretty teenager, long hair divided into bunches for this school photo. She's wearing a trace of mascara and eyebrow pencil, I think. Her nose is narrow and straight, and her small heart-shaped mouth is giving the photographer a hint of a smile. I tell Abigail what I saw, and she ponders on it.

'I can't think who she'd be afraid of at home. There's just her dad, her mum, her older brother Leo, who's seventeen, and her younger sister Bethany, who's four. Maybe the image you saw was of a sleepover at a friend's?'

Is she for real? Isn't it the case that family are always the first suspects? That's what Charlie told me, anyway. Maybe the fact that Lilly's the chief constable's daughter has clouded Abigail's judgment. Then I remind myself that so far there are no suspects.

The girl has gone missing. That's all. Apart from this one connection which showed me Lilly was scared of someone… 'A sleepover at a friend's? That's a possibility. You could ask her friends if she's had a sleepover with any of them recently.'

'Yeah I will. Are you going to try the other two items now?' Abigail's doing the teeth tapping thing, so I tell her to stop it and then I finish my coffee and concentrate on the photo.

Lilly's eyes draw me in and my hand trembles with static. A whirl of emotions spin in my head out of control. Lilly's emotions. I close my eyes to see a series of short images as the connection deals the playing cards and the emotions in my head settle upon them.

Snap.

Lilly younger, playing in the back garden with siblings. She's happy.

Snap.

Lilly older, walking to school with friends. She's relieved.

Snap.

Lilly now, throwing her phone on the bed, tears in her eyes. She's sad but resolute.

Snap.

Lilly on a dark street. Scared. Terrified.

The cards are put away and I open my eyes. I need a moment after the last one. I wish I could just reach my hands out into the image and pull her home safe. Abigail notes down what I tell her, then I pick up the rosette. It's blue silk, with '*2nd place*' on the middle in yellow writing.

Abigail tucks her hair behind her ears, goes to tap her teeth, then lowers her hand. 'Lilly's mad on horses, as I said. She has one of her own which they keep in a field behind the house, a little stable too. Lucky girl. This rosette was for a gymkhana event a few months back, her mum said.'

I ignore the comment about Lilly being lucky. I think she's far from that. I am also totally convinced she ran away from home. Home is not a happy place for Lilly. It's a while before anything happens with the rosette. Then just a short 'film' of her jumping a chestnut horse in a field runs on the back wall. I can't read her emotions. She looks happy enough. Then the film ends. I put the rosette down and tell Abigail what I saw. 'Not much help there, I'm afraid.'

'No. But we have with the other things. Thanks to you we have so much to go on than we did when I got here.' She goes over her notes. 'So, these things are possible. One, Lilly is perhaps scared of a friend's parent, or older sibling – maybe something happened at a sleepover. Two, she's maybe having problems with internet bullying, so she left her phone on the bed. One and Two might be linked. Three, she's probably been abducted by this person she's scared of, and the last image you saw could indicate she escaped, and is unable to find her way home. She could be in a different town.'

I'm incredulous. It's clear Abigail's judgment is clouded by who Lilly's father is. 'I'm getting something very different, I'm afraid. From what I've seen and felt, I'd say that Lilly was a happy as a younger child, but then something happened as she hit her teens. She was walking to school, relieved to be away from her house. Someone there is hurting her in some way. She left the phone on the bed because she didn't want to be contacted or traced. Lilly had made up her mind to run away, which made her sad, but she was determined to escape. The last one, I agree with you. I think she is in a strange town, terrified of being on the streets at night and the dangers all around. Poor kid. Wish we knew where. Have you been examining CCTV of rail and coach stations?'

Abigail shakes her head. 'No. She can't have run away because none of her clothes are missing, and the money she'd saved is still in the little box she kept in her bedside drawer. There was over two-hundred pounds. If she was running, she'd take that. And yes, we have people on CCTV just in case to cover all bases. It's not as easy as you see on TV crime dramas though.'

This information is not enough for me to change my mind. Lilly could have planned to run for some time and hidden clothes and money elsewhere. I don't know for sure, but it seems likely. What I am sure of, is that girl ran from home. Ran from someone at home. Abigail's scribbling in her notebook. A work of fiction. 'Look, Abigail, I know her dad is your big boss, but I think you need to interview the family again. Say you think you've missed something and need to—'

'Thanks, Nancy, but not just now.' Abigail's smile doesn't reach her eyes. 'It's frustrating enough for the Chief Constable as it is. They are a lovely family and been through such a hard time now and in the past. I can't tell you about that, because it's confidential. My boss is trying his best to keep everyone positive. He's obviously being kept informed of any progress, but he's not allowed to be involved in the case directly of course. Must be doing his head in. I'll take what we've found out, and get onto her circle of friends first thing. See if she's had a sleepover and go from there. We'll find her. Don't worry.'

I want to say that she won't be found if they don't look in the right places, but bite my lip and stare into the dancing flames of the log burner. I wonder what happened to the family in the past?

Whatever it was, it's helped to put Chief Constable Bradley on a towering pedestal. It's useless trying to convince DI Summercourt of the way forward. I need to have a think. And quick. Poor Lilly is God knows where, and I need to find a way of finding her before it's too late. Abigail's packing Lilly's things away and it's obvious this session is done. 'I was wondering how you'll explain what you know without saying where you got the information. I know the police mostly frown upon psychic help.'

'Yep. That's because it often leads us down the wrong path. I've heard of a few rare cases where it's helped, but it's a pretty hit and miss affair. I'll just say I was thinking of interviewing Lilly's friends again, as we've not much else.'

The way she'd averted her eyes when she'd said 'hit and miss affair' annoys me. I have a feeling she thinks the connections I made tonight might not be of much value, but she's not saying so. I collect the coffee cups and say, 'Yes. Often connections are hit and miss, because they are about messages, feelings and images. They can get mixed up, sometimes given to the wrong recipient, or misunderstood.' I walk to the kitchen and say over my shoulder, 'But I reckon my abilities are pretty bloody awesome to be honest. My friend Penny, who knows about these things, says I have a rare and extraordinary gift. She's never known anyone like me.'

Abigail follows me in. 'Oh, I know that. Look what you found out about my sister for me...you *are* awesome, Nancy. I just meant that it might not work every time and—'

She's bright red and babbling so I put her out of her misery. 'Don't worry. I know what you meant. Now, would you like some carrot cake for tomorrow?'

CHARLIE'S SPREAD-EAGLED in the bed when I go up later and snoring like a jack hammer. Knowing I'll wake him if I get into bed, I go next door to the spare room. It's past eleven, but I'm not tired. My brain hasn't allowed me a minute's peace since I left Abigail's three hours ago. My thoughts resemble the bread dough I used to make up in the huge mixer in the café kitchen on early mornings. Mechanical arms tossed and slapped, tossed and slapped, and then I'd turn it out onto a floured surface for a good pummelling. My thoughts remain half-baked, despite the heat of determination burning in my chest.

The moon slips free of a dark cloud, like a silver coin from a black velvet pocket. I sit on the windowsill and look at our little garden bathed in mercury, as moonlight spreads over rooftops towards the Camel. Where is Lilly tonight? Is she safe? Is she alone? In danger? There are a few things I could do, one of them is not sensible, or more importantly, likely to work. The chief constable could be found, visited and questioned by me, as could the rest of his family. I could pretend to be working with Abigail and Charlie. Mind you, coppers normally show up in twos, so that would look suspect straightaway. Besides. I'm only doing more to help if I'm asked. No volunteering. It would get back to Charlie and then all hell would break loose.

The more sensible option would be to put pressure on Abigail to keep an open mind about Lilly's family. Make sure she treats them in the same way she would any of Lilly's friend's family…if she finds that Lilly did indeed have a sleepover. It could be a step forward in finding out why she ran. But it would leave us standing still in terms of *where* she ran. I leave the window and flop down into bed. The quilt cover's a bit stiff and the mattress has a dip in it. Poor me. Lilly would kill to be in it right now, I expect. Thirteen-years-old and on the streets because she feels unsafe at home. Doesn't bear thinking about. Except I can't do anything else at the moment.

Trying to get comfy, I thump the pillow and imagine it's whoever drove Lilly away. Those hazel and green eyes haunt me when I close mine, and draw in a big breath – try to regulate my breathing, make myself relax. Then I open one eye and realise I forgot to close the curtains, but I really can't be bothered to get out of bed now. I'm beginning to feel sleepy at last. As I'm drifting off, I feel something brush my cheek. Bet it's a bloody spider. I flap my hand about and turn over with a sigh. The same thing happens again, but this time there's a trace of static following the arc around my cheek to my chin. My eyes fly open. Standing by the moonlit window, is the figure of a little girl in pink pyjamas, around seven-years-old. She's holding a yellow stuffed rabbit by the ears in one hand, absently stroking its fur with the other.

I sit up in bed and the girl points at me. 'You must go. Go to the place of the big clock.'

'The big clock?'

The girl nods and twists the end of her dark plait round her finger, which hangs over one shoulder. 'The town with the big clock.'

She looks so tiny, vulnerable and alone. A sucker punch of grief, and the injustice of one so young having her life cut short, renders me almost mute. I take a moment and a big breath. Then eventually I manage to make sense of what she's said. There's only one town with a big clock. 'London. Is that where I must go?'

The little girl scrubs at her nose. Looks unsure. 'Ben.'

'Big Ben?'

'Find Lilly.' The girl looks out at the moon. Her small frame is bathed in its light, silver down dusts the curve of her cheek.

'Where in London shall I look? Can you tell me anything else?' The girl turns her back, starts to pixilate. 'No don't go yet!' I say jumping out of bed. 'Wait!' But she's gone…I'm left talking to a square of moonlight on the carpet.

Chapter Twenty

Charlie looks more like Charlie when he comes down at six-thirty the next morning. The rest has made a huge difference. I feel the opposite. Sleep claimed me eventually at around three, and I woke at six from a dream about me wandering round London, with the girl in pink pyjamas calling for Lilly at the top of our lungs. I've decided to keep my connection with her from my husband, but I'll tell Abigail as soon as he's gone to work. My brain might be frazzled, but I can see no other way forward. Somebody has to go to London. I need to tease some information from Charlie too. The more I know about Lilly's family, the better.

'Morning, love. You should have woken me. I need to get going after a quick cuppa.' Charlie shoves his hand through his hair and yawns. 'Did you have a nice time at the candle thing last night?'

Guilt at having to lie sends a heat arrow to my cheeks, and I run water into the sink to avoid facing him. 'Yeah, not bad. But nothing to write home about.' I make tea and put crumpets in the toaster. Inside my head in the background, I'm having an argument with myself about whether to ask a question. I have to ask it in such a way that he won't suspect I've been talking to Abigail. I put the crumpets in front of him, and though he protests he hasn't time to eat them, he's soon wolfing them down.

'Abigail might want me to sort through Lilly's friends again this morning. I'll do ringing round and hopefully find a lead that we didn't have before. You were right. I do feel more positive this morning after a good night. Not rocket science is it? Some might say I was stubborn.' He gives me a smile and wipes melted butter from his chin with the back of his hand.

I lean against the counter and nibble the crunchy edge of my crumpet. I say, 'You know you said the other day, that the theory so far is that you think Lilly was taken, rather than run away?'

He nods. 'Yeah. Because she hadn't taken any clothes or money and her phone was on the bed. Phones are like another appendage to youngsters.'

'Hmm. Something bothers me about it though. I know I've not had any connections or anything, but I have a feeling she wasn't abducted at all. I'm getting a sense that she was running from the house...that she was afraid of someone who lives there.'

'Eh?' Charlie says through a full mouth, soggy bits of crumpet pattern the front of his dressing gown. 'Who'd she be afraid of? They're a lovely family.'

Here we go. 'You've met them?'

'Yes. I went over with Abigail one day to get a few items of Lilly's. The chief is such a brave guy. He nearly broke down once or twice, but he held it together well.'

'Right...and Lilly has two siblings, one older and one younger.'

'Yeah. Lovely kids too.'

I finish the crumpet and drink my tea. What I'm about to say is important, but I try to make it sound casual. 'When I was chatting to Abigail about her evil sister the other day, she told me a bit about Lilly's case. She said her heart goes out to the family, because they went through another awful time in the past.'

Charlie glances up from his plate, his expression full of surprise. 'She did? Did she say why?'

'No. I interrupted her about something else, and I've only just remembered she didn't finish telling me.' Heat rises up my neck at this outrageous lie and I turn to back to the sink to hide.

'It's not like the boss to just drop something like that into conversation. She obviously trusts you. Okay, this stays within these four walls,' he says to my back. 'But four years ago, I think it was, they lost a daughter. She was about seven. A couple of years younger than Lilly. This girl was the youngest at the time…Chloé, I think her name was. Her mum was pregnant with little Bethany when she died. Awful, awful tragedy.'

The heat in my face is cooled by a chill sense of dread in the centre of my chest. I turn round to face him. 'What happened to her?'

'The poor kid fell from a window while climbing out to save the family cat. Bloody thing had got stuck in a tree opposite her bedroom.' Charlie sighs and drains his cup. 'At least it was quick, the fall broke her neck.'

I stifle a sob, because I know her straight away. Poor little Chloé – the girl in the pink pyjamas. I was so, so sad when I met her last night. But now I know her story, I'm devastated. What a tragic and senseless loss. My heart goes out to her, as I picture her sad little face bathed in moonlight at my window last night. Why does life have to be so cruel? Her poor mother, pregnant at the time. What hell she must have suffered. Then without warning, Sebastian's loss kicks me in the gut, keen and as fresh as it was on the day he died. I realise I'm crying as Charlie comes over with tissues.

'Hey, Nance. I'm sorry, I shouldn't have said anything.'

'No, I did ask. It's okay…it's just so awful And I always think of Sebastian at times like this.'

'Yeah. Me too.' Charlie holds me tight and kisses the top of my head. 'Okay, I'm off to work. I'll keep in touch.'

I wipe my eyes and kiss him on the lips. I so wish he could stay. As he gets to the kitchen door I say, 'You will get dressed before you leave? Not sure a tatty old dressing gown covered in crumpet crumbs will create the right look.'

He does the lopsided smile that melted my heart all those years ago at the school dance. 'I'll have you know tatty old dressing gowns are *in* this season.' Then he blows a kiss and goes upstairs.

'YOU'RE NOT SERIOUS?' I say into the phone and begin to pace up and down the summerhouse. My stomach's doing acrobatics, and I plop down in a chair feeling quite giddy all of a sudden.

'I've never been more so,' Abigail replies. 'You'd be perfect.'

'There must be lots of female police officers who could go. People who know what the hell to do in missing person cases.'

'But they aren't psychic, are they? They could show up in London and have no clue what to do next.'

'So could I! And what the hell would I tell Charlie? I told you, I want him none the wiser about my involvement in this case. I only called you to pass on the latest about seeing Chloé, and that she told me about London and that she was Lilly's deceased sister.' I cross my fingers behind my back. Another whopper. 'And also to repeat that I'm convinced Lilly's run away. She's run away because she's scared of being at home for some reason…whether you like it or not.' The snappy tone in my words can't be helped. This is a serious matter.

'Okay, okay. No need to get arsey.' Abigail says with a sigh. I'll go with your theory for now. This visit from Chloé tells me you're on the right track. And we're wasting time. I'd love to come with you, but I don't know how I'd explain my absence. You must go. If you get a lead, I'll have to come. I'll make something up…no idea what.'

'No. And I don't know what I'd tell Charlie either. The whole thing is ridiculous. I'm not a copper, or a real investigator. The 'PI' on my leaflets is just to attract attention…' The acrobatics of my stomach is turning to a deep nauseas churn. 'I didn't sign up for this. Why don't you go? Say you had an anonymous call from someone who thought they recognised her.'

'Because it might lead nowhere. I know you've seen Chloé, but what if Ben turns out not to be Big Ben? It might be a wild goose chase for someone like me who's not tuned into…' She sighs and I hear a tapping sound. That'll be her fingernails on her teeth. '…What do you call it, otherworldly stuff like you. Besides, if I went, I'd have to inform the Met. They'd want to take it over. It wouldn't work, Nance.'

'And it might not work if I went either.' I'm beginning to feel backed into a corner.

'No. It might not. But you're the only real lead we have, Nancy. Surely you want to help us find this poor girl.'

'Hey, that's not fair.'

'Life isn't.'

At these curt words, the temptation to end the call is almost overwhelming. 'Yeah. I know. It's not been all roses for me, you know.' Abigail doesn't respond. Perhaps she's hoping the silence will get too much I'll break it with a few rash words like – Okay, I'll do it. I think of Lilly out there somewhere, lost and alone. And Chloé. The little girl who never got to see her eighth birthday. The desperate plea for help. I heave a deep sigh down the phone and say, 'Okay. I'll do it.'

MY HEART'S THUMPING in my chest as I look out of the train window at the countryside whizzing past. Charlie will blow a gasket if he ever finds out…I must make sure he never does. I haven't called him yet. I'll do it when I'm in London. The latest lie will be that my mum called and she's feeling a bit low. So…I decided to go up to Aberdeen and cheer her up…on a whim. It needs work.

My brain chastises me for my decision every half hour or so, like a parent who needs to assert dominance over a wayward child. My gut tells it to shut up. My gut told me to pack a bag and buy a ticket to Paddington, and I'll be there in about five hours or so. That's the trouble living in Cornwall, it's so far from everywhere, but I wouldn't change it. I unzip the side of my rucksack and look into Lilly's hazel eyes peering from the dark interior. Abigail sent the image through and I printed it and stuck it in a poly-wallet. I'll be needing that when I get to the town with the big clock. Despite all my misgivings, I do feel a little excited.

The river of adrenaline feeding my rush of excitement slows as the journey progresses. Thinking about it, the photo is all I have. Besides Big Ben, I've no idea where to begin my search in London. Lilly could be anywhere. Let's hope she is in London and that I didn't misinterpret Chloé's message in some way. The child didn't say Big Ben, she said Ben. What if Lilly's been held captive by someone called Ben? What if Abigail was right all along when she said that Lilly was abducted, not run away?

RUSH HOUR ON Westminster Bridge sweeps me along, helpless against a tide of business-suits, bustling tourists, exhaust fumes and traffic horns. The contrast between the Capital and my little fishing port is bewildering and brutal. My levels of tolerance for such a metropolis have been learned and experienced over a number of years. I'm here for a purpose with a full belly and money for a hotel room. But poor Lilly's on the run from everything she ever knew, at the tender age of thirteen. This city is vast and alien to her. How must she be coping?

Near the end of the bridge, I look up at the face of Big Ben obscured by scaffolding due to the restoration. Then I look the other way, across the gravy-brown Thames to the London Eye. Charlie and I went on it a few years ago and I remember the sightseeing boats bobbing at its feet, while other tourists marvel at the slow rotation of historic London from the top of the wheel. Every day, all this is going on, while hundreds of homeless people and rough sleepers patiently wait on street corners, and in tube stations. Hidden in plain sight.

Hefting my rucksack further up my back, I lean my elbows on the bridge and stare down at the water, then turn round to watch the passing feet, the people who've stopped to scroll through their phones, the ones who are just looking around like me. I wish I could see a little girl in pink pyjamas. I try to empty my mind and concentrate on Chloé, but she remains elusive. Big Ben. He's all I have to go on, so I'll go there first. Negativity tries to suggest it's all been a waste of time, so I close my ears and make for the clock.

I wander around the immediate area below Big Ben, but see and feel nothing. There's no hunch, not even an inkling of where Lilly might be. I sit down on a bench and watch the traffic grumbling by. Where would I go if I were her? I might try and find other kids like me on the street. If I went to a homeless shelter, I might worry that those running it would try to phone the police because of my age. I've no idea what the policy is. If they do report anyone under-age to the police, kids wouldn't dare go there. Therefore, they would be at more risk out on the streets. At least if they were accepted with no worry of being reported, the organisers would have more chance of talking them into getting help. But if they didn't report, it might be seen as negligence and encouraging children to run away. It will be worth asking someone who'd know.

The thump of footsteps echo along the underpass near the Houses of Parliament as people rush through, and a faint whiff of urine wrinkles my nose. There's a homeless man not far from the entrance, with a small white dog curled up on a filthy blanket by his side. I put a few pounds in the pot at his feet and hunker down nearby, my back to the tiled wall of the underpass. He jabs a couple of fingers through a tangle of dark matted hair, gives his head a scratch, glances at me, away, and then back. 'You don't look like you belong here, lady.'

I smile and hold his gaze. In my head I say to him – And you don't look as old as I first thought when I saw you from a distance. Your kind green eyes are supported by lines and wrinkles etched by weather, not age. You have much pain inside you and your spirit's battered…but not dying. Yet. There's hope for you just around the corner. It's not too late.

These words come as a shock to me. I've heard of psychics that can look at someone or hold a person's hand and get connections about their past and future. But so far, it's never happened to me. Maybe I'm just reading his face and surmising. Anyone could do that…

I say, 'I'm looking for someone.'

'Aren't we all, love?' A throaty laugh reveals a close relationship with cigarettes.

'Would you mind if I asked you to look at a photo?'

'No. Knock yourself out…unless it's porn. I know your type.' I get a cheeky wink and have to laugh.

'This girl's been missing five days almost. She's my friend's daughter and I'm helping to find her. She's from where I live in Padstow, Cornwall—'

'Padstow?' The man's eyes light up. 'I've been there many times…mind you, that was when…' The light dies and he stares at the floor. 'Lovely part of the world,' he finishes. I say nothing and hand him the photo. He studies Lilly's face and says, 'Yeah. I've seen her about. She was wearing a shit load of make-up when I saw her, so it took me a while looking at this photo, because she looks so much older in real life. Her hair's lighter too. The eyes gave her away. She's got that same shy look as she has in this picture.'

Hope floods my heart and I take the photo back with a trembling hand. 'Are you sure?'

'Yeah. I'm sure.' He gives the little white dog a stroke. 'She had a sleeping bag and warm clothing, but asked about homeless shelters and I told her the nearest one. The next day she came back to thank me and said she'd been just been hassled by some street kids. Said they'd get her some gear to sell. If she didn't, they said they'd make it hard for her. I told her if they threaten her again, come to me.'

'Oh my God. When was this?'

'Nearly two days ago, I think. Not seen her since.'

Shit. I lean my head back against the wall and close my eyes. Lilly could be anywhere by now. But if this man is the only one who's been kind to her, she might not wander too far from him.

And I was right that she'd run away. If she had a sleeping bag and warm clothing, she must have been planning to run for a while. Maybe she hid everything somewhere until she was ready. The heavy make-up and dyed hair, could explain why the officers examining the CCTV footage hadn't found her too. I open my eyes and smile at the man. 'Thanks for helping her...er?'

'Ben. And you are?' He sticks his hand out.

Ben. Of course. What else would you be called? I grin and say, 'Nancy.' Then I shake his hand. It's rough with dry skin and calluses. To my surprise, in the short time my hand is joined with his, I see a nineteen-thirties semi-detached house with a red door and a black car parked on the drive. I know Ben used to live there. The car is electric. No idea why that is significant. And the idea that help isn't too far away from him comes to me again, and I know I can't leave yet. 'Ben. Tell me about how you came to be here.'

'Same as we all do. The sperm meets an egg and then grows into a baby in the mother's womb. Then...' Ben looks at my deadpan expression and the nicotine chuckle follows a finger-jab through the air between us. 'Thought you'd know about the birds and the bees at your age.'

'You don't have tell me if you don't want to. I'm just being nosy.'

He says he doesn't mind and tells me a tale of his fledgling business that failed unexpectedly, and spectacularly, devastating his comfortable life in the suburbs along with his marriage. The house had been tied to the business, so he lost that. His wife was appalled that he'd mortgaged the house to facilitate the business without telling her and went to live with her sister nearby, taking the kids with her. At the age of thirty-seven, Ben ended up reduced to sleeping on a series of friend's sofas and floors. After failed attempts to get a decent job, he'd started smoking again, cigarettes and other stuff – turned to drink too, because his wife had met a new man and moved in with him. The drinking got worse and his self-esteem so low, that he didn't even try looking for work anymore. His wife said she wanted him nowhere near the children. He'd fallen so far, so fast, and was in no fit state to be a parent.

Ben sighs and strokes the little dog. 'So it's just me and Snowy now. Been on the streets two years.'

I can hardly respond. My hearts swollen with compassion and sorrow, and it's squashing any words I might have, labelling them inadequate and trite. You see on documentaries and on the news, that all of us are only a few steps away from being like Ben. But until today, I hadn't really understood how easy those steps could be. And once again the extent of my abilities has amazed me.

Many psychics hold the hands of people to make connections, but I never have. It must all be part of the fact that I'm using it properly now. Believing in myself. I smile at Ben. It's a big risk, but I decide to tell him about my psychic abilities. He doesn't exactly sneer, but raises an eyebrow. 'I know it's hard to take in, but this is how I ended up in London.' I tell him about Chloé.

'You reckon this ghost told you about Big Ben and me too, possibly?'

'Yeah. You told me about Lilly, didn't you?'

'But that information hasn't done you any good has it? Not really?'

'It's told me that she's not dead. That she's around here nearby, hopefully. I'll book a hotel room locally and keep my eyes peeled. Maybe you will too?'

'Yeah of course.' He shrugs. It's the shrug of a man who thinks I have no chance of finding her, and that he also thinks I'm a bit flaky.

I give him an intense stare, and his brows attempt to shield his suspicious green gaze from mine. 'Ben would you be more open to my abilities if I told you that the house where you used to live was a nineteen-thirties semi-detached with a red door, and that you used to have a black car on the drive?'

Ben's furrowed brow becomes two high arches stretching up to his matted hair, and from pursed lips comes a slow whistle. 'Wow…How the fuck did you know that?'

'When I shook your hand just now, I saw a snapshot image. If you like, I'll take your hand and see what else there is waiting in your future.' I hold up a finger. 'I must warn you though. I haven't done this type of connection before.'

Ben's hand trembles as he covers his mouth. He says through his fingers. 'What if you see something bad? My body floating down the Thames, for example?' A smile curls his lips, yet there's no humour in his eyes, just apprehension.

'Then I'll keep it to myself.' He nods his agreement and I swallow hard, hoping I'm able to do this. Shuffling further along so I'm right next to him, I hold out my hand, palm up. He hesitates, then places his big grubby paw over it, and I give it a squeeze. I draw in a deep breath, then wish I hadn't, as the sour odour of Ben's unwashed body coats the inside of my nostrils.

With some relief, I feel the familiar static run down my arm into our joined hands, and immediately my head is full of pictures. I relay them to Ben as they translate themselves into sentences. 'Your business was something to do with plastics and recycling.'

Ben nods, his eyes round with wonder.

'It's complicated and not really clear to me…but I think that businesses could use your recycling ideas to reduce cost while still being green?'

The nod again.

'It worked, but at the time it wasn't as popular as it is now. The plastic thing I mean. Not enough companies got on board.'

Ben just stares, open mouthed.

'Your wife Harriet is a shallow person who cares more about her own comfort than the good of the planet. She hated the electric car, because it wasn't sporty enough. You should have told her about tying the house to the business, but she would have left you anyway, if the money had dried up. You aren't compatible. Your children miss you.'

Ben's eyes are bright with unshed tears.

'A man gave you something recently as you sat here in the underpass. He is the key to getting yourself back on your feet. You must contact him, Ben. There is hope for you, I promise.' I let go of his hand and my shoulders slump. The effort of what I've just done leaves me drained for a few moments.

He scrabbles in a tatty old coat under his sleeping bag and pulls out a business card. Holds it up in wonder. 'This is what you mean. A smart guy in a suit put twenty-quid in the pot last week. Then he sat where you are, asked me my story. I told him, and he was fascinated by my recycling ideas. He said if I wanted to talk further, I should ring him. I laughed at that. I haven't got a bloody phone. Then he said if I knew what was good for me, I should use a sodding phone box. The guy brushed his suit down, gave me a cheeky wink, and went on his way.'

He places the card in my hand and I know straight away that this is the hope for Ben I'd seen. 'Do it, Ben. Ring him.'

'I just thought he was a do-gooder. A bit of a dreamer...'

Ben's looking at the card as if it's the Holy Grail. I give it back to him.

'No. He's the real deal.'

'Shit...I'll ring him then, shall I?'

I laugh and stand up. 'Might be an idea.' I look towards the end of the tunnel and a chill wind blows in, dragging the end of the day behind it. Time I looked for somewhere to stay tonight. Must contact Charlie before he lists me as a misper too. He's texted me already. 'Okay, Ben. Will you be here tomorrow if I come back in the morning?'

'Yeah. I'll stay in the shelter tonight, see if I can get cleaned up, make myself look presentable. Then I'll ring this man tomorrow. I'll keep my eye out for Lilly. Tell her you're looking for her.'

My heart lurches. 'No. Don't do that. I don't want her running off. If she's scared of a family member, she won't want me popping up and dragging her back home. Just try and find out where she goes in the day. Once I've got somewhere to stay, I'll go to the shelter and see if I can find her tonight. Tell me where it is.'

As I'm walking away, Ben calls, 'Thanks so much, Nancy. For the first time in a long time I feel like something good might happen to me tomorrow.'

'It will. Believe it.' Then before I can talk myself out of it, I dig my purse out of my rucksack and walk the few steps back to him. 'Here. Take this.' I shove a hundred pounds into his hand. 'I know it's not much, but you can buy some cheap clothes and smarten yourself up a bit. Show him you're serious.'

I hurry away with the sound of his thank you echoing after me through the underpass and hope that something good might happen to me tomorrow too.

Chapter Twenty-One

I'm in a Premier Inn with a great view of the London Eye. It has an eye-watering price too, and I'm hoping I find Lilly sooner rather than later, or I'll need to rob a bank to pay for it. I check my phone and find two missed calls from Charlie and three texts. I've already passed the latest on to Abigail and she says she's coming up to lend a hand if I get any closer. But Charlie…God. If I don't phone him in a minute, he really will start to worry. It's only just gone eight o'clock, but it's not like me to miss calls and texts. I scroll down to his name and my gut screws into a tight fist of apprehension. I've delayed so long because I hate lying, especially to him. He's going to be so surprised to say the least. Can't be helped though.

I sit on the bed and look at the twinkly red lights coming on around the wheel of The London Eye. It's not dark yet, but it's been a chilly and overcast day for the time of year, and the lights lift my mood. Now for Charlie…

'Nancy! Thank God! I've been at my wit's end. Where are you?'

I picture him either in the office at work, or in the kitchen, pacing, raking his fingers through his short spiky hair. I decide to just plunge in. 'Sorry, for worrying you, love. But I couldn't call you earlier as my phone died. And I didn't message you before I went, as I wasn't sure you'd be too thrilled.'

'Eh? Where are you?'

'Aberdeen.'

'Aberdeen! What the hell for?'

'Because Mum's descended into one of her dark times. She really needed to talk, and sometimes the only person who understands her is me.'

'So why did she bugger off to live up there then? She couldn't get much further away from you and still be in the UK.'

'I know. While I'm here, I'll try and persuade her to come home for good. She's not happy here. Not really. Admitting it would seem like failure to her. You know what she can be like.'

'Hmm. So how long are you going to be there?'

Now what? 'Um, no more than a couple of days or so.'

'Right, good…and how did you get up there?'

Yeah how, Nancy? I wouldn't be there yet by train and the car's at home. 'I flew.' Please don't let him check the flights from Newquay. I've no idea if there are any at this time of year.

'How much did that cost?'

'Not that much.' I say quickly and switch the subject. 'Anyway, how's the case going?' Cringing I look out of the window again. I know exactly how it's going, don't I? Because at the moment I have the only lead. He waffles on about Lilly's school mates and that they are none the wiser after speaking to her best friend again. I end the call with a promise to ring him tomorrow to tell him how Mum is. Poor Charlie. He'll be tired, hungry, despondent and all alone in the house, apart from Scrappy. Hope he's keeping close by.

It occurs to me that I should message Mum. I need to tell her not to answer calls or messages from Charlie. I doubt very much he would call, but I have to cover all bases. I quickly fire off a text and stress to Mum there's nothing to worry about and I'll fill her in in the next few days. Predictably, Mum messages straight back asking if Charlie and I have split up. I reassure her again and flop back on the bed. What on earth have I let myself be talked into? I've dragged my mum into it all now, and lied big-time to my husband. Then I shake myself. Come on. No use getting side-tracked by Charlie. I'm here to find Lilly, and that's what I'll do.

THE HOMELESS SHELTER is in part of what was an old school, and outside, a little way off, there's a few hooded teenagers leaning against a wall smoking. Is Lilly amongst them? I scan their faces, well, what I can see of them in the half-light and under hoods. No. She's not here. As I walk past, one lad says, 'You a copper?'

I shake my head and try not to feel intimidated. They're just kids. I dig in my bag and pull out Lilly's photo. 'No. I'm looking for a young girl called Lilly. I'm a friend of her family.'

The youngsters gather round and look at it. The lad who spoke to me says, 'Might have seen her, might not. If I had, I wouldn't tell you, copper.' He narrows his dark eyes and blows smoke at me. His skin's greasy and he's wearing a beard of spots across his chin.

'I told you, I'm not a copper.' My level stare back is supposed to be no-nonsense, but he sucks his teeth and spits on the floor by my feet.

'Whoever you are, this girl doesn't want to be found, so do one.'

I'm about to reply when his phone rings and he hurries away down the street his phone clamped to his ear. The other kids look less sure of themselves now and I walk past towards the door of the shelter. As I'm about to go in, I feel a tug at my sleeve and turn round. It's one of the girls I noticed at the back of the other kids. She looks about fifteen and not as rough around the edges as the others. 'Let's have a look at that photo again.'

After a few moments of silence while she studies it, I say, 'Has she been to the homeless shelter here?' I know she has at least once, because Ben told me.

'I'm not homeless, am I?' she snaps. 'A few of us hang round here, that's all.'

'Right. I didn't mean to suggest you—'

'Why are you lookin' for her?'

'As I said. I'm a friend of her family and—'

'Then you're no friend of hers.' She thrusts the photo back at me.

'You know her, then?'

'I reckon. She had more make-up on though and looked older. But yeah that's Zoe. Felt sorry for her 'cos Sticker scared the shit out of her the other night. Said he'd make stuff hard for her. Zoe's not cut out for this game.' The way the girl squares her shoulders and pouts says, 'not like me.'

My heart goes out to her. If she's not homeless now, chances are she might be, the way things are going. And Lilly's using the name Zoe. Could be helpful, if indeed this girl isn't mistaken.

'Sticker?'

'The one who asked if you were a copper.'

'Right. What did you mean by saying I'm not her friend, if I'm a friend of her family?'

'She said she'd run from home 'cos she was scared of someone who lived there. Not telling you who.'

This information indicates the girl probably isn't mistaken. 'Okay. I did wonder if it was someone at home…do you know where Zoe is now? I promise I'll help her and not make her go home, if that's what she wants.'

'Hmm.' The girl turns her mouth down at the corners, looks over to the others and back. Shifts her weight. There's a feeling of readiness about her. Either she's ready to tell me something, or ready to walk away.

The next few words out of my mouth have to be right or I've lost. 'The thing is, she's not cut out for this game. I reckon you've got to be tough, have your wits about you, like you. She's not as street smart as you. Not by a long way.'

Pride flits across her eyes and she nods. 'Damn right. She's just a kid.'

'Yeah. She's thirteen.'

'You shitting me?'

I shake my head. 'Can you tell me where she might be?'

One of the older boys shoves two fingers in the corners of his mouth, gives a piecing whistle and beckons her over. She hesitates, and then says quickly, 'When Sticker rocked up, I might have seen her run round the back of the shelter.' Then she hurries away.

Walking slowly away in order not to alert the youngsters to my intention, I skirt the shelter and then once out of sight, my heart thumps faster than my feet as I scoot up the alley adjacent. A flash of green by a row of bins at the end stops me in my tracks. Is it a rucksack? Flattening my back to the wall, I move sideways towards the bins stepping over litter and a tangle of weeds. Soon I can make out a crouched figure, furtively peering round the corner of the alley and then back. It's wearing a dark hoodie and yes, a green rucksack with a rolled sleeping back slotted through the top straps. It's Lilly, I can feel it. I can also feel the smack of frustration as adrenaline makes my feet clumsy.

The figure's head snaps round at the crunch of a plastic bottle under my foot. 'Who's there?' her voice is as taut as a wire.

Shit. Nothing for it now. I step away from the wall, show myself. 'Lilly, I'm a friend. Don't be afraid, I'm…'

Lilly's off like a hare before I can draw breath. Damn it! I give chase as she runs out of the alley and up the hill away from where the youngsters were. Even with the heavy rucksack on her back, she's already about forty meters ahead. I have just a small handbag, but no matter how much I power my legs forward, I'm never going to catch her. I stop, cup my hands to my mouth and yell after her up the hill, 'Lilly! Lilly come back!' But of course, she doesn't. I see her dash to the left and then she's gone. *Shit. Shit!* I lean forward, put my hands on my burning thighs and take a moment. Then I hurry on up the hill in the direction of where she disappeared.

At the top of the hill I turn left into a park. The path runs through a swathe of trees and a kid's playground is a little way off to the right. Though night is falling fast, I can just make out two figures on the swings. One has a little white dog at its feet. My heart lifts. Ben! Please let it be Ben. I hurry along the path and one of the figures sees me and gets up, starts to run, but the other calls out and they stop. When I get close, I can see it definitely is Ben and Lilly. Thank God!

'Hi Nancy, just been explaining to Zoe…or I should say Lilly here, who you are and about your unusual abilities.'

I smile my thanks and give his shoulder a quick squeeze.

Lilly folds her arms, gives me a brief sweep of her heavily mascaraed eyes and looks towards the park entrance. 'I'm not going home,' she says to the sky.

'I'm not surprised. Someone there is making your life intolerable. But running to London and living in fear isn't the answer either,' I say.

'So why are you here if you've not come to force me home?'

'To help you. We can get you a safe place to stay back in Cornwall, while we try to get to the bottom of it all.'

'Who's we?' Lilly twists her painted lips to one side and narrows her eyes.

'Me…and people who can help.'

'The police you mean. No thanks. I know *all* about them.' Her words are acidic.

The feeling her father is not the great guy everyone thinks he is hits home. I have to try to keep her calm. 'Not just the police, Lilly. There are professionals who work with young people all the time. Yours won't be the first case they've come across, and—'

Her eyes flash. 'My case? You don't know *anything* about my case!'

'True. But your sister Chloé asked me to help you. So here I am.'

Lilly's mouth drops open and then her face contorts with anger. 'My sister is dead!'

'I know. Sometimes I can talk to those who have passed,' I say in a down-to-earth way hoping to make it sound as normal as possible.

Lilly's bottom lip trembles and her eyes fill. 'What did she say?'

'How about we go for a cuppa and I'll tell you all about it? You can tell me why you ran. Promise I won't call the police.'

Ben pats her on the shoulder. 'Go on, Lilly. I told you how Nancy helped me. She'll do the same for you.'

Lilly nods, and I release a breath I didn't know I'd been holding. Me and Ben have a quick chat. He tells me he was just passing the park on the way to the shelter to get a good night's sleep and cleaned up, when he saw Lilly run past. What a stroke of luck. I wish him plenty of that for his phone call tomorrow, and give my contact details. Then Lilly and I walk towards the main shopping area.

LILLY LETS ME buy her a burger and milkshake, and I wait in silence while she demolishes the burger at the speed of light. She still has some money, but she's rationing it – so this burger is all she's had today, apart from a packet of crisps and a half-price sandwich. Then she tells me that she planned to run away for ages, and has been saving her Christmas, birthday and pocket money up. She sold some of her old toys and a bike without her parent's knowledge, and she left behind the proceeds – two-hundred pounds, to make it look like she'd not run away. The phone was left deliberately, for the same reason, and as I suspected, to make sure she wasn't traced.

Now comes the big question and my mouth goes dry as I gear up to ask it. 'Who is hurting you at home, Lilly? I know someone is, because I made connections with some of your things.' I tell her about Abigail. Charlie too.

'So now I find you're married to a policeman. There's no way they will believe my story. They all stick together that lot.'

'I'll believe you. Just tell me.'

Lilly shoves her hood back and rest her chin on her fists and looks at the table. 'The chief constable is not what you think he is. He's a bastard. An evil bastard. He's been touching me where he shouldn't.'

My worst fears are realised then. I'd suspected something like this, but I had thought it could have been the elder brother for a while, which is bad enough. But this is worse. So much worse. 'Oh, Lilly. I'm so sorry.'

She continues as if she's not heard me. 'It all started after Chloé died. Not long before she did, she told me he used to go into her room at night and 'cuddle' her and she didn't like it. She told him she was going to tell Mum one night, and the next day she was dead. I saw her fall. I heard her yelling and ran into her room. He had her by the arm at the window, she had one leg balanced on the tree branch, and the next minute she was gone…he said afterwards that he was trying to stop her from falling, and she slipped from his grasp, but I don't think I believe it now. Not after the way he's started to be with me. He wanted to shut her up.'

The shock of her words takes my breath, as does the sudden pixilated appearance of Chloé in her pink pyjamas seated next to her sister. She says, 'The daddy is a bad man. The daddy pushed me. Killed me.' She reaches a hand to Lilly's face and rests her head on her shoulder. The longing in the little girl's face, and the keen loss of her sister is almost tangible. Why was she taken like this? This is so cruel. So unfair! Once again, I can hardly function because of the weight of sadness swelling my heart. Then Chloe does the off switch and I'm looking at the empty red plastic chair-back. 'Oh…my God.'

'Yeah. I know it's a big thing to accuse him of. I don't know for sure of course but—'

'No. You don't understand. Chloé was just here…she said your dad pushed and killed her.'

Lilly's hand flies to her mouth and tears well in her eyes. 'I knew it! Is that what she said word-for-word?'

I close my eyes and think. 'No. She said the daddy is a bad man. The daddy pushed me. Killed me.'

Lilly releases a sob, and then covers her mouth with a napkin as if to stop more. Tears pull black rivers of mascara after them down her cheeks, and she gives a shuddering sigh. 'Yes. We always called him 'the daddy' behind his back. Not Daddy.'

'Why?'

'Because he's not our dad. Our dad died when we were too young to remember him much. I do remember bits. Like being held up to put the star on top of the Christmas tree, and touch the twinkly lights. But not much else.'

More tears come and I take her hand across the table. It's taking all I've got not to join her. So, he's the stepdad. Does that make a difference? Does it matter? Is it better that he's not her biological father? Maybe. But whatever he is, he's a murderer, on top of being a filthy child molester. 'Lilly.' I push the milkshake towards her. 'Here, have a drink. Try to calm yourself, lovely.'

'I think he knew I suspected him, you know?' She takes a sip of her drink and stares beyond me at something only she can see. 'He was so nicey-nicey after Chloé. He bought me a pony, and then later a horse. Spoiled me rotten. Then when I'd just turned eleven, I went to the field to get Major, my horse, and my stepdad came with me. He put Major's head-collar on and gave me a boost up onto his back. He had no saddle on 'cos he was in the field and we'd just gone to get him. My stepdad started to lead Major up the field towards the stables, and then he told me to get off, because he said he'd heard that there were some insects on horses round here that could cause a disease. I got off, and he told me to pull down my trousers and knickers so he could see if there was anything there. He told me to do the same with my top. I knew that this didn't feel right, but I was so scared because he'd got a funny look in his eyes…so I just did as he said. Then I got back on Major and that was it.'

The coffee I've just swallowed wants to come up and I close my eyes, regulate my breathing. If that bastard were here right now, I would not be responsible for my actions. Lilly tells me he told her not to mention any of it to her mother, because she'd worry about the disease and not let her have a horse anymore. It was a year or so after that he did anything else. He would causally put his hand on her breast and brush her bottom as he went past in the kitchen. Then, one night last autumn, he'd come in her room and pulled her onto his knee. He said she was beautiful and kissed the side of her breast. Lilly falls silent and wipes her panda eyes.

'Did you tell your mum?'

'No. Because I'd told him to stop and that I'd tell Mum. He said if I did, I'd be very sorry. He said if she knew, they would divorce, and Mum would have to work two jobs to provide for us. We'd have to live in a bed-sit, and we would probably eventually be taken into care. Mum would never forgive me for causing such a fuss. And didn't I understand that it was just because he loved me so much that he wanted to be close?'

I shake my head. 'What a vile man.'

'He is. I made my mind up then to run away as soon as I could get it all planned. I hoped he was lying about what would happen if Mum knew, but I couldn't chance it. And after what had happened to Chloé, I was terrified I'd end up the same way. But then he backed off a bit. He still brushed against me in the kitchen and stuff, but he didn't come to my room again. I thought it had all stopped until a few weeks back…he came to my room and…' She shakes her head and covers her face.

Oh God. I can't bear it. 'He…raped you?'

'No…but…' Her mouth works but no words come out. She rubs her arms as if she's cold. And now that her make-up's gone along with the bravado, she looks like the scared little child she really is.

'Don't worry. You don't have to say more. Come back with me to my hotel. I have a twin-bedded room. You can have a shower and a good night's sleep without worrying. Everything will look better in the morning,' I say. Cringing at how trite that sounded.

Surprisingly, Lilly quickly agrees and an hour later she's sound asleep. I watch her as she sleeps, thanking God that I found her and she's safe. I imagine sleep won't find me as easily tonight. My thoughts are in turmoil. What will Charlie and Abigail say when they find out about their boss? Will they make Lilly go over everything again? I know the answer to that. I hope they are gentle on her though. The poor kid has suffered enough. And there'll be the terrible fall-out when the bombshell hits the family.

In the bathroom, I clean my teeth and look at the dark smudges underlining the green of my eyes, my milk white face surrounded by a mess of red curls. I look like the wild woman of the woods. Must have been all that chasing up hills and through parks, plus the trauma of listening to Lilly's story. I put my pyjamas on, and the word *murder* spins to the front of my consciousness. Proving Chief Constable Bradley killed little Chloé will be practically impossible. There's only Lilly's word for it. But after she tells everyone that he's a paedophile he'll lose his job, wife and family. Hopefully he'll be put away too. That's if she's believed. I heave a sigh and slip into bed. In the end, the main thing is that she's safe and well. It could have been very different if I'd not found her in time. With a sense of relief, I realise that lying to Charlie big-time was justified. Then I get back out of bed. No rest for the self-satisfied. I need to make sure Abigail is updated.

Chapter Twenty-Two

What a fool. What a bloody fool I've been! I slump down onto Lilly's empty bed and re-read the note she left me on the back of a room service menu:

Sorry, Nancy, I know you are a nice person and want to help, but I can't go back. My stepdad is the chief constable as you know, and he will find ways to make me look like a liar. He's very clever. My mum won't believe me when he's finished with her. I'll be punished and then he'll come to my room again. I'd rather die. I'll find a way to make a life here. Sorry again. Bye x

How did I sleep through her leaving? It's only six o'clock now, so what time must she have left? Damn it all! I ball my fists and scrub them at my eyes. I want to cry, rage, scream. Lilly was found. She was safe. Now she's gone again, and this time it will be much harder to find her. If I was her, I'd go somewhere far from here. Why did I ever agree to play the detective all by myself? I should have insisted Abigail come too. Fuck! What a mess.

I sit and think for a while and then with a heavy heart I pick my phone up. I rang Abigail in the bathroom last night, after I made sure Lilly was still sound asleep. I updated her, including Chloé's appearance, and she was knocked sideways when I disclosed Lilly's news about the chief constable. Abigail said she'd get to London before the end of the day. Now this.

'Abigail…I'm so sorry… but Lilly's gone, and I need your help.'

'Shit! Do you think she heard you talking to me last night in the bathroom?'

'I don't know. It's possible.' I tell her about the note.

'Okay. I'll get onto the Met. I should have done that last night to be honest. I'm sorry for snapping, Nancy. It's me that's fucked it up, not you. As you said before, you're not trained. What was I thinking?'

Her words are like a punch in the throat. Instinct tells me that getting the local police will be a very bad idea. Panic takes hold. My thoughts jumble together, crash into each other while she's rabbiting on about me meeting her at a particular police station near me, until I silence her with, 'No! Stick to the plan. You come up here to help me find her without telling anyone, Abigail. If the Met get involved, Bradley's got more of a chance to talk his way out of it. We need her to come home. Come forward of her own volition and tell her local police. Which is you and Charlie. Let Lilly put the finger on *him* instead of her being captured and dispatched, like she's a criminal.'

Abigail sighs. 'It wouldn't be like that, Nance. They would handle it sensitively. Besides, we have to do things by the book. Anything we do wrong in this case might count against us and hurt her chances when it comes to court.'

'Sounds like you believe her story if you're talking about court?' I cross my fingers and hold my breath.

'It sounds pretty outlandish. But I'm keeping an open mind. I hate to think of it being true…but…' she sighs. 'In the end she's a frightened child. Why would she lie? Run off like that – put herself in danger, if it weren't true?'

'Exactly. But the thing is, Abigail, you can't do things by the book, because I'm involved. You couldn't tell the truth about me, as you'd get it in the neck because you brought Lilly's things to me to make connections. In fact, you might lose your job…and so might Charlie if they thought he was in on it.'

There's another huge sigh and then silence for a few moments. Then she says, 'Look, I'll leave the Met for now. I'm coming up. I'll fly. Should be there by late morning, early afternoon. Don't do anything until I get there. Promise me?'

'I promise.'

WHEN I SEE Abigail's face at my door after lunch, the emotion that has been submerged under a calm exterior, bursts through, and I cling to her like a limpet, blubbing all over her.

'Hey, hey. It's okay,' she says, awkwardly patting my back. 'I'm here for you. Don't worry. We'll find Lilly together.'

'But how?' I wail. 'She could be at the other side of London now. Or even on a train heading God knows where.'

'Or she could be still round here. Just calm yourself and we'll have a think.' She comes inside, hands me a tissue and a bottle of water.

Once I've calmed down, I ask her how she managed to get out of work, and she explains that she said she had food poisoning and would probably be away a few days. It was a huge step, but Abigail's fully behind me and trusts my judgment.

'If we haven't found her by tomorrow, I'll tell the Met that I've had a tip off that Lilly's been seen around here, and then it's out of our hands,' she says.

'Thank God we have another chance to find her and persuade her to go back,' I say, swigging from the bottle. 'But where to start.'

Abigail's reading the note Lilly left and then she flicks it with her finger, looks across at me with a smile. 'Call yourself an investigator?' I frown and ask why. 'She says in the note that she'll try to make a life here. That means in London, so she's not on a train.' Abigail fans herself with the menu and stares across at the London Eye. 'If I were her, I'd go back to those kids you saw last night. This Ben told you she'd been threatened. If she didn't sell drugs, it would go hard for her. Maybe she's opted to do that.'

I can't bear to think of it, poor Lilly, living on the streets getting into all sorts. I sigh. 'It's possible.'

'I'm afraid it is. So many kids end up like Lilly. Too many. I think our first call is the homeless shelter you told me about. See if we can speak to that girl again.' She throws the menu on the bed and I get an idea.

'I might as well try and make a connection with that note and the pen she held before we go. It's worth a try.'

The menu tells me nothing. The pen shows a single snapshot of the London Eye. I tell Abigail that her idea seems the best, as I think my connections are messed up because of the stress of losing Lilly.

She looks out at the Eye through the window and says nothing for a few moments. 'I reckon we go there first. Your connections might be messed up. But then again, they might not. I've got every confidence in you.'

My nose tickles and a lump rises in my throat at this unprecedented praise. 'Really? That means such a lot after I've buggered everything up…' The rest of the sentence catches in my throat and Abigail pats me on the back again.

'Hey, come on. Don't cry. I'm more to blame than you. As I said, I should have come with you. And I've come to the conclusion that your connections are remarkable. There's too much evidence to prove otherwise. You found Lilly when half the police force in the south west couldn't. Okay, she got away again. But not for long. Come on. Let's go and find her.'

Abigail's words mean more than she could ever know, and I don't have the right ones to tell her. So instead, I slip my shoes on and we hurry out.

IT BEING A Friday and wall-to-wall sunshine, there's so many tourists around the London Eye we can hardly move. Our walking pace is frustratingly slow, but at least, in a crowd we're harder to spot, if Lilly's hanging round here. The last thing we want is for her to clock us and do a runner. After a while we decide to split up and meet back at the river cruise area in half-an-hour. I'm just walking past The London Dungeon, when I glimpse a flash of pink clothing as a child slips through the crowd. Somewhere in my mind, there's a nagging sense of recognition in that pink. It's not just any old pink. It's the pink of Chloé's pyjamas. She's here.

Pushing my way through a gaggle of girls posing in front of selfie sticks, I swing to the left away from the Eye and shield my own against the sun. Lots of kids with their parents, an elderly couple, a group of teenagers led by what looks like a teacher, but no little girl in pink pyjamas. I turn in a full circle but no. She's gone. Then my phone chirrups. It's a message from Abigail saying *no luck this end what about you?* Would it be helpful to say I'm looking for a ghost at the moment? I text back *Nope. Fraid not.*

I walk on looking for Chloé, while keeping a watch for Lilly by the side of the river, on a bench, near the queues for the Eye and boat trips. Sweat trickles between my shoulder blades and down my back. My long-sleeved top's sticking to me. I didn't come prepared for weather like this. In fact, I didn't come prepared at all. Just chucked some stuff in a bag and off I went. I peel off my top and tie it around my waist. Luckily, I'm wearing a vest underneath, but unluckily, the sun's baking every inch of exposed skin and I need a drink. Stopping by the river, I wipe the back of my hand across my forehead. This is hopeless. I'll call Abigail and tell her we may as well revert to Plan B. Go and see if the gang of kids are up by the shelter. Then a cool little hand slips into mine, and I look down to see Sebastian aged about four, his hair's dark and curly and he's wearing jeans and a yellow shirt.

He's smiling up at me, and though his mouth doesn't move, I hear him say, '*Come with me, Mummy.*'

My heart swells with love for him and I want to pick him up, never let him go. Scoop him up, take him home to his daddy. I want to call Abigail, get her to come and meet him, but I know all that's not possible. Sebastian leads me through the crowds to an area with trees, and from an expanse of green comes the sound of children playing. A sign reads *Jubilee Park* and inside, there is a huge climbing frame in the shape of a pirate ship and beyond that, swings and other playground equipment. Sebastian points a finger towards a seating area and there's Chloé, sitting next to a girl in a dark hoodie. Despite the heat, her hood's pulled low over her forehead and she's staring vacantly at the ground between her feet. Lilly.

Sebastian slips his hand from mine and runs to Chloé. She stands up, puts her arm around him and smiles over at me. My little boy has a friend. Thank God he's not alone. I can't bear to think of him alone. An ocean of tears push behind my eyes, but I can't give into them. I must help the living. I call Abigail and tell her to come quickly. Then I walk over to Lilly and slump down beside her. My legs won't hold me up any longer. When she sees me, she immediately springs up and looks around. Perhaps she's expecting to see an army of police closing in.

'Please, Lilly. Sit down and let's talk,' I say, but already can see that she's preparing to run.

Then Chloé says to me, 'Tell Lilly I love her. Tell her Anna must go back. The bad daddy will be punished.' Then she and my boy smile at me and walk away hand in hand, pixilating as they do.

'No. Sebastian, don't go!' Tears roll down my cheeks. Through them, Lilly's concerned face looks like it's behind bevelled glass.

'Sebastian?' Lilly says.

I nod and blow my nose. She sits back down, and I explain about Sebastian and what Chloé's just said. 'Hope that makes sense.'

Her eyes copy mine. 'Yes…it does make sense. I was always Anna and she was Elsa from the film *Frozen*. We played it all the time. And I'm so sorry about your little boy.' She breaks down and leans into me. I put my arm around her and hold her tight while she sobs. And this is how Abigail finds us a few minutes later. Lilly's understandably shocked by her just appearing like that, but we both convince her that we won't involve the Metropolitan Police.

'Look, Lilly. Our main priority is to get you back to Cornwall. I'll hire a car and we'll all drive up now. You can stay with us tonight until we can work out a plan of what to do,' Abigail says.

I say nothing, but very much doubt her staying with us is doing things 'by the book.' It seems like the best plan though. I couldn't bear her to be with social services tonight. Going at it from a different angle, and mindful of her feelings, I say, 'You do want to come home, Lilly? Chloé certainly wants you to.'

'I never wanted to leave in the first place,' she wails. 'I had no choice.' She takes a tissue from me and blows her nose. 'But yes. I will come back and tell what he did to me. Chloé says he will be punished, and I believe her.'

Abigail tucks her hair behind her ears and presses her lips together. I can tell she's being affected by the fact Sebastian and Chloé were here, as well as what a despicable creature her boss is. 'Good girl. We'll say you decided to come home by yourself…just walked into our station and told us what had happened to you. We can't mention Nancy's involvement. Her detective skills are not what you'd call normal.' She gives her a smile. 'And not everyone would understand. She might even get into trouble for not turning you in as soon as she found you. Is that okay? Are you happy to keep quiet about my friend, Lilly?'

'Yeah. I won't say anything. Nancy is lovely.' She puts her hand in mine and I give it a squeeze.

'You're not so bad yourself, kid.'

'I am though. I did a bad thing today,' she says, her bottom lip trembling.

'It wasn't so bad that we can't mend it, I'm sure,' I say.

She looks under her lashes at Abigail and her cheeks turn pink. 'You might arrest me if I say.'

'I very much doubt it,' Abigail answers.

A heavy sigh. 'I agreed to sell drugs for Sticker. I've got them in my pocket now. Someone's supposed to come to meet me here in ten minutes.'

Abigail looks around. 'Come on. Let's go. They'll just have to find their kicks elsewhere.'

'But what about the drugs?' Lilly asks.

'What drugs?' Abigail says, standing up. 'Give them to me. I'll make them disappear.'

IT'S ALMOST DARK as we pull up outside Abigail's house. We agreed it would make sense for me to stay too, because I could hardly go home to Seal Cottage, could I? As soon as the hire car's wheels had crossed the border into my beloved Cornwall, all the tension of the last few days that twisted my gut and had my shoulders up by my ears, began to dwindle away. There'll be more tomorrow, once Lilly goes to see Abigail's boss and the brown stuff for Lilly's step-father hits the fan, but for now, I'm home and all's well. Lilly's been asleep for the last three hours, but opens her eyes once Abigail cuts the engine.

'We here?' she asks rubbing her eyes.

'We are indeed,' Abigail says. 'We'll get our bags in, and I'll make us some beans on toast, yes? And you can meet my wonderful cat, Paddington. Yes, I know that's a bear's name, but he looks like one. He's huge, brown and fluffy.'

'I love cats!' Lilly says, then her face falls. 'We aren't allowed any animals as my stepdad doesn't like them.'

'Never trust a person who doesn't like animals,' I say leading the way inside.

LILLY AND PADDINGTON hit it off straight away, and a little while later she settles down under the quilt in one of the spare rooms with the cat at her feet. I miss my own bed and I miss Charlie. It seems ages since I slept in my own home, and little Chloé first came to me, but it's only a few nights ago. The moon's still full and shines a silver path across the carpet. I go to close the curtains, but Lilly asks me to leave them open a crack. Unsurprisingly, she hates the dark. She smiles at me as I hand her a glass of water, and I tell Paddington to make sure he doesn't wake her in the night.

The feel of Sebastian's little hand in mine today re-awakened my maternal instinct, and his loss is a physical ache in the centre of my chest. I so wish I was a mother. I know Lilly's not mine, but it's wonderful to be with her. Even for a short while. I hate that we've made her promise not to mention me to anyone, as she's been told to keep secrets before – by him. But this time the secret is for a good cause. She's safe, cared for, and very soon she'll be reunited with her mum. All that's down to Nancy Cornish PI, with a little help from my good friend Abigail, dear Ben, and a few special ones who are no longer present in this world.

'Night, Lilly. Sleep well, and if you need anything, you know where I am.'

'Night, Nancy…and thank you so much for everything.' Then she sits up in bed. 'I know I can't tell anyone about you. But can we still keep in touch?' Her expression is a blend of hope and melancholy.

'Of course we can. We'll find a way.'

Lilly settles back down with a sigh of satisfaction. And I go downstairs to tell Abigail how much I appreciate her going out on a limb. I just wish I could tell Charlie all about it, and how much I love him.

Chapter Twenty-Three

They say what a difference a day makes, don't they? Things in the last twenty-four hours since we came home have moved so fast, it feels like three days rolled into one. Abigail took Lilly to Truro the next morning and watched her go into the station. Charlie collected her after reception called him. Lilly walked up to him and said who she was, why she ran, and that she decided to come back to disclose everything. Later she was questioned by Abigail (who'd made a miraculous recovery from her food poisoning). and various others; social services, child protection too. After which, Chief Constable Laurence Bradley was arrested and taken from his home into custody.

Mrs Bradley apparently collapsed with shock when the police officers came for her husband. She was incoherent for some time, and then grabbed a kitchen knife, said she was going to the police station to kill him. Once she'd been calmed by the attending officers and recovered a little, she was desperate to have her daughter home. After some more checks and red tape, Lilly was eventually allowed back into the safety of her mother's arms.

Charlie took her back home, and he described that evening (I'd made an impromptu return from Scotland as Mum was much recovered). to me how Mrs Bradley had held her daughter on the sofa, sobbing into her hair and rocking her like a baby. He was so choked up, he could hardly get the words out. Laurence Bradley is suspended from duty while the investigations are ongoing, and if he is let out on bail, he's not allowed within fifty yards of his house.

I wish I could phone Lilly for a chat, but of course that's not possible. I expect we'll find a way over the coming days and weeks, as contact with Abigail and Charlie will be inevitable during the investigations. It's doubtful that the chief constable will be charged with Chloé's murder, as there's no evidence, apart from Lilly's testament. There's Chloé's testament too, but of course that wouldn't be admissible in court. Whatever ends up happening to Chief Constable Bradley, it won't be good. And nobody deserves it more.

June has turned my garden into a riot of wildflowers and is, so far, flaming. My south facing kitchen has turned into an oven. I'm wondering whether to get a fan or two for the summerhouse, because the sun streams in through the French doors like molten lava in the afternoons. Thinking of which, it's time I went down there and wrote up the notes for Lilly's case while they are still fresh in my mind. Scrappy at my heels, I wander down the path towards it, noting that my two beautiful blue agapanthus look so tall and majestic planted at either side of the doors. Horticultural bouncers stopping insects from entering. Charlie laughs at my pet name for them. Aggie Panthers. But to my mind, it just fits them perfectly. Aggies are sometimes hard to grow, but this year they have bloomed early, and look set to stay for summer's duration.

I open all the windows and pin back the doors with two heavy pots. It's warm but not unbearable. Scrappy comes and sits on my desk to watch me write. I'm just a few lines in when my phone rings. I don't recognise the number…might be another case. I answer it.

'Nancy, it's Ben. How's things with Lilly?'

My hearts soars. I'm so glad he kept his promise to ring. I tell him all the news. He's overjoyed that she's been found and home again. Then I ask, 'And now you know all my news, any news of your own?' I cross my fingers.

'My news is that my life has changed in the last few days beyond my wildest dreams!' There's a chortle running through his voice like a river. 'Nathan, the guy I told you about, arranged to meet me, and we talked through all my recycling ideas. He was blown away. I agreed to work for him and he set me up in a lovely apartment overlooking the Thames. It has a communal garden too, so Snowy is a happy little dog! Nathan's a multi-millionaire, Nancy. But luckily for me, one who's committed to saving the planet!'

'Ben! That is amazing! I can't tell you how happy that makes me. This is what I saw when I made the connection with you. Well, not exactly this, but I saw an incredible change happening for you. So pleased. It couldn't happen to a nicer—'

Excitement rushes Ben on, as if he's worried his words only have a set time limit to come out into the world. 'And it has three bedrooms, so if the kids want to come and stay, they can! I know it's early days, but if I can prove to a court that I have a stable home and I'm a good father, it could happen…And Nancy, if it hadn't been for you, I would still be in that underpass. I'm not sure how long I'd have been able to carry on like that, to be honest… I can never ever repay you for what you did for me. Ever.'

Ben's voice whispers the last word and I hear a sniff. 'Ben. You've repaid me already. You helped me to find Lilly and persuaded her to come with me that night in the park. You've also made me very happy knowing your life has taken a turn for the better. I had a small part to play in that, which makes me feel useful and needed. No thanks necessary.'

'Oh, I think there is. When I'm properly on my feet I'll send you a photo of me, and hopefully one with the kids. Maybe we'll come down for a holiday? I'd love to go back to Padstow one day.'

'I'll hold you to that! Charlie and me will show you all the best places.'

We agree to be Facebook friends once he's set up an account and then we end the call. There's a giggle in my stomach that I need to release. I want to shout from the rooftops and rejoice. Popping my head through the door, I check nobody is around and then do a mad dance around the summerhouse whooping like a banshee. Scrappy is not sure what to make of it. He jumps from the table, curls up on the sofa and pretends to be asleep. This makes me laugh out loud, but laughter turns into a shriek as a quiet voice behind me says,

'Have you been on the wine already? It's not even noon, Nance.'

'Penny! You scared the shit out of me!'

Penny's helpless with laughter for a few moments. Then she sits on the sofa next to a bemused Scrappy. 'You actually jumped. Jumped!' she says and sets off giggling again, her cheeks red from the hilarity and the heat. Fanning her face, she says, 'Go and get an old woman a drink before she expires, would you?'

I feign aloofness. 'I see no old woman here. Just a cruel vixen intent on shortening my life.' She frowns at my lack of humour, but then my lips twitch at the corners giving me away.

She smiles. 'And a biscuit or two wouldn't go amiss. Or cake, it you've got it.'

TEN MINUTES LATER, we're demolishing a sizeable piece of a chocolate cake I made last night, and sipping homemade lemonade. I nod at her plate. 'Hope that meets madam's requirements.'

Penny closes her eyes and savours the cake. 'It's a good job you're my friend and can pop round here for my fix, now you've left The Whistling Kettle. Because God knows what I'd do if you weren't.'

'You only want me for my cake and lemonade.'

'Yup.'

'Nice.'

I tell her about my latest case, but leave out the names and job description of Lilly's dad. It wouldn't be ethical. I'll tell her when it's all over. I also say mum's the word as far as Charlie's concerned. Chocolate icing lines the edges of Penny's lips and I hand her a bit of kitchen roll. 'Can't take me anywhere.' She smiles, scrubbing at her mouth. 'I don't care though. Getting messy is totally worth it.' Then she gives me an intense stare. 'You know you are doing so well, Nance. I'm so proud of you. And as I said before, I'm in awe of your talents. You're worth your weight in gold.'

'That's a lovely thing to say. But talking about gold – I still feel awkward about accepting payment.'

'Look. Either you see yourself as a professional psychic investigator or you don't.' I say nothing. Think about it. 'Well?'

'Well, yes. I do.'

'Therefore, you don't work for nothing.'

'No, but—'

'No buts.'

IT WAS SO good seeing Penny. I've been so busy lately I've neglected our friendship. But that's the thing about good friends, isn't it? Even though you don't always see each other, the friendship's just as strong as it always was. After Penny has gone, by late afternoon, I've washed and dried the laundry, cooked a chicken for dinner to have with salad, done a bit of weeding and written up the notes from Lilly's case, including Ben's success. I can't stop marvelling at his change in fortune. It would make a good TV drama. Thinking of that makes me wonder how Alison is getting on with her novel. I must ring her some time.

I'm in the summerhouse contemplating a sneaky glass of ice-cold pinot to celebrate finding Lilly, when I hear voices. One of them is elderly, querulous and shouty.

'Yes, I'm sure this is her address. She told me if I ever needed her, to just walk down the side of the house, down a path and the office is at the end of the garden. Why do you always imagine I'm mistaken about things, Kathy!'

I smile. I know that voice. 'Dot. Kathy. Welcome,' I say, stepping through the French doors and giving them a wave.

Kathy raises a hand, her anxious expression softening with a smile. 'Phew! Mum was right then. You do live here,' she says, clearly relieved.

'I'm always right. You should know that by now.' Dot smiles at me and does an eye roll at her daughter. 'We were outside on the pavement for ages, because Kathy thought it was rude to just walk down someone's path unannounced! I *told* her it was perfectly fine.'

I laugh. 'It's lovely to see you both. Would you like a cuppa?'

Kathy says, 'Oh, no thanks We only just stopped off to—'

'That would be grand, thank you,' Dot elbows her daughter to one side and sets off towards me leaning on her stick. 'Is that the summerhouse office you told me about? It's like a mansion. And it has your name and everything above the door. Louisa told me about it but I didn't realise just how marvellous it was.' She's at the door now and peers round me. 'Oh. You have a kettle, little kitchen and everything, can I go inside and have a nosey?' Before I can answer, she's up the step, surprisingly fast with 'her knees' and oohing and ahhing all over the place.

Kathy comes down and peeps in at her mother, now sitting on the sofa stroking Scrappy as if she's known him forever. 'Hope this is alright?' Kathy says to me in a loud whisper.

'Oi. Whatever else I am, I'm not deaf. If it wasn't alright, Nancy wouldn't have asked us in for a cuppa, would she? And I expect she has cake too. She used to work at The Whistling Kettle. They have the best cakes.' She stares me straight in the eye.

I say it's all fine and Kathy sits down opposite her mum, while I hurry up the path back to the house. Dot is a real spiky character, but I think she's wonderful. I'd liked to get to know her better. Luckily, I have a bit of chocolate cake left in the tin. I'm not sure Dot would let me forget it if I hadn't. And after all this cake today, I'll need to build an extension on the summerhouse for my belly.

Dot approves of the cake, thankfully. We talk about Frank's medals, Frank and Ken. Much to Dot's pleasure, Kathy's not at all 'put out' about her mum being friends with Ken. She's happy that it all ended so well. Dot nods. 'And it's not as if we'll be getting married at our age! I'm not sure we'd last the wedding night.' This turns Kathy's face pink and Dot flaps her hand at me, her wheezy laugh becoming a cough. After a sip of tea and a few deep breaths, she says, 'Right. I want to show you this.' From her bag she pulls a framed black and white photo of a man in uniform. 'This was Frank in 1939. Is this the man you saw in the charity shop?'

I take the photo. He's got dark hair, twinkly eyes and a smile that would break your heart as my mum would say. His heart must have broken at the horrors of Dunkirk. In this photo he was blissfully unaware. And yes, it was the man who pointed up the hill marking out the fishermen's cottages. 'That's the man I saw, Dot.' I give her the photo back with a smile.

'Oh, I'm so pleased,' she says, a catch in her voice. 'Frank knew Ken had the medals and that we would remember each other if I went to his house to get them back. He must approve of our friendship.'

'Of course he does, Mum. Dad would want you to be happy.'

'Yes. He would, bless him.' Dot rummages in her bag again and pulls out her purse. 'And this is for your trouble, Nancy. I don't know what I'd have done if my Frank's medals had been lost forever. It's not as much as I'd like to give, but I'm not the bloody queen of Sheba!' She stuffs some notes into my hand and holds it closed. I half expect her to say, 'and don't spend it all at once.'

I'm about to decline, but remember Penny's words from earlier. I have to take myself seriously. 'Thank you, Dot. That's very kind.'

'How do you know? You haven't counted the bloody money yet!'

'I don't need to. Whatever you gave me is—'

'There's a hundred quid. Kathy said give fifty, but she's a skinflint.'

Kathy's mouth drops open. 'I didn't say that! I said are you sure fifty wouldn't be more affordable for you.'

'Same difference.' She tips Scrappy from her knee unceremoniously, and brushes hairs from her navy trousers. 'Right, we'd best get gone. I said I'd pop round to see Ken before tea.'

With a face like thunder, clearly smarting from her mother's remarks, Kathy mutters, 'You want me to drop you round there, you mean.'

'Not if you have some terribly pressing engagement, dear.' Dot sniffs. 'I can easily get a taxi.'

Kathy grabs her bag, sighs but keeps her counsel. I stand and help Dot to her feet. 'Well, it's been lovely to see you both,' I say, as she takes my arm and we walk to the door.

'It's been marvellous to see where the great psychic detective works, Nancy. And the cake was delicious too.' Dot pats my shoulder and takes her daughter's arm as she steps onto the path.

'Thank you for everything,' Kathy says. 'We're so pleased to have Dad's medals home.'

'You're most welcome,' I say. 'And don't be a stranger, Dot. I want to know all your news.'

As the two women make their slow way up the path towards my house, Dot waves her stick and says over her shoulder, 'Be careful. You'll never see the back of me now!'

Once they disappear around the corner of my house, a pang of yearning for my own mum unexpectedly stirs a pot of emotion. Old Dot and Kathy, on the surface, are at each other's throats, or more accurately, Dot is at Kathy's. But they wear their love for each other like a second skin. I'm guessing they don't normally articulate that to each other openly, but it's always there. And as such, words are unnecessary. In my case, words *are* necessary. My words are crucial. And now seems like the perfect time to say them. I can put it off no longer. I hurry indoors and pick up my phone.

Chapter Twenty-Four

I'm in the kitchen making pizza and feeling a bit sorry for myself, because the last four weeks have been dead. Nobody has called, phoned or emailed about a new case, and a tiny part of me is beginning to worry that Nancy Cornish PI is over. Charlie says it's to be expected. People are away on holiday and the kids are off school which makes things slow. He said it will all get back to normal in September, and that word of mouth is bound to make a difference soon. Nevertheless, I will make some new flyers and do a trip round town with them in the next few days. I chop a red onion, slice peppers and remind myself that apart from the business, there are two wonderful things to look forward to in the offing.

The first of the wonderful things, is that Mum has agreed to come back from Aberdeen with a view to moving back for good. The day Dot and Kathy came over, I phoned Mum. There was much relief on her part, once I'd explained the reason for the cloak and dagger thing over Charlie calling when I was in London. She had been very worried, and I apologised for that.

Then I told her how much I missed her and begged her to return to Cornwall. Mum admitted that she had been thinking along those lines for some time, but wasn't sure what to do for the best. Making a permanent new life there had been her goal, and she'd obviously failed to put it in the back of the net.

I said she *had* made a new life for the past three years. But now it was time for her to return to her old one. I was her only child after all, and she'd never forgive herself if she left me any longer. I said I'd phone social services or report her to Childline if she said no. She'd laughed then and said that might be the clincher. It was a daft joke we'd shared when I was growing up. Sometimes if she'd told me off, I'd threaten her with Childline. She said she'd give it some serious thought. And today she confirmed it. She's coming back to Cornwall. No idea when, but it will be in the near future.

As well as Mum's home coming, there's Louisa and Mark's wedding to look forward to in a couple of weeks. It will be wonderful. Summer in Tintagel is always stunning. Like a treasured work of art, upon a green hill, the ancient church sits stark against the azure sky. And below the cliff, a wide horizon threads a navy line, welding sky to ocean. I wonder what Louisa will wear. Whatever it is, she'll be a beautiful bride. I'm nervous, but thrilled about giving her away. Such a great honour. My joy is reflected in my placement of peppers in the shape of a smiley red mouth on the pizza, and I dot some sliced olives in a circle for eyes.

'HEY, NANCE. I'M home!'

'In the kitchen, love!' I call.

'Smells good!'

I'm at the sink, when Charlie comes through after getting changed. He comes up behind me, encircling my waist and drops a few gentle kisses on my shoulder and the back of my neck. 'The dinner smells delicious,' he whispers in my ear. 'But you smell better. Want to delay eating for a while, my beauty?'

I laugh. 'Maybe later. But that pizza won't wait, and I'm starving.'

Charlie sighs. 'Actually, I'm starving too. And look at that smiley faced pizza!' He tries to steal an eye, but gets a slapped hand as usual. He never learns.

We sit at the table and he pours us a glass of merlot. He nods at his glass. 'I've been looking forward to this, almost as much as seeing you today.' Then he takes a big mouthful. 'Ah…that's nearly as good as it tasted in my imagination.'

I smile and slice up the pizza. 'Get your laughing gear round this.'

He bites into a slice. It's a hundred times better than any you can get in Dominoes. 'You could get a job in an Italian restaurant in your spare time, Sweetling.' He dabs garlic oil from his chin with a bit of kitchen roll.

Bless him. I reply through a mouthful of pizza. 'You haven't called me Sweetling in years!'

'Have I not? I forgot. I'll call it you more often now that you're the best detective in the south west.'

'I am?'

'You am.'

'Why do you say that?' I ask, passing the big wooden salad bowl.

'Because I found out that you didn't go to Aberdeen at all. You went to London at Abigail's request after a lot of cajoling, and even a bit of begging on her part, she told me.'

My mouth drops open and a bit of pizza crust drops onto the table.

Charlie laughs. 'It makes a change for someone else other than me to make a mess while eating.'

I'm not laughing though. I'm not even smiling. There's a thunderstorm brewing in my chest and I can scarcely breathe. How could she? 'Abigail. Abigail told you about it all! Why the hell—?'

He holds his hands up. 'No. No it was Lilly. She'd come in this morning to clarify a few things. She let something slip about trusting you, next she went bright red and started babbling. Then she refused to say anything. Abigail tried to help her cover it up, but I wasn't having any. They eventually came clean.'

I can't believe this. My shoulders slump and I take a big slug of Merlot. 'Fuck. I'm so sorry, Charlie.'

'Don't be! I'm not at all upset. In fact, I'm touched beyond words that you cared about my feelings enough to keep it all a secret. To go through all that on your own.' Charlie takes my hand. 'God knows what Abigail thinks of me now, mind. I bet she thinks I'm a monster.' He does a monster stance and contorts his face.

I force a smile, but my eyes moisten. '*You* aren't a monster, but your dad was. He made you insecure and worried about not being good enough. I didn't want to add to that. And believe me, Charlie, I didn't want to go to London at all. As I said, I have my own way of helping people, and it shouldn't involve me working with the police. But as you say, Abigail practically begged.'

'I know all that. And I'm grateful to you and so proud of you for doing it.' Charlie's voice trembles. 'And the strength of your love for me is without question...but I honestly don't feel belittled or jealous like I did over the Proctor case. Talking to you about my dad really helped get stuff out of my system. I'm over it now…' I raise an eyebrow. 'Okay, not completely, but I'm well on the way – I'm working it through.'

I get up, and put my arms round his neck. He tucks a few strands of hair behind my ear so he can kiss my tears away.

'Whatever my dad thought of me, I can't be all bad. Because you wouldn't love me so much otherwise.'

'You're not bad. You're lovely. Promise you'll still talk to me if you have any future worries? That you won't bottle it up?'

'Of course I will. And guess what else!'

'What?' I sit back down and take a forkful of salad.

'Leo, Lilly's seventeen-year-old brother came forward last Friday and said his stepfather touched him inappropriately too, when he was in his early teens. I didn't tell you, last week, because I was waiting for the fall out. And boy did it fall out today!'

I nearly choke on a tomato. 'But why didn't he say so straightaway when his sister came back from London?'

'He was ashamed. Leo felt dirty, to blame somehow, and guilty that he'd not spoken out before. Because if he had, he might have saved his sisters from harm. Bradley had apparently kept him quiet by saying the same vile stuff to him that he had to Lilly. That their mother would be alone and practically homeless – that they would be taken away by social services. Bastard.'

'What an evil, evil man. Poor boy must have gone through hell.'

'Yeah. And let's hope that Bradley rots in that place shortly. It will come to court in the next few months, and he's going down for a long, long time. He changed his story once the stepson came forward. Broke down and admitted it all.'

'What? That's astonishing.'

Charlie nods, leans across the table, eyes round. 'And, Nance, this next bit will blow your mind. He even admitted to murdering little Chloé!'

I put the bit of pizza down. 'Eh? Bloody hell! How come?'

'Said he was ashamed. Said that an evil overtook him when he pushed her from the tree. This evil drove him to molest his stepchildren and lie and threaten. He hated himself and the person he'd become. He said if he didn't confess, after he died, his soul would roam the desolate underworld condemned to eternal pain and misery.'

'He said that?'

'Yeah. I memorised it especially for you.'

'Is he trying to plead insanity?'

'Might do. He's no chance though. It had been going on for too long and he was leading an otherwise perfectly normal life.'

'My God.'

'I know. We couldn't have wished for better really.'

'Well done, sweetheart. And well done to Abigail too.'

He traces my cheek with his fingers. 'We only wrapped it up. It was all down to you, my love. You deserve a bloody medal. But you won't get one, because you're invisible. It's so unfair.'

'I don't need medals. Just the satisfaction of knowing I helped.' I squeeze his hand. 'And talking of medals. I forgot to mention that Dot is coming to Louisa's wedding, them being neighbours, and—'

Charlie holds up a finger. 'Can I stop you there? I want to hear about your day, but I want to tell you my idea before I forget. It came to me just now when I came in. The commissioner came to our office unannounced this evening, not long before I left, to thank Abigail, me and the team for all our 'fantastic and incredible' police work.' There's pride in his eyes at the memory of it. 'So I was thinking. What do you say to the idea of me having a word with him about you? Telling him your part in Lilly's case with a view to you helping out in misper cases in future? Serious assault and murders too, maybe? You might even get paid.'

My gut doesn't like the sound of this. Tied to the police by a wage? I'd feel pressure to 'perform' and my gift isn't a side-show. 'I don't know, Charlie...I mean, I'm grateful for your faith in me. But as I keep saying, there are so many other cases not connected to the police. Like the medals, the missing cat, the cheating estate agent and lovely Mark and Louisa's story. If I was working with you lot, I wouldn't have time for all those types of cases. They are so important. Not in the grand scheme of things compared to Becky's and Lilly's case, but—'

'Okay, I admire your conviction, your passion. But how about you don't close the door on the idea of me speaking to Commissioner Whitelaw? You could just do it now and then when you haven't too many other cases? You were saying the other day you have nothing on at the moment.' The sag of my lips tell him the last remark was not helpful. 'But I know it will pick up soon. How could it not? Nancy Cornish PI is the best in the business.' He finishes with a big clown smile.

'We'll see, okay? Don't say anything to the commissioner yet. I want to see how the next few months pan out.'

As I LIE in Charlie's arms later after making love, contentment soothes my tired body like a warm bath. I can't remember when I was last so happy and hopeful for the future. Then I remember something. 'Oh, Charlie. With all the excitement of your news, I almost forgot the other wonderful thing that happened today.'

'Really? What's that?'

'Well, you know I've been on about phoning Mum and asking her to come back here?' I feel him tense up, but he makes an interested noise. 'I got round to it a few weeks back. Seeing Dot and Kathy together made me realise how much I miss her, and guess what?'

Nothing.

'She phoned today and said she's coming home for good! I told her she could live with us until she finds a place of her own. Isn't that fantastic?'

Again. Silence. 'Charlie? It is okay, isn't it?'

'Er it might take a bit of getting used to, but she's your mum. I wish my own parents were still alive, even Dad. And it won't be for long…with any luck.'

He twines his fingers through my hair and pulls my head back down onto his chest. 'So, it's okay?'

'Of course it is, love. I'm glad you made the call.'

Chapter Twenty-Five

Cecil Merryn's ruddy round face, jolly disposition and cheerful smile is half the reason I've been going to *Merryn's Butchers and Farm Shop* for the past twenty-odd years. The other half of the reason is because his meat is sourced locally, outdoor reared and free range. Cecil's sausages in particular are second to none. He never tires of proudly telling customers that *they've won awards, you know. Best in all of Cornwall, some say*. Gloria, his late wife used to help make them. Apparently, she always added a secret ingredient that was only know to herself and Cecil. Cecil hadn't even shared it with his son Talan, and his grandson Ruan who work alongside him. The old butcher told me recently with a cheeky wink, that his Talan would only get to know the secret when Cecil hung up his butcher's apron, and that wouldn't be for a while yet.

I hurry along down the steep hill from Seal Cottage into Padstow, and thread myself as best I can through the crowds swelling the narrow streets and alleyways. The July sun is high in the sky which is a welcome relief from the torrential rain we've had the past few days. But the sun's a magnet for the holidaymakers – they're out in their droves. Mustn't grumble though, a busy summer season puts food on the table through the winter months for many shopkeepers. At the end of the street on the pavement, I see the wooden board in the shape of a pig wearing a chef's hat outside Merryn's. I've been so busy these past few weeks that I've not managed to pop in, but today, I just fancy some of those award-winning bangers for dinner.

There's a queue inside, predictably, but it's always busy no matter what the season. Talan and Ruan are busy serving, while Cecil's at the far counter, his back to me, chopping something up. As I get closer to being served, I notice through the glass front of the display section that the sausages look different. They're thinner and are labelled – *Finest Pork*. They aren't the ones I usually buy – they've always been called *Cecil's Special Sausages*. When Cecil turns round to bring a tray of chicken legs to the cabinet, I'm shocked by his drawn, pale face. He looks like he's lost a stone in weight at least, and there's dark circles under his eyes. His white hat, usually set at a jaunty angle across neat grey hair, is jammed on tight and smeared across the brim, is a thin streak of what looks like animal blood. His ready smile is a grimace, and his normally sparkly green eyes are the colour of algae under dirty pond water.

I watch him place the tray and move a near empty one of pork chops to the front. Then he thinks better of it and moves it back. His hands are trembling, and I can see he's really not on top of his game. His eyes flit to the customers and then to his son, wide with apprehension. When he bites his lip and blinks a few times mumbling something under his breath, I worry he's going to lose it. He raises a hand to his hat and then lets it flop to his side, repeats this action a few times. It's as if his arm doesn't belong to him at all, and someone's operating him by remote control. I'm reminded of a malfunctioning robot. The poor man looks totally bewildered and frightened.

Stepping round the counter at the end of the queue I pat his arm, say, 'Hello, Cecil, how are you? Not seen you for ages.'

Cecil startles at my touch and then recognition dawns. 'Hello, Nancy. Tired you know? Very tired.'

Talan looks across at his dad, worry etched across his forehead and gives a strained smile. He furrows his thick dark brows. 'You wanna take a break, Dad? Me and Ruan can manage for a bit.'

'Break? Er…' Cecil looks round the shop, seemingly unsure of what this entails.

I say to Talan, 'Do you have a back room with a kettle? I could make us a drink. Have a chat.' Cecil's back is to me again and I mouth to Talan, '*he doesn't look right.*'

Talan nods, his relief palpable as he ushers me and his dad through a meat preparation area into a small kitchen with a sink, kettle, cupboard, table and a couple of chairs. He grabs some mugs from the cupboard and a packet of biscuits. 'Kettle's there. Thanks so much, Nancy. Sure Dad would welcome a chat,' he says in a too bright, too loud voice. Then in a low voice as he passes on his way back to the shop, to me he adds, 'I'm worried about him if truth be known.' I give him an encouraging smile and turn to Cecil who's staring out of the window at a brick wall. His hands hanging loosely by his side.

'You sit down and have a rest in that comfy chair.' I pat the chair when he stares at it, and through me. Then after a pause he does as I suggest. 'Tea or coffee, Cecil?'

'Tea...I think.'

Now and again I glance at him while I organise the drinks. He's examining his nails which look none too clean, red like the smear on his hat. Not washing hands thoroughly is certainly not what's needed after food preparation. I'm sure Cecil would be horrified normally. But anyone can see that he's not normal today, poor man. 'Want to wash your hands before we have our tea and biscuits, Cecil?'

He obeys me like a child, but after he's finished, he leaves the hot tap running over his hands until they start to turn pink. He just stares vacantly at them, seemingly unaware of the temperature. I switch the tap off and hand him a towel, lead him back to his seat. I hand him his tea. 'Thank you, Nancy. You're very kind.'

I sit down opposite and watch him blow across the surface of his drink and take a sip. 'Why do you think you're so tired, then?' I ask, offering him a biscuit.

He declines, takes his hat off and attempts to smooth the grey tufts of uncombed hair. 'I don't sleep much. Lie awake half the night. Started when Gloria left.' He makes it sound like she just decided to live elsewhere. Probably hasn't had the courage to say the word *died* out loud yet.

'Really? No wonder you're tired, Cecil. Gloria's been gone…what…?'

'Six months on Saturday.'

'That long…it only seems—'

'Like yesterday?' I wasn't going to say that, but keep quiet. 'Not to me. To me it seems like an eternity.'

'It must.' I push unwelcome thoughts of been separated from Charlie in the future to a deep dark hole and drag a heavy weight over it.

We sit drinking our tea and say nothing for a while. I want to give him time to say what's on his mind. Cecil takes a biscuit and crunches into it. Then he grabs another. A bit of colour comes back into his cheeks after a few minutes and I wonder how long it is since he's eaten. 'The thing is…as well as the not sleeping lark, I think my marbles are on their way out.' He puts a finger up and a spark of the old Cecil twinkles briefly in his eyes. 'They aren't lost yet, mind,' he says with a brief smile.

'Good. And if you're not sleeping, everything will seem out of kilter. Especially if you've not been getting quality sleep for months at a time.'

'Yes. But you see…' Cecil pauses, and through narrowed eyes looks me up and down, as if gauging whether to allow his words out into the open. 'People say you're one of them side-kicks. Before you say anything, I know the word's psychic.' A little twist of the mouth – another glimpse of the old Cecil. 'Don't normally hold with it myself, ghosts and stuff…but you might believe more than most what I reckon's happening. Even though it's baloney, I can't get it out of my head.'

'We side-kicks are good listeners, Cecil.'

He finishes his biscuit and sets his mug on the table. 'Thing is this. As you know, we used to make the best sausages in all Cornwall, so some say. Me and my Gloria made 'em I mean. *Cecil's Special Sausages*, a bit of a tongue twister. We thought of that… me and her. Made it a bit of fun, memorable too.' He stares longingly at a framed photo of Gloria on top of the fridge, holding a tray of sausages with a red rosette propped on top. She's outside this shop, sun on her curly dark hair, a beaming smile on her face. 'They won awards.' He points at the photo. 'That was taken thirty years back when we won the first one. People come from Tintagel, Wadebridge, Fraddon, Indian Queens, St Columb Major, and even as far as Newquay to get 'em…or used to.'

'Yes. I did wonder where they were today. I always buy some when I come in. What's happened?'

'Right. I'll tell you. Bear in mind I said I think my marbles are on the way out.' He gives me a hard stare before continuing. 'When I get up in the morning to make the sausages, they're already made and in the fridge. Yeah, I swear to you. Already made!' He jabs a sausage like finger through the air at me. 'And if that's not crazy enough, they're bloody awful. There's too much water and breadcrumbs, not enough sage or pork, too much seasoning and no secret ingredient.'

317

I don't know what to say to this. Maybe Cecil is making them and then he's not remembered, because of the stress of losing Gloria and lack of sleep. 'That's certainly a mystery, Cecil.'

'You're not bleddy kidding, maid. And guess what else? I can't even remember the secret ingredient. But I know it's not there 'cos of the taste of 'em.' He turns his mouth down at the corners. 'Wouldn't feed 'em to our dogs.' He takes his mug, drains it and bangs it down. 'I'll get to the ghost bit now. I reckon it's my Gloria, coming in the night and making a batch of duds. Maybe she's mad at me because I'm still here and she's not. Maybe she's just playing a joke to let me know she's still around. Make sure I don't forget her.' He looks at the photo and says with a catch in his voice. 'As if I ever could. She was my life…'

Gloria's doing it? Even for me this sounds a bit 'out there.' As far as I know ghosts can't make sausages, or anything else come to that. There has to be another simpler explanation. 'Hmm. I think that might be a bit of a stretch, Cecil. Look. How about I have a hold of that photo up there and see if I can make a connection.' I explain what I mean by that. Let's try to solve this mystery, eh?'

Cecil draws a big breath and blows it through his nostrils. 'No. No I don't want her disturbed. It's all a bit much for me to be honest.' He stands up and takes his black and white striped

318

apron off. 'I've made a decision. Come the end of next week I'm hanging this up for good. If I stay, I'll just make a balls-up of everything. I'm too tired to think straight, and I know my boy and his boy are fed up with covering for me. I keep making mistakes, with the till, with the produce, you see. All sorts. My mind's going.' He sniffs and sticks his chin out. 'Still. I've had a good innings. I'm going before they have to cart me off. At least I'll have my dignity.'

Merryn's without Cecil is unthinkable. I watch his proud expression fighting with defeat and say, 'You've got many good years in you yet, Cecil. You'll be so much better with a good few night's sleep under your b—'

'No. My mind's made up, Nancy. Besides, I'm seventy-one. I said I'd keep on until seventy-five, but it's time to go.'

Then before I can say anything else, Cecil gets up, grabs his coat from a peg and leaves through the back door. Poor, poor man. I hurry after him, but see his hunched figure is just disappearing round the corner through the narrow alleyway. I go inside again and find the shop isn't as busy. The lunchtime rush for pasties and pork pie has abated a little. Talan sees me and comes over. I beckon him through to the kitchen and I tell him what's happened.

Talan takes his hat off and ruffles his curls. I can see Gloria in him. 'Thanks for trying Nancy. He's walked off before and not come back in for a few days. And I knew Dad was struggling, but I had no idea that's what he was thinking about the bloody sausages. I thought he was making them and just forgetting about it. Why he was messing them all up though, I've no clue. I do know that losing our mum was like him losing his right arm.'

'It must have been. And for you too.' I take the photo down from the shelf. 'I'm not sure if you know that I've set up as a psychic investigator?' Talan looks a bit wary, so I push on and explain. I also tell him that I asked his dad if I could try and make a connection and he said no. 'But if you were willing, I'd give it a go. I wouldn't do it without your say-so, but it can't hurt, can it? I'm just so worried about Cecil.'

Talan sticks his hat back on and gives me a that cheeky wink, obviously learned at his dad's knee. 'I can't pretend to go along with all that malarkey. But be my guest. I have to get back to the shop now, so is it okay to do it without me?'

I smile. 'Of course. Probably better without an audience anyway.'

After Talan's left, I take a few deep breaths and clear my mind. Then I sit in Cecil's chair, close my eyes and hug the photo to my chest for a few minutes. Next, I hold it in my lap and look into Gloria's eyes. 'Are you making the mystery sausages, Gloria?' I ask out loud. Very slowly, warmth seeps into my fingers from the frame and I hear distant laughter. A woman's laughter. Gloria was always laughing. Like her husband, she'd a cheerful way with her – a joie de vivre. The laughter stops, and on the fridge a rolling film of Gloria and Cecil in a kitchen begins. They're making sausages and laughing all the while. Then I hear her say, *don't forget the cinnamon. We need to order more…can't have Cecil's Special Sausages without that.* Then I'm looking at a white fridge door again. Short and sweet.

Cinnamon's the special ingredient? Now I think about it, I can remember a hint of that spice in them. I'd never have guessed if I didn't know, though. But I'm no closer to solving the mystery of who's making the awful sausages. About to put the photo back, from the corner of my eye, I see the shadow of a figure by the door. I turn to see Gloria polishing the door handle, and then she sighs and shoves a duster into her floral apron. She looks at me, hands on hips. It's a younger Gloria, maybe thirty years back. I have noticed this before with some older spirits. They like to appear younger – revert to the age they were most happy with. Maybe they're given a choice when they meet their maker. But with my Sebastian, he appears at different ages. Perhaps it's because he never got the chance to experience what it was like to be two, three…older. But why didn't he appear in London recently as the teenager he would have been if he'd lived? Maybe he decided not to be a teenager…maybe…Gloria interrupts my ponderings.

'This place is going to the dogs.' She runs a finger across a shelf and examines her finger. 'Needs a good clean. Go and see Cecil…find out about the sausages. And tell him the answer to his nightly question is…' Her big brown eyes fill with tears and she dabs a tissue at the corners. 'Tell him the answer is forever and always.' Then she pixelates through the wall.

I go through to the shop and tell a sceptical Talan what I've found out, but don't tell him about the cinnamon, or about the last thing his mum said.

'You're not going to tell me what the special ingredient is then?' he asks.

'Not my place.' I shrug my coat on and give him my best cheeky wink. 'Besides, you don't believe in all that malarkey, do you.'

'Er…no. But I might be open to persuasion.'

'Sorry. My lips are sealed. Oh, can I have your dad's address so I can do as Gloria asked? I can't go round today though, as I have errands to run.'

Talan jots it down on the back of a paper bag. 'Don't be surprised if he doesn't let you in, Nancy. He can be very stubborn.'

'Don't worry about that, Talan. I'm used to stubborn men.' I laugh and say over my shoulder as I walk through the door, 'I married one.'

Chapter Twenty-Six

The next day I'm back on the job. Talan told me his dad's unfortunately still not back at his, so I set off to solve the mystery of the sausages. A wiggle of apprehension worms through my belly as I draw up outside Cecil's lovely cottage by the sea. What if he won't let me in? I sit and look at it for a few moments before getting out. It looks like it used to be two fishermen's cottages knocked through. It's very chocolate box. Wisteria hugs the length of its whitewashed stone walls, its lavender froth framing the windows and green front door. The back of the house faces the ocean, the sunsets must be spectacular.

I walk up the little path and give a tentative rap on the wood. Nobody comes. Out of the corner of my eye I think I see a curtain twitch in an upstairs window. I wait. Nothing. There's no sign of movement or sound from inside. Shall I just give up? After all, I can't help someone who doesn't want to be helped. If Cecil wants to hide himself away in his bedroom, then so be it. Gloria's words won't let me abandon this mission, however, and

I rap on the door again. And again, much louder. The thump of footsteps on stairs is followed by, 'Okay, keep your hair on!'

The door opens and Cecil's grumpy face thrusts itself at me. His hair's stuck up in tufts and he's wearing striped yellow and blue pyjamas. Pyjamas that look like they could do with seeing the inside of a washing machine. 'Morning, Cecil. Just popped over to see how you are. You weren't yourself the other day.'

'I'm not myself most days, as I told you. I was just trying to take a nap, having been awake again most of the night.' His expression leaves me in no doubt that I have interrupted that attempt and he wishes me far away.

'Well, it's only eleven o' clock, plenty of time for a nap later. I'm here because Gloria asked me to come and see you.'

'Gloria? What are you saying to me?' Cecil's eyes narrow and his anger is as strong as his suspicion. I can feel it coming at me in waves…along with the unwashed pyjama odour.

'Let me in and I'll tell you all about it.'

He mutters something under his breath and stands to one side allowing me access. Good. That's the first hurdle over. We walk through a large, bright, well-equipped kitchen which looks like a tornado's been through. Dishes piled in the sink, flour over the big farmhouse kitchen table, sticky jammy finger-marks around the door jamb. Gloria would be appalled if she could see it. She wasn't too pleased with the cleanliness of the shop, and I imagine this house would have been her pride and joy. The living room has two big patio doors opening onto a sweep of lawn and a stunning view of the ocean. But like the kitchen, the room's not seen a cloth or a duster for weeks, and judging by the trail of biscuit crumbs, a vacuum either.

Cecil stands by the patio doors and folds his arms. 'Sit down if you like.' He inclines his head to the only chair with no rubbish piled on it.

I sit. 'Okay, Cecil. I can tell you don't want me here and you mentioned the other day that you don't 'hold' with all this psychic stuff. But I am worried about you. And because I care, Talan gave me permission to have a chat with your Gloria.'

He throws his hands up. 'I said to leave well alone.' I say nothing. Then he scratches the grey stubble on his chin. 'Right. I don't mean to be rude, but let's be hearing what you've to say and then you can be on your way, Nancy.'

I tell him that it wasn't Gloria who made the sausages and that she told me the secret ingredient. 'She also said the shop needed a good clean. I move a plate with dried on egg to one side with my foot, and raise an eyebrow at him.

Cecil's not giving much away. He perches on the arm of the settee. 'What's the ingredient, then?'

'Thought you said you didn't hold with all that—'

'Don't play silly buggers with me, girl.'

I smile. 'Cinnamon.'

His mouth drops open and he just stares. 'That's it. You're right…cinnamon. How could I forget?'

'Because you're dead on your feet – not sleeping and heartbroken about Gloria. It's not surprising.'

'And I'm losing my marbles. Don't forget that small detail.' Cecil snorts and looks out of the patio doors.

'I doubt that very much. That's why I'm here to see if we can get to the bottom of who's making the sausages.'

'And my Gloria said for you to do that?' he says to the ocean. 'Yes.'

'Seems unbelievable to me.' Cecil looks back at me, scratches his stubble again. 'I supposed you could have just guessed about the cinnamon…you having the sausage so much in the past.'

'Unlikely, but yes, I could. But I didn't. Now, I think the best bet is for me to just hold your hand and see what happens. It worked for me recently, and something's telling me this is the right approach.'

'Now you're just flirting.' Cecil does his wink and that melts the frosty barrier he's built between us.

I go over, move a newspaper and a pizza box and sit on the settee. 'Okay, here we go.' I take his hand, trying not to wonder when he'd washed it last. 'Don't think of anything in particular. Try to relax.'

'Not much chance of that with all this spooky carry on.'

'Shush.'

I feel the weight of his big butcher's hand in mine, fingers like the sausages he used to make, folded loosely over my palm, and closes my eyes. I see the scene of him and Gloria making the sausages like I saw in the shop. They're larking about and laughing. Then it's just Cecil. It's him in the messy kitchen I just walked through. It's night, the darkness lifted only by a little lamp. He's throwing ingredients in a bowl and tossing flour on the table. He has a metal machine on the side, sausage skin dangling from a tube. But he looks odd. He looks like he's not present mentally, even though his body is making sausages. Concentrating on his face I realise what it is that's wrong. He's asleep. Eyes open…but asleep.

'What's up?' Cecil interrupts. 'Your face is twitching.'

His voice breaks my concentration and the scene's fading to the edges like a sepia photo. I shush him again. 'Not much longer now.'

Focussing for a few seconds, the scene becomes clearer again and I watch Cecil fully asleep making sausages. Or rather making a mess of the sausages. He piles them on a plate and shoves them in the fridge leaving a trail of destruction in his wake. Then like he did in the shop the other day, he runs his hands under the hot tap until they turn red. That's got to be uncomfortable, but he doesn't seem to notice.

I open my eyes, let go of his hand and give him an encouraging smile. 'I have the answer to the mystery of the special sausages, Cecil.'

'Hmm, really. I'm just glad your face has stopped twitching. Looked like a bloody rabbit to be honest.'

The scepticism in his voice prods me towards an irritable response, but I ignore it. 'I had no idea I twitched, I'll try and work on it.' I move over a bit, get comfy. 'Okay, it's you who's making the sausages and—'

'I knew it! In my heart of hearts I knew it wasn't Gloria, 'cos I don't hold with all that. Just proves I've lost my marbles. I mean, what kind of sane person makes sausages – makes bad ones at that, and doesn't remember the next day?' Cecil thumps the sofa cushion next to me and stands up. His eyes are wide but his mouth's pressed together in a grim line.

'The kind of person who's sleepwalking. Or sleepsausaging in your case.'

His mouth becomes as wide as his eyes. 'Eh? Sleep whating?' I tell him what I saw. 'But why the bloody hell would I be doing something like that? And washing my hands until they're red hot too? Makes no sense.'

'I'd been thinking about that and I think it makes perfect sense in the light of what you said the other day. When you told me it was Gloria making the sausages, and making them badly, you said maybe she was playing a joke, or punishing you because she'd had to go, and you were still here.' I get up and squeeze his hand briefly. 'What you're doing is out of guilt and grief. Guilt because you're still alive and she's not. Also, Gloria was as much behind the success of those sausages as you. Perhaps you don't think you deserve success without her. So, you ruin them. And grief, well that's obvious. She was the love of your life. Add to that the fact that you're dead on your feet through lack of sleep, it's not that hard to believe, is it?'

Cecil stares through me while he chews this over. 'No. I don't suppose so…but why the hand washing?'

'Again, you're punishing yourself.'

His eyes come back into focus and he nods. 'Yes. I can see how that would be the case.' Cecil walks over to the window and shoves hands in his pyjama pockets, speaks to the patio. 'Not being funny, Nancy…but you could be making all this up to help me feel better. Maybe Talan's had a word. Asked you to do this and convince me not to hang up my apron. If I'm right, I thank you, but it won't work. My mind is made up.'

Expecting this, I answer, 'I could be making it all up, but I'm not. The only way you'll believe me is if I give you proof. When Gloria told me to come here, she also told me to tell you that the answer to your nightly question is "forever and always."'

Cecil spins round to face me so fast he nearly topples over. He stretches a shaking hand to a chair back and grips it. Tight. 'Oh my God…my God…'

He's gone ashen, so I guide him to the sofa and he flops down as if his legs won't support the weight of him. 'It's okay, Cecil. These things can be a shock sometimes. Take a few moments to let it sink in.'

I sit next to him, tell him to take some deep breaths. After a while he looks at me and blinks back tears. They refuse to be staunched and trickle down his cheeks into his grey stubble. There's something helpless about him. Despite his age, he looks like a lonely child who's lost his mum. 'My Gloria…' he whispers. 'My Gloria and me, we used to love this old song from our courting days. A duo sang it. One of them sang, 'how long will you love me? The other would answer…always and f-forever. Each night of our married life when we went to bed at night, one of us would ask the same, and the other would answer. And now I'm alone…I still ask the question before I get into the bed I shared with her for nigh on fifty years. But no one answers, of course. My beautiful Gloria…I miss her so much.'

Cecil stops and sobs into a cushion and my throat's so tight I can hardly get my words out, so I put my arm around him. 'But Gloria does, Cecil. She answers just the same as she always did. She told me so it would bring you some comfort.' I rustle up a tissue from my bag.

He gives his nose a mammoth blow. 'Yes. Yes, it would seem so,' he says, bewildered.

'She clearly doesn't resent you, Cecil. She loves you just as much as she's always done. She'll be waiting when your time comes.'

'She will? How do you know…and where do we *actually* go?' Cecil wipes his eyes.

I just know…and the rest isn't shown to me.'

'Well I'll tell you what, maid. There's no denying all this side-kick stuff now. I'm a believer after today. Now I've heard it from the horse's mouth…'

We talk about Gloria and how happy he is that she's content and watching over him. I joke that as she is, he might like to get the house tidied and himself too. When he sees me to the door, Cecil's more like his old self. His real old self with the cheeky wink and the ready smile. Halfway down the path I turn and ask, 'Will you reconsider staying on at the shop?'

'I'm saying nothing for now. I'll have a big think.' Then in a loud voice he says, 'But what I will say is thank you from the bottom of my heart, young Nancy. You've made an old man very happy.' He glances to his left at his neighbour's open window and lowers his voice. 'And that will give old Nellie Gardner something to gossip to the WI about.'

LATE THAT NIGHT as I turn over in bed, I wonder if Cecil is asking his nightly question but this time hearing the answer. I also wonder if he'll be making those special sausages for a few more years. I do hope so. But then I put that to the back of my mind. Tomorrow is the wedding day of Louisa and Mark, and I can't wait to see them married in that little church on the hill.

Chapter Twenty-Seven

For once, the weather forecast is totally accurate. The sky is blue, the sun's shining and with only a gentle breeze on the top of the hill by the ocean, the collection of wedding hats, long dresses and pashminas are likely to remain in their placed positions. Charlie has wangled a day off, and is looking very smart in his charcoal grey suit, white shirt and blue tie. I do like a man in a suit. Especially Charlie. He doesn't know Louisa and Mark, but I wanted him to meet them, and of course to accompany me.

I agonised over to whether to wear a fascinator or not this morning. My green silk dress looks good with my red hair left loose, but the fascinator with all the coloured feathers looked like a dead parrot had landed on my head. I decided against. I wish I'd decided against these shoes too. Heels and me don't get on.

The wedding is at one o'clock, and we drive up the winding narrow lane and park the car overlooking the Atlantic at twelve-forty. There are already quite a few people milling about outside the church and in the churchyard. They all look so colourful and animated, like a carpet of wildflowers rippling in the breeze. I think I can see Mark talking to a huddle of guests near the ancient arched entrance. Charlie's fiddling with his tie and checking his phone, so I link arms with him and drag him towards the church. 'Oi what's the rush?' he says, still thumbing his phone.

'No rush. I just want to have a quick word with Mark before it all kicks off. Ask him how Louisa is and stuff.'

Charlie stops. 'Bugger.' He shows me his phone. 'Abigail says she's got my wallet. I left it on the desk last night.'

'But surely you checked before we left just now?'

'No. You were rushing me so much I forgot.'

'I was not rushing you, Charlie Cornish. Just checking you were getting ready.'

'Anyway. I need to go and get it from hers. I'll go after the wedding, but before the reception.'

This is very annoying. Charlie will get caught up in shop talk and be late back and I'll be husbandless. 'Why can't she drop it to the evening do after the reception dinner? I'm sure she won't mind. It would be nice to see her too.'

'Won't Mark and Louisa mind?'

'I doubt it. They probably won't even notice. It's not as if she'll be eating, just having a drink at the bar.' Charlie looks like he's going to argue, so I add, 'I'll message her. Hang on.' I get my phone out, send off a text and get an instant reply. 'All sorted, Charlie. She says she'll be there and it's no trouble.'

Mark sees us coming towards him and holds his arms out to me. I walk into them and he says to the people he was talking to. 'This woman here is a miracle worker. If it hadn't have been for Nancy, none of us would be here today!'

I turn pink as all eyes focus on me, but I can't help feel a sense of satisfaction. It's true, Nancy Cornish PI brought two lost lovers together again. 'Thanks, Mark. I can't tell you how happy I am for you both.' Then the little huddle start firing questions at me and I have to tell them how it all came to be and about my connections. Mutterings of astonishment, admiration and surprise follow, and two people ask for my card. They have a case that I might be able to solve. Excellent. At last there is more work in the offing.

The vicar comes out just then and asks us all to take our seats. From the corner of my eye as we walk towards the door, I see the wedding car sweep round the corner. My heart leaps with excitement and I place my hand on the ancient sun-warmed stone arch. It feels alive somehow. This church with its ancient tower and windows must have watched people pass in and through over the ages, their hopes, dreams, happiness, grief, longings, love and regrets alive in the stones.

I say to Charlie, 'Put your hand on the stone and tell me what you feel.'

He frowns but puts his palm against it. 'I feel the rough stone, the warmth of the sun in it and the work of a chisel. Great craftsmanship.'

'But can't you feel anything else?'

'Like what?'

'Well like…' I have a think to sort my words through before I say them. '…A sense of peace, and of those who have gone before, their hopes – dreams?'

'Not as you'd notice. I'm no psychic, Sweetling.' Charlie looks over his shoulder. 'Come on, we're holding everyone up.'

Sometimes I wish Charlie was more spiritual. I know he can't be psychic, but he often closes his mind when it should be open. Mind you, I can't really grumble, considering what he used to think about my connections. We go in, and in front of us on the floor is a tall vase of white lilies, their intoxicating scent heavy in the air, just as it was the day I came looking for Mark. Perfect. We walk down the aisle to an organist playing a gentle tune, as the sun splashes a kaleidoscope of colours through the stained-glass window onto the stone floor. I wonder how many weddings this place has seen, and conversely, funerals. My mind sweeps such morbid thoughts to one side as we sit on a pew near the front and wait.

Mark walks to the front a few minutes later and then the organ stops and is replaced by the opening notes of 'The First Time Ever I Saw Your Face'. This is my cue to go back to the door and escort Louisa. We agreed we'd do it like this, because she wanted to arrive on her own. Something about being alone with her destiny. Already my throat's struggling with a lump as I remember the couple in their youth. I see again the photo Louisa showed me in the hope that I might make a connection, of herself with Mark in 1977 on the harbour at Porthleven, their backs to the sea. Her face full of youthful excitement, her jet-black hair lifting on the breeze and Mark looking adoringly at her, while she's grinning at the camera. And today, in this wonderful place, at last they will accomplish what they failed to, so many years ago. Charlie sees me blinking away tears as I get up and he whispers, 'God knows what you'll be like when you see the bride.'

At the door, I watch Louisa walk towards me. The beauty and radiance surrounding her takes my breath, and I have to press a tissue under each eye. The dress is in her usual boho style. Shoestring twists of fabric on her shoulders sweep to a deep bustline, from which long flowing swathes of light blue and cream reach almost to the ground, with little silver bells sewn along the asymmetric hem. Woven through her long grey hair are delicate wildflowers. The blues of forget-me-nots and lemon of buttercups, and a soft pink of a flower I can't identify. The same flowers join a few yellow roses in her bouquet. Stunning.

We smile, but no words are necessary as she takes my arm, and together we walk the final steps towards the rest of her life. The faces of those gathered are full of joy as they watch her pass. But something outshines all of this. As Louisa takes her place next to Mark and they look into each other's eyes, the love that surrounds and bonds them charges the air. It's tangible.

'How in love and wonderful they both look,' I whisper to Charlie as I re-take my place beside him.

He takes my tissue and dabs it along my eyeline. 'Yes. You, on the other hand, my darling, look like a panda.'

This turns my tears into laughter, which I pass onto him. We sit like naughty children in assembly, trying not to giggle as the vicar reads the vows.

IT'S OVER ALL too quickly, and the congregation file out behind the bride and groom to the tune of 'We've Only Just Begun'. I do deep breaths and the thought of pandas helps to keep the emotion from rising to my throat this time. Charlie and I walk to the edge of the gathered crowd while the photographer does her job. The two of them against a backdrop of the ancient church, blue sky and ocean will make some stunning photographs. Louisa spots me and waves her bouquet like she's frightening bees. I blow her a kiss and send a big smile.

'You scrub up well,' a voice says behind my left shoulder.

'Dot!' I say, turning around. She's smiling up at me, a vision in turquoise leaning on her stick and the arm of Ken. Her peach hat's so big and floppy that the brim's rippling, lifting and falling on the breeze, and I'm reminded of an exotic jellyfish propelling itself through the shallows. 'How are you both? You look lovely, Dot.'

'I am lovely.' She nudges Ken. 'Aren't I?'

'You are, that.' He winks at me, cups one hand against his mouth and says in a stage whisper. 'I have to say that, or she'll push me over the cliff.'

'You cheeky bugger!' Dot shrieks and gives him a poke on the shoe with her stick.

I introduce them both to Charlie and Dot questions him for the next ten minutes about what it's like to be a policeman, and has he caught any baddies recently.

When she stops to draw breath, Charlie gives me a 'help-me-for-God's-sake' look. So I come to his rescue. 'Looks like the bride and groom are moving off for more photos by the ocean. We'll see you at the reception, no doubt.'

'Oh yes. I wouldn't miss it for the world!' Dot says. 'I need to find our Kathy, because she's taking us. Where is that girl?'

I see Kathy a little way off standing behind a large gravestone. To the untrained eye, it might look like she was deliberately hiding from someone.

As they walk from the churchyard, the photographer whispers something to Louisa and she turns to the crowd. 'Okay. Who wants this bouquet?'

A few calls of 'over here', and 'yes please' go up and Louisa draws her arm back while the photographer waits to get the shot. As if in slow motion, the bouquet leaves Louisa's hand and from nowhere, Dot springs forward and knocks it from the sky with her stick. The flowers turn a lazy circle in the air and land in her outstretched arms. A cheer goes up and Ken looks on, as astonished as I am. Dot's knees must have miraculously healed at the crucial moment.

THE RECEPTION IS in the Metropole Hotel overlooking stunning views of the Camel Estuary and Padstow Harbour. The food is delicious, and I'm so pleased we're seated near Mark and Louisa, so I have time to have a long chat with her about what she and

Mark have been doing. They are going on a walking tour around the south west coast path, to raise both money and awareness for a charity which helps those suffering from domestic abuse. I'm in awe of these two. Not just content with at last finding happiness, they want to make sure they do something to help others too. Mark said it would be a way of healing the past and forging a strong path for the future.

A little while later, Mark stands and taps on his glass. He's going to say a few words. His few words tell the story I already know about him losing Louisa all those years ago. Some of the guests know too, but not everyone. A few tissues come out and flap at faces like paper butterflies. Next, Mark turns me scarlet yet again as he says, 'And I can't reiterate enough how much this woman, Nancy Cornish means to me and my wife.' He points his finger at me. 'If it hadn't been for her extraordinary gift, today wouldn't have happened.' Then he tells the story of my involvement and at the end he makes everyone stand to toast me and give me a round of applause. I glance up at Charlie and note his eyes are bright. The pride in his face sets me off, and I make a mental note to reapply my mascara in the ladies as soon as I can.

Five more people come up immediately after the meal is ended and ask for more information and my card. They promise to be in touch, but I don't find out what their problems are, as the wedding reception is neither the time nor the place. But so as long as they keep their promises, including the ones who seemed interested outside the church, that's maybe seven possible cases. Things are looking up. And as Charlie said the other day, word of mouth should make a huge difference.

THE EVENING 'DO' is well underway. I'm contemplating another drink to give me courage to ask Charlie for a dance. I'm not a natural dancer, but the joyful atmosphere today has given my feet wings. That and the wine. I laugh at Dot wiggling her bum to the 'Macarena'. And tapping his feet nearby, Ken looks more like Father Christmas tonight than ever before. He's sitting on a chair smiling at Dot with his hands folded over his tummy, his face flushed from the heat of the summer evening, and maybe a few beers too.

Unbidden, a sobering image of the D-Day landings flash in my mind again and I marvel at the courage of people like Ken. He belongs to a fast disappearing generation. A generation of fighters. The things he lived through in the war, both at home and abroad. The things he must have seen. Dot's made of stern stuff too. I smile as she drags poor Ken to his feet and makes him do one or two dance steps. They certainly broke the mould when they made that one.

I'm about to drag Charlie up too, when an attractive woman in a clingy red dress, with long dark hair comes over and sits by my side. She looks to be in her thirties and very much like Louisa when she was young. Similar intelligent grey eyes and strong jaw. 'Hi, I'm Vicky,' she says offering her hand. 'I'm Louisa's niece.'

'I did think you were related. I saw a photo of Louisa when she was young, and you're quite like her.'

'Yes. My mum is her sister and she looks like her too. She's over there somewhere with my dad.' Vicky smiles and takes a sip from her glass. 'I just wanted to say how very grateful I am to you for helping my aunty find Mark. Happiness has been a long time coming, but, it's never too late to find 'the one' is it?'

'It isn't. And have you found the one?' I ask, thinking she must have a long list of admirers if she wasn't spoken for.

'Sadly, no. I've had a few relationships over the years, but not found my soul mate yet'.

I'm about to ask why she thought that was, when Abigail comes over and kisses me on both cheeks. 'Hi, Nancy. Have you seen Charlie? Just gonna give him his wallet and go.'

I look round and see Charlie's missing. 'He was here a moment ago. Why not stay for a while? We could talk about how fantastic I am at surfing!'

She laughs. 'Love to – but it's been a long day catching the bad guys, I'm afraid. I'm knackered.'

Vicky says, 'Bad guys? You're a police officer?'

'Yeah. A DI.' Abigail tucks her blonde bob behind her ears and smiles.

Vicky pats the chair next to her. 'You can stay for one drink, surely?'

'We-ll…'

'Go on, Abi,' I say. 'One won't hurt.'

I go to the bar to get Abigail a drink but there's a queue so I'm a good fifteen minutes. When I return, I find the two women deep in conversation. They seem oblivious to my presence until I sit in the vacant chair between them feeling like a gooseberry. 'Thanks. Nancy,' Abigail says, taking a sip of the cyder. 'Vicky here is a journalist on the local paper. An interesting job by the sounds of it.'

'Not as interesting as yours,' Vicky says, her eyes fixed on Abigail's in a way that…

Charlie appears then, interrupting my thought pattern and Abigail stands up, digs his wallet out of her bag and they start chatting about something that happened at work. While they do, Vicky comes round to my chair and kneels next to me. 'I don't suppose you know if Abigail has found 'the one' yet, do you? She told me all about how you helped her and how grateful she is to you.

'So she told you she's gay, but not about her wider personal life?'

'Yeah.' Vicky's eyes stray to Abigail and back to me. 'The thing is, I'm gay too. But I don't want to tread on anyone's toes. You know. If she's in a relationship.'

This day just gets better and better. I think Vicky would be perfect for Abigail. She's a nice woman, I can sense it. 'As far as I know, she's single. I'd go for it if I were you,' I say, standing up and linking my arm through Charlie's. 'Come on, old man. Let's see what you're made of on the dance floor.'

Charlie shakes his head. 'No thanks. Me and Abigail are just discussing the—'

'Not anymore you're not.' I say. 'Abi and Vicky were having a nice chat until you came over. Sit in my chair, Vicky, and have Charlie's chair, Abi. We might be some time.' Still protesting, Charlie allows me to lead him onto the dance floor while I whisper in his ear why I want the two girls left alone.

As we smooch to 'I will Always Love You', I sneak a glance over his shoulder at Vicky and Abigail, and find them laughing and staring into each other's eyes as if they're joined by invisible hooks. Charlie kisses my neck and says in my ear, 'It's been a great day hasn't it?'

I nod and kiss him on the lips. 'It has. The best.'

Chapter Twenty-Eight

I pull the duvet back, flop into bed, and wait for Charlie to finish brushing his teeth in the en suite. While my body is tired, my mind is still whirling to the music of me blowing my own trumpet. On the way home from the reception at the hotel, I was thinking about the day and how well it's gone. Mark's praise could lead to a number of new cases and that led to me assessing the wider success of my business. Nancy Cornish PI has only been up and running a few months, but so far, I've had no unsolved cases. There will be some in the future, it's just a simple law of averages, but for now, I can give myself a huge pat on the back. The immediate future looks bright.

A few minutes later Charlie comes into the bedroom and turns the light off. 'You awake?' he asks slipping into bed beside me.

'Yup.'

'I forgot to mention something I found out the other day. Something to do with Scrappy.' He gives a long sigh.

My heart plummets. Does he have owners? I couldn't bear it if he was taken from us now. 'What did you find?'

'Those flyers I made you put in the shops with his photo and our phone number, when we first found him?'

'Yeah?'

I saw one in the pet shop when I went to get his treats yesterday. And you'll never guess what...our phone number had two incorrect digits.'

From his tone I can tell he's rumbled me, but say, 'Really? Oh dear. It's a bit late to do anything about it now, isn't it? He's settled here with us.'

'Hmm. I suppose it is a bit late.' He elbows me and laughs. 'Sneaky lady.'

I laugh too. 'You wouldn't be without him, though would you? Not now.'

'No. He's grown on me.' We lie there quietly for a few moments, then he asks, 'Why are you wide awake, anyway? I thought you'd be out for the count when I'd finished in the bathroom, with all that wine you put away.'

'The cheek! I didn't have that much. It's because I'm thinking of all the people I've helped over the past few months since I've been a PI. I can't tell you what a huge sense of achievement that is for me – how happy it makes me. I feel useful, Charlie. A real part of our community.'

'More than you were when you worked at the café?'

'Of course. I know the café is a great place for people to meet and catch up, but I didn't feel like I was helping people in the same way. I didn't feel like I was making a crucial difference to their lives.'

'Your chocolate cake makes a difference to mine,' Charlie says with a laugh.

I sigh and say nothing.

'Hey, Nance. I'm joking.' Charlie turns to me, props himself up on his elbow. 'You know what I think of your connections. I told you the other day when Lilly's case was closed. If it was up to me, you'd be properly respected for your work, instead of us having to keep you hidden like some dirty secret.'

'Oh Charlie. That's a lovely thing to say.' I curl my hand around his neck and pull him close for a kiss. Then I run my hand down his chest. 'I love you.'

'Are you trying to have your wicked way with me?' he asks, moving his hand to my breast.

'Might be. Now shut up and kiss me again.'

A LITTLE WHILE later, Charlie's soft snoring is the only sound I can hear, apart from the fading notes of my trumpet blowing. I close my eyes and say a silent thank you to all those who have gone, that helped me to help those still here. Sebastian, Chloé, Dot's Frank, Alison's Jack, Adam the estate agent's Granny Alice, and Cecil's Gloria. Then I silence the trumpet and settle down to sleep with a light heart. I need to get some rest, because tomorrow there'll be a new case to solve. I can feel it.

Case Notes – Updated

7 August:

Cecil popped round to ours with a big basket of sausages, pasties and a whole selection of goodies. He's been back in the shop for a good few weeks, thankfully, and back to his cheeky old self. He's sleeping well and making the best sausages in the whole of Cornwall again, some say. When I've popped in, I never mentioned payment for helping him, because I don't think he realises I'm a 'proper' business, and I don't like to ask. I'm happy to have helped. Once we'd had a cuppa and a chat, I started to unpack the big basket, thanking him for each item. But he suddenly got flustered, said he had to get on and hurried off. At the bottom of the basket I found an envelope with five-hundred pounds inside, and a card which said I had a lifetime's supply of Cecil's Special Sausages. I don't know who was most thrilled, me or Charlie!

15 September:

Alison dropped by the summerhouse this afternoon and brought cake and flowers to say thanks and to tell me her news. She looked so different from the nervous, brow-beaten woman she had been when we first met. Her bitten down fingernails have been professionally manicured and painted by the look of them. She's not shoving her hands under her armpits as she used to. Rufus is doing fine, and he brought a stray kitten home a few weeks ago – so she's got two now! She's called the kitten Duster. And she shared her fantastic news. Her agent got her a two-book deal with a big publishing house! I was over the moon for her. We promised to keep in touch. What a lovely morning!

2 October:

Lilly popped round with Abigail! I had just finished baking scones, so we had those with clotted cream and jam. Lilly had begged Abigail to let her see me, but sensibly, Abigail had asked her mum first. A half-truth had been told about me being helpful to her case, but not the detail. She'd said that I'd been understanding and helped Lilly to feel confident enough to go to the police.

Lilly seemed so happy. For the first time ever she'd been able to ask friends to hers for sleepovers, when before she'd always been worried about her stepdad ogling them, or making inappropriate comments. She'd also started a journal to get a lot of the awful things that happened on paper and out of her system. They would never leave her completely of course. This will be something she'll live with. But it will get easier over the passage of time. Lilly had been researching psychic phenomenon for a school project, and hoped that she could maybe contact Chloé again one day. She and her brother had also been trying to help her mum to come to terms with it all, and made sure she knew she wasn't to blame for any of it. I am so proud of the strong young woman she's becoming.

22 November:

Ben phoned and asked if he could meet me at the Whistling Kettle because he was up here for a short break. I was over the moon and of course said yes. Imagine my surprise when I walked in. The first surprise was his appearance. He was clean shaven, had a stylish haircut and was very handsome. It took me a while to recognise him to be honest. The second surprise were the two children he had with him. They clearly adored him. I was so happy he was allowed to see them again! Apparently, they stay with him every other weekend and as a special treat, they were having a three-day break in Cornwall with him.

His new partnership with Nathan is going well and he really feels he's back on his feet now, both financially and mentally. The children gave me a card they'd made to say thank you for saving their daddy's life, which had me in bits. And Ben gave me a beautiful jade necklace which he said reminded him of my eyes, and a large envelope which he dropped into my shopping bag and said to open later. I opened it when I got home and was in total shock when I counted the five-thousand pounds inside. When I phoned him to say it was too much, he said I deserved every penny and more. The card the children made spoke the truth. He owed me his life.

14 December:

Abigail and I met for a drink and a catch up. She was pleased to tell me that Vicky and she are in a serious relationship and are thinking of moving in together in the New Year. Her parents have come round to accepting who she is a bit more, and have invited her over on Christmas day with Vicky. Abigail declined Christmas lunch as that would feel a bit forced and awkward, but agreed to go for drinks in the afternoon.

Abigail's brother had a lot to do with it. He'd apparently said to his parents that they talk about the glory of God's love a lot, so what about Abigail? Doesn't she deserve to be loved? To have a partner to share her life with? Or is love just reserved for heterosexual people. He said what they believe is against human rights and they should be ashamed. If they believe God made us all, then he made Abigail too.

As for Abigail's sister, it will be a long time before they speak again, if ever. She's in disgrace with her parents too, but still sees them often. As does her brother. They are trying to guide her forward, but she's in a bad place. A small part of Abigail wants to help her, but the bigger part can't bear to breathe the same air. We agreed to go out over Christmas with Charlie and Vicky. That should be fun. I love my job and I love my life!

Acknowledgements

There are so many people to say a huge thank you to. Each and every one has been a brilliant support.

The first person to see *The Cornish Connection* in its very early stages was my good friend and fellow writer, Celia Anderson. She thought Nancy's story was a breath of fresh air, and made me really believe it could be a winner. Fabulous editor Charlotte Ledger saw it too early on, and was similarly impressed. Another lovely friend and writer, Chris Stovell further cemented my resolve to carry on, with her enthusiastic words of encouragement, and constructive advice. Jane Johnson, amazing writer and friend who cheered me up one day unexpectedly, and encouraged me to get this book out into the world. And to Mel Brown, writer and friend whose good humour and Yorkshire straight talking, had me laughing out loud in Waterstone's cafe on a few Saturday mornings. Thank you all. You all helped in different ways, far more than you know.

Next are the wonderful people who were early readers of the finished book. Some writers, some bloggers, some who just love to read my books that I've met along the way. I am happy to say that each and every one is a friend, and huge support in my writing journey.

So in no particular order, thank you so much, Trish Dixon, Anita Waller, Livia Sbarbaro, Yvonne Bastian, Glynis Meloy, Kathryn Wainwright, Sue Kinder, Linda Stacey, Anne Mackle, Sue Curran, Diane Warburton, Sharon Sawford, Kelly Florentia, Zoé-Lee-O'Farrell, Anne Boland, Diane Thompson Waterston, Tina Jackson, Linda Huber, and Tina Dorr.

And a big thanks to anyone who has given me advice via messenger or email, on a myriad of things in recent months. You know who you are. Linda Huber in particular must have sore ears by now!

And last, but not least, a special mention must go to Emma Mitchell from Creating Perfection for her fantastic formatting and techie expertise. My mind boggled at what was required to get a paperback ready to launch on the world. And also to Debbie at The Cover Collection, for her fantastic cover design!

Also by Amanda James:

A Stitch in Time

Cross Stitch

Somewhere Beyond the Sea

Summer in Tintagel

Behind the Lie

Another Mother

Deep Water

The Calico Cat

The Cornish Retribution

The Feud

Dark Deception

Printed in Great Britain
by Amazon

41640374R00218